MOTIVE IN SHADOW

MOTIVE IN SHADOW

LESLEY EGAN

DOUBLEDAY & COMPANY, INC.
GARDEN CITY, NEW YORK

All of the characters in this book
are fictitious, and any resemblance
to actual persons, living or dead,
is purely coincidental.

Time driveth onward fast,
And in a little while our lips are dumb.
Let us alone. What is it that will last?
All things are taken from us, and become
Portions and parcels of the dreadful Past.
                    —Alfred, Lord Tennyson
                    "Choric Song"

MOTIVE IN SHADOW

ONE

"I just don't know how to thank you, Mr. Falkenstein," said Lillian Keller earnestly. "You've been awful good to me." Her spaniel eyes were brown and moist. Jesse should have felt sorry for her, but he was merely irritated. Silly dreep of a woman, meekly putting up with a bully who regularly beat her and the kids, until a strong-minded sister bullied her into a lawyer's office and divorce court.

"You'll be all right now," he said inanely. The decree had just been issued by a bored judge. And he'd be willing to bet that if she took up with another man it would be just the same kind; she was a born doormat.

The sister nodded grimly at him and bore her away; Jesse headed for the side entrance of the Hall of Justice, which gave onto the parking lot, and stopped to light a cigarette on the steps.

He was feeling stale and bored with life in general. The usual run of daily business was dull: the eternal paperwork, a handful of litigious clients, a damage suit which would probably never get to court. Unlocking the Mercedes, he gave himself a mental shake; life was treating the Falkensteins rather handsomely at the moment, and he ought to be enjoying it. Old Edgar Walters' dying last year—and he still missed the old reprobate—had left him quite a bundle of money. Nell had found her sprawling old house up in Coldwater Canyon, and was having fun remodeling and redecorating: some day it might be ready to move into. Even the weather was behaving itself, after a wet and wild winter; March had come in sedately, producing mild and pleasant days, and was surrendering to a milder and warmer April.

And Jesse felt stale and fretful. Perhaps this was what happened as you got into the mid-thirties and realized that there was probably only a lot more of the same thing in store down the years.

It was just past noon, and he had an appointment at one-thirty with a man who wanted to make a will, and that was all for today. Catching the light at Temple, he yawned and sighed. Stop somewhere for lunch, and unprecedentedly have a drink first?

But when he went into the restaurant a block from his office on Wilshire there was a discouraging crowd waiting, and the bar was packed. Allergic to people *en masse*, he settled for a milk-shake at a fast-food cubbyhole in the next block, and got back to his office at one-twenty, the handsome new office on the third floor of the tall new office building.

His invaluable twin secretaries, Jean and Jimmy (Jamesina) Gordon looked up from file cabinet and reception desk as he came in. There was a client—the man about the will?—waiting in one of the comfortable deep green armchairs Nell had chosen.

"Mr. Manning," said Jean formally. The one-thirty appointment. The Gordons, of course, could run the office without Jesse; Jean was reminding him that the paperwork was up to date and he might as well see the client now: nothing else on hand.

"Yes," said Jesse, and looked at the client, who stood up and looked back at him. He was a good-looking man, about fifty, as tall as Jesse, broader, with heavy shoulders; he had a good square jaw, intelligent dark eyes—it was an individual face. He was conservatively—and at second glance expensively—dressed in a navy suit, immaculate white shirt, discreetly patterned navy and gray tie; his squarish tortoiseshell glasses conformed to what the well-dressed businessman should wear. He had a briefcase in one hand. Jesse shepherded him into the inner office and indicated a chair, sat down at his desk. He was still getting used to the big, new L-shaped desk, the spacious new quarters. He swiveled the desk chair around to face the client and idly met the stern dark gaze of Holbein's portrait of Sir Thomas More on the paneled wall opposite the window. "I understand you want to make a will, Mr. Manning." More busywork.

"No," said Manning. "I said it was about a will." He had an un-expectedly deep, full voice. He looked at Jesse consideringly, doubtfully; he opened his mouth, shut it, and said after a moment, "Tregarron suggested your name. It seems he knows your father, who I gather is also a lawyer. He said you should be—er —sound. I don't know. I don't know what we can do— You see, I couldn't ask Tregarron to act for me, because he's named executor of the will, and besides we've used Tregarron and Weekes on all the legal business of the company for twenty years, he's—an interested party. My God!" said Manning, and sagged back into the chair and passed a square manicured hand over his face. "What a goddamned mess—and I ought to be furious, I am furious—but mostly I'm still feeling so damned astonished—" He let out a long breath. "Short and sweet," he said. "My mother's will—we'll have to contest it. I haven't the least idea how you go about it, but—"

Jesse sat back. "Very tricky thing in law, Mr. Manning. You could spend some money and get nowhere. On what grounds do you want to contest?"

"I don't know, damn it! I can't—Mother! Mother, doing a thing like—" Manning hoisted the briefcase onto his lap, opened it. "This has—it's like seeing four suns in the sky, or, or waking up on Mars. Nothing like this happens. It can't be happening. But it seems to be. I'm not making much sense, am I?" He took a little sheaf of papers out of the briefcase and laid it on the desk. "That's the will," he said. "We knew where her will was, of course—in Tregarron's office. She made a new one a little over five years ago. She—she died ten days ago, and Tregarron was starting all the paperwork—getting it into probate—but there was the safe-deposit box to clear. We had an appointment with an I.R.S. man on Monday—and there was this thing on top of everything else. Made three months ago." He sat back. "You'd better read it first."

Without comment Jesse picked up the papers. It was a Xerox copy of the original. The outer sheet was labeled *Last Will and Testament of Claire Elizabeth Manning;* below that a line was crossed out, *has been deposited for safekeeping with,* and below that was *Peter J. Kellogg, attorney-at-law,* with an address on Melrose Avenue. Jesse folded the first sheet over and was confronted with a single succinct page.

I, Claire Elizabeth Manning, a resident of Los Angeles County, state of California, do hereby declare this to be my

last will and testament and revoke all other wills and codi-
cils previously made by me.

First, I declare that I am a widow.

Second, it is my intention hereby to dispose of all my
property, real and personal, which I have the right to
dispose of by Will.

Third, I give, devise and bequeath the following bequests
to the following persons:

The sum of ten thousand, three hundred and forty-two
dollars and seven cents ($10,342.07) to my son John G.
Manning, resident of Los Angeles County.

The sum of ten thousand, three hundred and forty-two
dollars and seven cents ($10,342.07) to my grandson James
J. Manning, resident of Los Angeles County.

My home residence on Valle Vista Place, Hollywood, and
all its contents to my son John G. Manning.

All other property of which I die possessed, real and personal, I leave to my third cousin Adam Pollock, resident of
Middlesex County, New Jersey.

I name Arthur Tregarron sole executor of this Will.

There followed the signature, in a fairly neat backhand, Claire
Elizabeth Manning. On the third sheet was more typescript:

On the seventh day of December, 1979, Claire Elizabeth
Manning declared to us the undersigned that this foregoing
instrument was her last will and testament, and requested us
to act as witnesses to the same and to her signature thereon.
She thereupon signed said will in our presences, we being
present at the same time. And we now, at her request, in her
presence and in the presence of each other, do hereunto
subscribe our names as witnesses.

Below this was a careless, big scrawl, *Peter J. Kellogg residing
at Hollywood, CA,* and a neat, tiny script, *Emily W. Vickers residing at Glendale, CA.*

Jesse put it down and said, "Short and sweet all right. What's
the matter with it, Mr. Manning?"

"My God," said Manning. He opened and shut his mouth

again, and then reached into his breast pocket and handed Jesse a card: C.M.R. Management Company, an address out on Sunset in West Hollywood. Mr. John G. Manning, President. "I can't tell you within a few thousand what we're worth, but we grossed seven and a half million last year. We own fourteen office buildings. We manage about forty others. We've gotten into condominiums the last ten years. It's a private company. The family business."

Jesse's brows shot up. "That's 'all other property of which I die possessed'?"

"That's what I mean," said Manning. Suddenly, as if he couldn't sit still another moment, he plunged to his feet and began to pace back and forth in front of the desk. "My God, my God, why? *Why* should she do such a thing? Why? There was nothing—no reason—I don't even know who this goddamned Pollock is! The whole business, the whole shebang that she worked to build up, that I worked for— It doesn't make sense!" He stopped short and stared at Jesse bitterly. "Ruth—my wife— says she was crazy. It's easy to say, and you'd never prove it. I never knew a shrewder woman than Mother."

"The other will—the one you thought was valid—how does it read?"

"It all came to me. Naturally. It's the family business, for God's sake. There was never any question— Not even any special bequests, she knew she could leave it to me to do the things she wanted—five thousand to Mrs. Hawes, and Jim was to have my father's diamond ring. Why in God's name she did this! My God," said Manning, "how many times has she said to me, when I'm gone and you're in charge—"

"Could you supply witnesses to that?" Jesse got up to find a book in the rank of shelves behind the desk.

Manning nodded, pacing again. "I was doing some thinking along that line. Very probably. Fowler—he's our head accountant—must have heard her say something like that a good many times. And Hansie, of course. I suppose the family wouldn't count."

"Within the last two or three months, since this will was made?"

"Oh, God, no. I've been in charge the last five, six years." For the first time he gave Jesse a small fleeting grin. "Whatever, she was quite a gal, my mother, Mr. Falkenstein. You couldn't beat her—you couldn't get her down. She was in charge, in spades, up to then—at her desk all day five days a week, knew everything that was going on. It was her baby, she knew the business backward and forward—"

"'Scuse me," said Jesse, "you put up with getting ordered around? Don't strike me as a milquetoast, Mr. Manning."

Manning laughed briefly and sat down again. "I wouldn't like to think so. It wasn't exactly like that. God knows when I was a brash kid just out of business administration at U.S.C. I clashed with her a few times—but I found out she usually knew just what she was doing. And she never tried to keep me under her thumb while she bossed everything—I served time in accounting, and then on to investments, until I knew the whole business as well as she did—that was the general idea, that I should take over. Actually I'd been running the business for ten years and more, only she liked to come in, keep an eye on what was happening. Then she broke her hip, and that finished that. Though she surprised everybody, including the doctor, how she came back. He didn't think she'd walk again, but she was on her feet in three months, slowed down a bit but just as sharp as ever."

"Um," said Jesse, leafing over pages. "There hadn't been any difference of opinion between you at all?"

"Nothing," said Manning. "Nothing. I—when we came across that thing, and read it, Tregarron and I must have just goggled at each other for five minutes before— It's a monstrosity, nothing that could happen. Everything—the whole business, all the property—and Jim just out of college and in his first job in the accounting department— There wasn't any damned reason! I suppose Mrs. Lightner could testify that we were on perfectly amicable terms, and Mrs. Hawes—though I wasn't often there when she was—"

"Mrs. Lightner."

Manning finally stopped turning a cigarette around in his fingers and lit it with a little vicious click of a lighter. "Housekeeper," he said. "Nurse? When she broke her hip—she couldn't be alone any longer. That white elephant of a house—but she never would consider leaving it, going into an apartment. They'd only just built it and moved into it when my father was killed. That was nineteen thirty-five. Of course I lived there, after college, until Ruth and I were married—that's twenty-six years ago. She'd lived there alone ever since, rattling around in the place. Had the cleaning woman, Mrs. Hawes, in a few days a week, to keep it in shape—she'd had her for years, twenty at least. She was still driving then. Then she fell down the back steps and broke her hip, and when she came home from the convalescent place she had to give in, have someone with her. She—was a woman who valued her privacy, and she didn't like it, but there it was. And Mrs. Lightner's been more than satisfactory. A practical nurse really, but she took over the housekeeping, did everything for Mother."

"What," asked Jesse, "did your mother die of, Mr. Manning? Did you notice any—even slight—mental disability?"

Manning stubbed out his cigarette. "It said cardiac failure and thrombosis on the death certificate. You might as well say old age, I suppose. She was getting on for seventy-six. All I can tell you is that, yes, she'd slowed down a good deal—but she was still all there mentally, if a little absentminded sometimes. But I think that was mostly because she missed having a regular routine—the way it had been, all those years, every day at the office—"

Jesse watched him, letting him talk; he prowled the office restlessly.

"Oh, God, I hate like the devil even having to think about it— Mother, incompetent? Off the rails enough to do a thing like this —the whole business she's spent a lifetime building up— People to testify we were on the usual affectionate terms," and he shook his head, collapsing into the chair again. "I really don't know. I respected her more than anyone I've every known, you know. But she wasn't a—a demonstrative woman. I—if you don't mind a little family history—"

"We might have to look at some."

"Yes. She wasn't a woman to live in the past, either, but just in the course of learning the business I heard a certain amount— and Hansie could fill in between the lines—"

"Hansie."

"Miss Wilma Hansen, she's retired now, but she was Mother's

secretary for years—as long as I can remember. Nice woman—I suppose you could say I got as much mothering from Hansie as from Mother," said Manning heavily. "You don't, well, think of your parents having romantic feelings and deathless love affairs, but looking back at it—I don't know a great deal about my father. Mother was brought up in New Jersey—Passaic, I think it was. For some reason my father went there on his way to California. She was an only child, her mother was dead, and I gather there was quite a row when they eloped. All I know about my father is that he came from somewhere in New York and his family was all dead then. He had an idea there was money to be made in Southern California land. Money!" said Manning. "A gold mine. Southern California in the twenties—the thirties. My God, was there money. That was in 1925. They came out here, and he was with a real estate firm in L.A., doing all right, when her father died and left her a bundle of money—it wouldn't amount to a hell of a lot now, but then it was a nice piece of working capital. They were so lucky, you see, up to a point. All they could see was land investment—when the bundle came, it was in gilt-edged stock, and they sold it all out to realize the capital—and that was just before the crash in twenty-nine."

"Oh, yes, I see," said Jesse. "And after that—" Talk about gold mines. Southern California in the thirties, just on its way to building one of the world's great cities: all the bare empty stretches of land west and east and north of Hollywood, property values depressed to record lows, but the potential—ten years later the great aircraft industry galvanized to growth by the war, and thousands of people flocking in. "Little joke, about the banks turning into real estate agencies during the Depression. All the foreclosures."

"That was the luck," said Manning. "Even a relatively small amount of working capital—it was just over two hundred thousand—gave them the edge to buy up rental property clear, buy up land to hold for future potential. One of the first goodies they held a deed to was a triple lot on Santa Monica between San Vicente and Robertson Boulevard—"

"Oh, my, how pretty," said Jesse. *"The hand of the diligent maketh rich,* according to Solomon. The profit on that alone—I can imagine."

"Yes," said Manning dryly. "They bought it in 1931 for fourteen thousand and sold it ten years later for two hundred and twenty grand. There's an office complex sitting on it now worth about seven million."

"You were talking about luck."

Manning got out another cigarette. "Up to a point. They were doing fine in the Depression, you can see. Other people's bad luck was their big chance. They'd accumulated enough, had enough profit coming in, to build that house—it was away out of town then—and they'd just moved into it, I should say we, I was six years old—when my father was killed. It was one of those senseless accidents—he was driving home up on Highland when a drunk ran a light and hit his car broadside. He was killed instantly. He was only thirty-five.

"And looking back on it—later on, when I knew more about it and understood her better—I could see that was when she changed, you know." Manning's tone was sober. "She never was a woman for—oh, the hugs and kisses and darlings—but I can just remember, when I was just a kid, her putting me to bed, singing lullabies. I can remember them laughing and singing together—they both liked music, and Hansie said they used to go dancing a lot. After he was killed—I can just barely remember him—there wasn't any more of that. I think it was as if something froze in her, and all the feeling she had left, for a long time, was a kind of fierce determination to go on and build up the business—pile up the money—just as he would have tried to do."

"Yes," said Jesse. "You're saying there wasn't much affection."

"No, no," said Manning impatiently. "It's hard to explain her to a stranger, Mr. Falkenstein. It makes her sound hard and cold, to tell you that she packed me off to military school and plunged into the business single-mindedly. She wasn't, exactly. She was always good to me, when I was at home. She talked to me— there were always birthday parties, and Christmas parties. I think it was when I was about sixteen, she took me to the office for the first time and explained what the business was, what they were doing—she'd turned it into C.M.R. Management then, you see, their joined initials just as if he were still there and they were working together. She told me then, she'd worked to build it all up because that's what Bob—my father—would have wanted—she was building it all for me, his son, and I was to learn all about it and take it over some day. It was as if—"

"Thirty-five years ago," said Jesse sadly.

"As if all her spontaneous love, any expression of it, had dried up, you know? But, if I can explain it, yes, there was affection. Family feeling. Maybe she didn't overwhelm Jimmy with grand-motherly kisses, but she was proud of him, how he did in school and college. And Ardeth—our girl. She didn't approve much of Jim going out for football—she'd grunt and say he'd better learn to use his brain instead of his brawn—but she got a kick out of that winning touchdown when they played Berkeley, all the same." Manning grinned reminiscently. "And on Ardeth's twenty-first birthday, she gave her a gold bracelet that had been one of my father's first presents to her. There was a lot of family feeling. We just didn't go around showing it much. She was very happy about Jim coming into the business. Of course he'd been brought up to the idea, but at one time he had some fool notion of going in for music—well." Manning sighed. "I don't know if I've gotten her across. She was—quite a lady, Mr. Falkenstein. Quite a lady. And I was never so flabbergasted in my life as when this will turned up. It's just—wild. Impossible."

Jesse looked up from his tome of California statutes. "This Pollock. You never heard of him?"

"I never heard the name. A long time ago, when I was in college, I asked her once if there were any relatives on either side of the family. She said, only some distant cousins of hers, they'd been out of touch for years and that was fine with her. So far as I know, she'd never seen or heard of them since she and my father came out here—of course that was five years before I was born." Manning shrugged.

"Would it be fair to say she was secretive?" asked Jesse.

"To some extent," agreed Manning unwillingly. "That is, she kept her affairs to herself all right. Made her own decisions. Why?"

"Contesting a will," said Jesse, "is a very chancy thing. I take it that Mr. Tregarron will be submitting this to the probate court right away."

"I'd better give you his address and phone number. He said he'd like to confer with you first. He knew her a long time too, and he was just as upset as I was about this. Couldn't understand it."

"Well, if we're going to contest it's always better to give notice of it before a will's in probate. Only we have to decide what grounds there might be. Now, we've got several choices—and we can use all of 'em. Mental incompetence—"

"I've got to say I can't see that. I don't think she was incompetent. She was as rational as you or me, up to a couple of hours before she died. She'd been failing—but only physically. The last six or seven months, since she'd been so ill last August, she'd been going downhill, but not mentally."

Jesse laid the book down. "You'd noticed a definite change in her in that time?"

"Yes," said Manning. "It was rather terrible to see her going like that, she'd always been so quick and sharp and—on the ball. She was a lot slower—and sometimes you'd speak to her and she wouldn't answer, and then she'd say, oh, she'd been thinking of something else. Like that. But she was quite rational." Manning was staring out the window. "We thought she was going then—last August. She caught a bad cold and it went into pneumonia —but she fooled the doctor then too. She came home, but she needed a lot more attention and help. Mrs. Lightner's been a godsend—I don't know what we'd have done without her. She was so tactful with Mother. Then—just two weeks ago yesterday—she had a seizure of some sort. Dr. Whymant said it was a stroke. She hated the hospital so—no privacy—but of course they could do more for her there. Ruth and I went to see her every day, afternoons and evenings. She just—faded away. We all knew she was going. I was with her—just before she went—that evening, a week ago last Saturday. Ruth had been there that afternoon, with Ardeth—but they had some long-standing date that night, a wedding shower for somebody. I was alone with her. She was too weak to sit up or talk much, but she held onto my hand and smiled at me. Once I told her she just had to hang on and we'd soon have her home again, and she said, 'Not this time, Johnny.'

She hadn't called me Johnny since I was a kid. She looked up at me for a while and said, 'You're so much like your father.' That was always the highest praise she could give me." Manning was silent and then went on, "A while after that she said all of a sudden, 'That old trunk in the basement, I should have got rid of it.' And then she squeezed my hand a little and said, 'You'll be all right, Johnny. Just go ahead with what you have the way Bob and I did.' And—that was all. She slipped into a coma a minute later and died about midnight."

"What do you suppose she meant by that?"

"I've got no remote idea," said Manning wearily.

"Well, it just could tie up to this other thing. These very odd sums of money. Very exact sums. Same to you and your son—ten thousand three hundred and forty-two dollars and seven cents. That looks like a mental aberration all right," said Jesse. "That figure mean anything to you?"

"Not a damned thing. Just a sum of money—and damned little these days. It's certainly funny that she specified that odd amount, but what kind of aberration—"

"Well." Jesse flattened the page again. "I'll want to talk to the doctor, everybody who was seeing her regularly about the time she made this will—and the lawyer who drew it up—the hospital nurses, probably. The devil of it is, if she had developed an obsession or hallucination of some kind, she was evidently rational enough on other levels to keep it from showing. And secretive enough. There is undue influence, of course. You don't know anything about this distant cousin. For all we know, he could have found out she had money and been getting at her in some way. It's far-fetched—"

"Far-fetched?" yelped Manning. "He seems to live in the East. I'd know if there'd been any strangers around, for God's sake—"

"You weren't there all the time, and I suppose Mrs. Lightner has some time off."

"Not much. Sundays, the occasional evening—she has a married daughter in Pasadena. When she was out for a day or an evening, there were a couple of other practical nurses to spell her—I didn't know all of them. But I don't see how it would have been possible—"

"We have to look and see," said Jesse. "He could have been writing to her."

"Mrs. Lightner would know."

"What's so difficult about this is the damned law itself, Mr. Manning." Jesse tapped the page before him. "Here's *Estate of Goetz, supra.* 'When the testator had a mental disorder in which there were lucid periods, it is presumed that his will was made during a time of lucidity.' In fact, the cards are stacked against you. In about seventy-five per cent of all cases of contested wills, the jury finds for the contestant, but if the decision's appealed—which it generally is—the higher court reverses the decision ninety per cent of the time, on technicalities."

"Thanks for nothing," said Manning. "My God, when I think—"

"But there's an ace in the hole," said Jesse, "in what's called Unnatural Provisions in a Will. 'This is defined as those giving preference to strangers rather than blood relations or to the natural objects of the testator's bounty.' Now, you can show clearly, with probably a good many witnesses, that your mother had for many years given evidence of intention of willing the business to you, and you and your family are her closest blood relatives. I think we can get a lot of mileage out of that. But it would help a good deal if we could get her motive in making this damned odd will. If we could show that she had developed some mental quirk—or, of course, that she'd been under the influence of this Pollock—"

"Nobody could ever influence her," said Manning.

"You can't be sure of that, Mr. Manning. She was old and, as you put it, slowed down. She'd got a little absentminded. How often did you and the rest of the family see her?"

"I dropped in when I could—maybe twice a week. And I'd phone her another few times. Ruth usually went by once a week or so, of course she's busy—Jim, well, I don't know, he's just got engaged. Ardeth's pretty busy working for her master's." Manning passed a hand over his still-thick dark hair. "Of course, she wasn't getting around the way she used to—Mother, I mean. She hadn't driven in five years—when she did want to go out somewhere she'd take a cab, but that wasn't often. We used to have her over to dinner once a month or so, but she'd got—the last year or two—where she really didn't care to go out much."

"Yes. She might have been feeling pretty lonely. And old people often remember things and people a long way back in their lives clearer than what happened yesterday. Suppose she'd started getting letters from this cousin, maybe recalling old times —it could have been."

"It still sounds far-fetched. She always had good sense," said Manning. "What they used to call horse sense. She was old and slow and a little absentminded, all right, but as far as I could tell —and I think I knew her better than anybody—she still had good sense. Or she was the world's greatest actress at hiding some sudden craziness. Well, so what do we do now?"

"You don't do anything," said Jesse. "You're the interested party. I'll see Tregarron, but he'll have to get this thing into probate, of course. I file the necessary papers to say you're formally contesting the will. It isn't going to come in front of a jury tomorrow, or next month—maybe not in six months. Tregarron will be getting into touch with this Pollock, and I'd like to find out more about him. I want to talk to a lot of people who knew your mother. If we could get at the reason— An old trunk," said Jesse, "in the basement?"

"Hell," said Manning, and rubbed his forehead, "I don't know what that was about. She'd lived there for forty-five years and she didn't like to throw things away. It's a big house—there is a basement. At least, even in that will, the damned house belongs to me. You go and look at anything you want to. Ask any questions."

"You haven't," said Jesse, "got anything to lose—sorry, that might have been better put. Are you willing to lay out some money on a private detective to sniff around this Pollock?"

"If you think we'd get anything useful. My dear God," said Manning quietly, "I never gave it a thought, you know, that everything was in her name. It's a private company. She more or less turned the management over to me—started to—fifteen, sixteen years back—it just gave her the illusion of still being boss, coming in to the office every day. When she broke her hip, she said it was time the old horse was turned out to pasture. And we'd do something about putting this and that in my name, on

account of the inheritance tax. And I didn't follow up on it then
—I thought there was time—she was sixty-nine, and well as ever
except for the lameness. It'd have underlined the fact that she
was finished with the business, and in a way it had been her life.
I—let it go. And time runs away before you know it." He got to
his feet. "Do whatever has to be done, Mr. Falkenstein. You'll
want a retainer—" He brought out a checkbook. "If you want to
talk to anyone at the office, just come in—I'll tell them to answer
any questions. You'd better believe the staff's upset too—most of
them have been with us for years. And I'll tell Mrs. Lightner to
expect you—she'll be staying on to look after the house until this
is settled."

"We'll see what turns up," said Jesse. "I think you've got a
pretty strong case on the Unnatural Provisions bit. I'll be in
touch, Mr. Manning."

Manning went out, and Jesse picked up the tome again. He
read over [§ 21.42] again: Unnatural Provisions in Will, Estate
of Ventura (1963) 217 CA2d 50. There was also Estate of
Warner (1959) 166 CA2d 677, 333 P2d 848.

He had forgotten about being bored with life. The dry legal
language was just thin covering for the eternal antics of human
nature, of erratic and foolish and beleaguered flesh-and-blood
people . . . "—it was held that provision for the decedent's only
son and his son's mother (his second divorced wife) and the dis-
inheriting of his fourth wife, who was supported under a decree
of separate maintenance and denied the decedent the divorce he
frequently requested during the last seven years of his life, is not
such an unnatural or unjust will as could be considered evidence
of the testator's alleged testamentary incompetence."

Estate of Warner, 1959. Jesse wondered idly what had happened to those people in the last twenty-one years.

But Manning had handed him a very pretty little mystery; forever fascinated with people, he wondered about the various pos-
sibilities here. What in the name of all sense had induced that
autocratic, shrewd, unbending old lady to make such an oddity
of a will? And given her secretive and stern nature—the stern-
ness had certainly showed through in Manning's story—would it
ever be possible to find out?

Because it was all very well to cite legal precedents and point to unnatural provisions and evidence of intentions. But if he could show a jury that Claire Elizabeth Manning had been laboring under a delusion or obsession of some sort, or had come under undue influence of this cousin at the time she made the will, there would be a hell of a lot better chance to rescue Manning's family business. And what a business.

And what an old lady, he thought. Quite a gal, as her son said. Unwillingly, remembering all Manning had said, Jesse found himself convinced that Claire Elizabeth Manning had known exactly what she was doing, and had had what seemed to her a very good reason for doing it.

It might not seem like a good reason to anybody else, of course.

He put a bookmark at page 908 of the California statutes tome and consulted the card Manning had left with Tregarron's phone number on it. Over the phone, Arthur Tregarron sounded elderly, pedantic, and flurried. "I have seldom in my life felt so upset, sir. I simply cannot understand it—of course, a very strong-minded woman—I scarcely know what to think. I should be very glad of an opportunity to discuss it with you, Mr. Falkenstein—ah, technically we shall be on opposite sides, but in actuality— Ten o'clock? That will be quite convenient."

Nothing in Tregarron, probably. He'd be able to testify that she had intended to leave everything to Manning, *vide* that other will—but that was six years ago.

Jesse got out the phone book and looked up Peter J. Kellogg, attorney-at-law, dialed the number. A pert female voice informed him that Mr. Kellogg was unavailable. "I'd like an appointment," said Jesse. "Sometime tomorrow?"

"Just a moment, sir." It was considerably more than that before she came back on. "We can just fit you in at three tomorrow afternoon. Your name, sir? And what matter did you wish to consult Mr. Kellogg about?"

Jesse reflected sadly on the state of public education. "It's about a will," he said gently. "Thanks very much."

He got home a little early, and in the entrance hall of the house on Rockledge Road murmured to himself, "Family feeling." Maybe it didn't lend itself to verbal description.

The table was set for six in the dining room, with Nell's best china and silver and a centerpiece with eight candles. In the living room his father was on all fours being a horsie for his namesake, year-old David Andrew, who was shrieking with glee. The enormous mastiff Athelstane was looking on excitedly, and as Jesse came in, excitement overpowered him and he pounced on Falkenstein senior, knocking him flat and dislodging his rider. David Andrew yelled, and Nell and Fran came rushing in, Fran holding a bottle of sherry in one hand and a fifth of Bourbon in the other.

"Why you harbor that damned dog—" Falkenstein senior sought a chair, feeling one leg.

"It's time he was in bed anyway—oh, Jesse, you're early," said Nell, giving him a quick kiss. "*Come* on, big boy—playtime's over, say good night to Daddy and Grandpa—" She whisked the baby up and departed. "If you'd just keep an eye on the hollandaise, Fran—"

The doorbell rang.

"That can't be Andrew," said Fran. "He had a zillion suspects to question on that latest heist. Jesse, I can't get this cork to *move—*"

Jesse opened the door to William DeWitt. Athelstane, who loved all humans, came eagerly to offer a massive paw. "Welcome to Bedlam," said Jesse. The baby was still howling at the back of the house.

DeWitt, as tall and dark and lank as Jesse, took the paw imperturbably. "I've got rather an interesting new tape for you. Quite an evidential session with Cora last night."

Jesse laughed suddenly. "If I thought one of your tame mediums could contact Claire Elizabeth—never mind. What the British call n.b.g.—no bloody good." It was a field of research he was interested in, and knew a good deal about, as unofficial supporter of DeWitt's Western Association for Psychic Research. But if he knew anything about people at all, whether on this side of life or the other, he could have an educated guess that that secretive strong-minded old lady wouldn't be remotely interested in communicating via any medium, to explain her feelings or motives or even aberrations.

And just what the hell had they been?

DeWitt had been invited to meet Falkenstein senior, who had conceived a new interest in psychic research. Jesse found the Italian corkscrew and opened the bottle of sherry for Fran. "Though who wants that damned stuff—"

"Nell and me and Mr. DeWitt," said Fran.

Jesse went out to the kitchen to build himself a Bourbon and water. Coming back, he said to his father, "I've gotten into a case with an Arthur Tregarron, who seems to know you."

Falkenstein senior temporarily abandoned DeWitt and automatic writing. "Oh, yes. Fussy old maid of a fellow. Very trustworthy at paperwork, but no good in court—no good at all."

"You don't surprise me," said Jesse, feeding Athelstane cocktail pretzels. The baby had stopped yelling, and Nell came back down the hall. She was looking very fetching, her glossy dark brown hair, never cut, in its usual fat chignon, her dress a pale green affair with a full skirt.

"Heaven knows how late Andrew'll be," said Fran. As usual, she was sleekly smart in coral silk, her dark hair shining. "There's just time now for a leisurely drink before everything's ready—"

But just then Sergeant Clock, LAPD, Hollywood precinct, arrived and was eagerly greeted by Athelstane; he staggered under the onslaught and made for a chair. Jesse brought him a double Bourbon and water. "My God, I need that," he said gratefully. "What a day! Unidentified bodies and heists all over the place."

"Sometime," said Jesse to his father, "I'd like to talk over this case with you. Rather a funny one. Contested will."

"People," said Falkenstein senior. "Thank God I'm just on the corporation side. The human factor—it does foul up the tidy legal cases."

"On the other hand," said Jesse, "there wouldn't be many legal cases if it weren't for human nature."

TWO

Jesse wasted an hour on Thursday morning in Arthur Tregarron's office, listening to him agitate. Women, said Tregarron huffily, were never to be trusted, that was the truth of the matter; flighty and suggestible, the best of them. He had certainly never known Mrs. Manning to be either, a very shrewd businesswoman, a woman of great character, but this just showed that in the end, well, women were women. Not to be trusted where money was concerned. She must have suffered small strokes, he understood it was a matter of lack of oxygen to the brain causing mental lapses; it was all very sad and annoying. It was going to make a good deal of work for both him and Jesse, and whether in the end— Tregarron went on shaking his head gravely.

One important aspect, of course, was the attitude of Adam Pollock. A formal letter had been dispatched to him: attached to the original will had been a memorandum listing all the relevant addresses. If he proved amenable to reason, some compromise— but that was unlikely, most unlikely: the unexpected acquisition of property of such value was not, he felt, apt to foster the spirit of compromise.

"If we could pin down her reason for it, whatever the hell reason she thought she had—"

"Women," said Tregarron firmly. "She must have had a brain lesion. And when I think of the entire estate in limbo, as it were, for God knows how long—" He actually groaned.

He was a short, stout little man with a bald head and a snub nose, but despite his naturally cheerful countenance he was a born pessimist. "I can, of course, get John a court order to continue administering the various properties, but the time and trouble—and all too likely to lose it all in the end to this—this unknown quantity— Women!" said Tregarron violently, and snatched off his rimless glasses to polish them on his handker-chief. "I had advised her last year to sign over the majority of it to John—avoiding the inheritance tax if possible, and she was getting on. She was quite willing, and then she got ill suddenly, had to go to the hospital, and when she was up and about again, and I went to see her, she refused to discuss it."

"Oh, is that so?" Jesse was interested. "You brought it up again, and she balked. On what grounds?"

"None—none. Certainly I brought it up—everyone had thought she was dying, and though she didn't, it certainly un-derlined her age and state of health, and in order to avoid inher-itance tax the property must be signed over five years prior to the death. She simply said, 'I don't want to talk about that now,' and that was that. If only she had—but she didn't, and here we are in this unholy tangle. I don't remember ever feeling more upset in my life."

"But she had been ready to sign it over, before that illness? That was around last July?"

"That's right. A brain lesion," said Tregarron. "During that ill-ness, undoubtedly." He groaned again. "And, damnit, we can't even try to prove it with an autopsy—she was cremated. A week ago Tuesday."

Jesse didn't think an autopsy would have shown anything con-clusive, but he didn't say so. He had the Gordons working on the necessary forms to file the formal notice of contest. Tregarron would be filing the will for probate on Monday.

When he left Tregarron and Weekes's rather shabby offices on Beverly Boulevard he drove up into old Hollywood, ambled up Hollywood Boulevard to the little side street just past the old Chinese Theatre, where Outpost Drive began. Valle Vista Place was a good way up above the many newer little residential streets here.

Finding the house after a few false turns, he contemplated it in surprise. When it was built, it must have been the only house up here for a while. It was in the thirties and later that midtown Hollywood had sprawled houses up the hillsides, up the long twisting canyons in the foothills circling the San Fernando Val-ley beyond. And this was a strange house to find in this particu-lar place; it looked as if it had been picked up bodily from some

sedate old Eastern suburb and set down this far away without
the slightest remodeling. It was a large two-story brick house
with a couple of tall chimneys. It was in the middle of about half
an acre of ground, back from the street; there was an expanse of
green lawn in front and at the sides, and a pair of enormous pine
trees flanked a straight walk to the front door. It was on a corner,
and the nearest house to it was some distance away, half hidden
by tall shrubbery.

There was a conventional door chime. The woman who
opened the door to him was tall and strong-looking, with a mass
of blond hair going gray done up neatly in a knot on her neck.
She was wearing a plain blue housedress with a little apron over
it, flat black moccasins; she might be in her early fifties. She had
a pleasant round face, a firm mouth, bright blue eyes behind
crystal-framed glasses.

"Mrs. Lightner?"

She glanced at the card he handed her. "Oh, come in," she said
at once. "Mr. Manning came last night to tell me about it, he
said you'd be coming to ask questions and I was to tell you anything I could. I can't get over it. Doing a thing like that—leaving
everything to somebody she didn't know!" She led him from a
spacious entrance hall to a large, gloomy living room. "Sit down,
we might as well be comfortable."

Jesse sat in an oversized upholstered chair with a huge
matching ottoman, and she perched on a long couch at right angles to it, reaching to switch on a lamp on the end table. "This
room's always dark, it's the trees in front. I just can't believe it.
I'm sorry for the Mannings, they're nice people. She can't have
known what she was doing—though—"

"You knew her—you lived with her here for five years, Mrs.
Lightner. Have you any idea what was behind it?"

She shook her head doubtfully. Unexpectedly she reached into
her apron pocket and brought out a pack of cigarettes; he leaned
forward to light one for her. "Thanks. Well, I knew her and I
didn't know her, Mr. Falkenstein. She wasn't an easy person to
know—sort of kept you at arm's length. A stiff sort of woman,
but always fair, and—you could trust her. I liked her, you know,
or I wouldn't have stayed this long. Oh, Lord knows it was an
easy job—I've been spoiled here all these years." She smiled

faintly. "It wasn't really a nursing job. She hated asking for help, having anyone fussing around her, and I know how she felt, I'd probably be the same way. I had to help her in and out of the bathtub—she could do everything else for herself. Aside from that it was just running the house, doing the marketing and cooking—there's a good cleaning woman comes twice a week." She drew strongly on her cigarette. "Mrs. Manning never confided in me at all."

"But you might do some guessing. You must have known her pretty well after five years."

"I don't know," she said musingly. "She had a lot of character. She was—somebody you had to respect, if you know what I mean. And in a way I suppose she had a reason to be—the way she was. Losing her husband so young—but another woman wouldn't have taken it the way she—" She broke off to look around the room. "This place. She told me about it, when I first came. It's an inconvenient old house, the stairs and all, and she laughed about it. She said her son wanted her to sell it and move into an apartment, but she never would, because it was Bob's house. Her husband. She said he'd been an orphan and never had much, and when they began to make money, he wanted a grand brick house like the ones wealthy people had, back East where he grew up. They'd just moved into it when he was killed. She told me about that too, how unfair it was. You'd have thought it had just happened the day before—she was still so bitter and hurt about it—not fair, she said, when they were just beginning to get places and have things, a whole life ahead of them."

"Yes," said Jesse. "Did she have many visitors?"

"Hardly any. Miss Hansen used to come every Saturday, they'd play cards and talk, but Miss Hansen hasn't been very well herself lately, she hadn't come in the last couple of months, just called on the phone. Mrs. Manning didn't have many friends —any, really, and that was natural enough too—"

"Why?"

"Well, it'd have been different if she'd had her husband. A couple, they acquire friends," said Mrs. Lightner a little vaguely. "Even if he'd just died a little while ago, there'd have been old friends. But I gather that—back then, she just carried on his business where he left off, it was her only interest, and she didn't have any social life at all."

"No regular visitors, then."

"The family and Miss Hansen. I don't think, even before she broke her hip and couldn't drive anymore, she was ever very social—going out much, entertaining."

"What about mail?"

"She never got much. She didn't write letters often."

"Would you have noticed what letters she got? You'd bring in the mail?"

"No." Mrs. Lightner smiled. "She had a—strong sense of property, should I say? It was one of her foibles—she liked to watch for the mail carrier and get the mail herself. Once in a while there'd be something for me, and she'd hand it over, but it was nearly always just ads and catalogs as far as I could see."

"Was that so just the last six months—her meeting the mail carrier, I mean—or as long as you'd been here?"

"Oh, as long as I'd been here." She put out her cigarette neatly in an ashtray on the coffee table. "The last six months," she repeated. "Mr. Manning said that will was made about three months ago. It's queer."

"Had you noticed any change in her in that time?"

"Oh, yes, certainly, but that was natural too. She was frightened," said Mrs. Lightner.

"Frightened?" asked Jesse sharply. "What about?"

"She knew she was going to die," said Mrs. Lightner quietly. "We all know we're going to die sometime, but when you're young and healthy it's a long way off and you don't think about it. And then something happens and it comes to you, it isn't so far off. She was sixty-nine when I first knew her, not exactly young, but she was feeling so pleased with herself at beating the doctors and walking without a cane, she was feeling fine, you see. The last couple of years she'd got slower and needed more help, and then in August she was very ill—she nearly died—and she knew then she didn't have much longer. She was frightened. Some people are. And of course she tried to pretend to herself she wasn't."

"She wasn't a religious woman at all?"

She shook her head. He decided that Mrs. Lightner would be

a very reassuring nurse in a sickroom; there was a kind of benign quietness about her that was soothing in itself. "That doesn't seem to matter, funny as it sounds. I've seen the regular church-goers scared out of their wits, maybe because they believe in hell." She smiled again.

"Well." Jesse lit another cigarette. "She must have been lonely —especially since she'd been used to a busy routine, up to five years ago. Did you sit and talk with her much? How did she oc-cupy her time—knitting, TV?"

"I'll tell you one way she passed the time just lately, and it's something rather queer." She accepted his light with a nod, blew a clean stream of smoke. "No, she didn't want me to talk with her. Patients are different—some of them like to get on first-name terms right away, and some don't. I asked her, right at first, if she'd call me Winifred, but she said she was too old and crochety to like the idea of first names as soon as you met some-body. That sounds as if she was unfriendly, but she wasn't—just formal. No, she didn't knit. She watched TV sometimes, only cer-tain programs—mostly dramas. She always read the paper through every day. And she had her music. It's a big house, or that might have driven me up the wall, but I couldn't hear it in the kitchen."

"What kind of music?"

"All the popular stuff from the twenties and thirties. She had stacks of records, and that thing." Mrs. Lightner nodded over his shoulder. Jesse looked, and was stunned to see, in the dim shad-ows at the side of the room, a looming old-fashioned Victrola, dating probably from the teens. "Mr. Manning said it was ridicu-lous, and he got someone to get all the records down on tape, and bought her a tape recorder. She'd sit and listen to it for hours. She told me once that it brought back the past better than anything—how they'd loved to dance to all that music. She'd been a musician herself—used to play the piano." Looming be-side the Victrola was a baby grand. "I suggested she might like to try it again, but she just laughed and said she'd forgotten ev-erything she knew about it. But what I meant to tell you—I told Mr. Manning last night and he didn't know what to make of it either—was about the books."

"What books?"

"Now that I couldn't tell you, and I was curious too," said Mrs. Lightner calmly. "You see, she wasn't a reader. There isn't a book in the place except those scruffy old ones about real estate laws and property management, in the den. She'd look at the *Reader's Digest,* or one of the picture magazines, now and then, that was all. I'm a mystery buff myself, I don't understand people who don't read for amusement, but she didn't. Until she came home from the hospital last August. Then she took to going to the library."

"I'll be damned," said Jesse. That was a break in the pattern: nonreaders seldom turned into bookworms overnight.

"She never went out much, once a week to the hairdresser's, once in a long while to shop. She'd call a taxi when she did. The first time, she'd gone out to the hairdresser's and she was late—I was a little worried—and when she came in she had a little wicker basket full of books. Four or five books, I think. And she didn't want me to see what they were, or talk about it. After that, she'd sit reading instead of playing with the tape recorder. A few times, when I came in—she usually sat right where you are—to ask something or bring her something, she'd put both hands across the book so I couldn't see the title or anything about it. But she was just automatically secretive, you know—" Mrs. Lightner smiled. "I scarcely think she was reading pornography."

"Queer," said Jesse. "Did you ever try to get a look?"

"She hated prying. We're supposed to be tactful," she said amusedly. "I couldn't, because she kept them locked in a drawer of the desk in the study—her husband's old desk. After that first time, she'd take the books away and bring more home about every two weeks. I do know they were library books because she dropped one once and didn't notice that her card fell out of it—a new library card made out to her. I just laid it on the table there for her to find."

"I wish to hell you'd got a look at some titles," said Jesse. "We're groping in the dark here, damnit. Anything that might have influenced her— Were there any left here when she had the stroke? Or have you looked?"

"I didn't have to." She looked a little somber. "She'd been out that afternoon, took the books with her, and didn't bring any back. She looked terribly tired, she didn't want any dinner, and said she'd go up to bed early. I got the bed ready, and turned on the automatic blanket—she felt the cold—and I was just getting out a clean nightdress for her when I heard her fall, in the bathroom. She was so thin, such a little woman— I got her on the bed and called the doctor and Mr. Manning from the upstairs phone. But she was conscious before the doctor got here, trying to talk. I tried to keep her quiet—"

"Do you remember what she said?"

"Poor thing," said Mrs. Lightner sadly. "The poor dear was frightened, just as I said. A woman like that—such a strong character, all she'd been and done. She wouldn't let go of my hand, and she kept saying, 'I'm afraid to meet her, if it's all true I'm afraid to meet them.'"

"I see," said Jesse. "I'd like to look over the house."

She got up at once. "It's what Mr. Manning calls it—a white elephant. And it's ridiculous for him to pay me nursing wages to be a sort of caretaker. Mrs. Hawes could come and house-sit until it's all settled and he can put it up for sale." At the door to the hall she glanced back at the living room. "I was sorry for her, you know. All that money that she'd given her life to making, and what pleasure did she get out of it? She didn't spend it on herself—clothes or jewelry or even nice furniture. I don't think anything's been done to this place, except painting and plumbing, since it was built. They fixed it up just the way Bob wanted it, and it's stayed that way."

Jesse turned to survey the living room, and realized that it might be a period piece in a museum, labeled *America circa 1935*. The furniture was mission oak, solid and heavy. There was an American-Oriental carpet not quite filling the room, its colors faded to muted gray. The Victrola was golden oak; the baby grand, ebony in need of polishing. There were three Maxfield Parrish prints, framed in heavy oak, on the walls. It was a dreary, sad room.

In the den, behind a cold-looking unused dining room filled with more mission oak, a massive old rolltop desk dwarfed a couple of armchairs and a steel file cabinet. Mrs. Lightner pulled out one of the bottom drawers; it was empty. There wasn't any comment to make. She led him through a square kitchen where, at least, modern appliances had replaced the originals, and up back stairs to a long hall. Four bedrooms and a bathroom opened off it. The three smaller bedrooms had dust sheets over all the furniture, so that they seemed tenanted by immobile unhappy ghosts. She opened the door to the left front bedroom, and said unexpectedly, "And she could have had so much out of life. If she could just have gotten over losing him—most women would have. But she—hung on to the grievance, how unfair it was. Like," said Mrs. Lightner, "tearing open a wound, never letting it heal. She'd have been very pretty when she was young, you know."

"Is there a picture? Was she?" He was hearing this and that about Claire Elizabeth, except what he wanted to know.

"I never saw any snapshots—Mr. Manning might have some. But she would have been. She had red hair, she told me once. That's the husband, of course."

The bedroom furniture was oak too, heavy and dark: a double bed, a long dresser, a vanity table with an oval mirror and a bench upholstered in gold velvet. The bedspread was gold velvet too, and the long curtains at the windows. A pair of low chests flanked the bed, a lamp with a gold shade on each, and on the one at the right stood a photograph, an eight-by-ten black-and-white print framed in an ornate gold frame.

Jesse studied it with interest. Robert Manning had been a vital-looking man, almost handsome; his son bore a distinct resemblance to him. Thick dark hair, a strong high-bridged nose, square cleft chin, and wide-set dark eyes with a little smile in them. Irrelevantly Jesse wondered just how different Claire Elizabeth would have been as an old lady if the drunk hadn't run that light forty-five years ago. Appointment in Samarra? It made you wonder.

"How were the household expenses paid?" he asked idly.

"Oh, Mr. Manning took care of all her banking, paying in whatever was due her, I suppose, and she wrote checks for the shopping and my salary, and for Mrs. Hawes." She watched him open the closet door. "How she'd have hated to have you prying like this." That was involuntary; she sighed. "It doesn't matter now."

"No." And probably the money had accumulated at the bank;

she hadn't spent much on clothes, at least. An old lady with no social life, practically no friends: neat and clean and going to the hairdresser's, but not clothes-conscious. The closet wasn't half full; a gray wool suit, several gray and black and navy dresses, a few lighter cotton dresses: six or seven pairs of comfortable old-lady shoes neatly aligned on the floor. He came back into the room. There was a leather jewel box on the vanity table. He opened it. Costume jewelry: a pearl necklace, a couple of gold brooches, a silver bracelet.

"The only thing she usually wore was her wedding ring."

"Yes." He discovered that the center well of the box was movable; it lifted right out, exposing another compartment below. It contained a few loose buttons, a pair of ancient silver cuff links, a handful of gray hairpins, and a much-folded paper.

He unfolded it carefully and after a moment said softly, "Well, I'll be damned."

"You found something."

"I did indeed." He was still looking at it. It was a receipt, dated last November. It bore a letterhead, *Arnold Chase Private Investigations,* and the same address on Melrose as the one he had for Peter J. Kellogg. A scrawl in the middle of the sheet read *received from C. E. Manning, services, $500.00.* "I did indeed," said Jesse.

He had probably delayed Winifred Lightner's lunch. He stopped at a coffee shop for a sandwich; it was two o'clock when he found a parking place down the block from the office building on Melrose.

This was an old, slightly tired area of Hollywood, and the office building had seen better days. It was six stories high, faced with tan brick, and looked dirty and shabby. The rents would be middling high because it was close in to downtown.

The board in the lobby listed Peter J. Kellogg, attorney-at-law, in Room 402, and Arnold Chase, Private Investigations, in Room 508. There was a small and noisy elevator; he rode up to the fifth floor.

The door labeled 508 was partly open, and somebody was typing inside, not in professional rhythm but hesitantly. Jesse shoved the door wider and went in, to a tiny reception office which held a small desk, a rickety office chair, a single file cabinet and a powerfully built middle-aged man in his shirt sleeves, hunched over the typewriter on the desk. He looked up.

"Mr. Chase?"

"That's me. Hell take all typewriters," said Chase cheerfully, swinging the chair around. He had a bulldog face and thinning gray hair. "I can't keep a receptionist for what I pay—they stay long enough so they can claim experience, and then off to greener pastures. They don't like all the reports to type either. Can I do something for you?"

"Probably." Jesse produced the receipt. "You remember anything about this?" He proffered a card.

Chase looked at both. "Sure," he said. "What's your interest?"

"Mrs. Manning is dead. She left a—mmh—rather unexpected will, which her son is going to contest, and we're sniffing around for some plausible grounds. Could probably get a subpoena, but it might be friendlier if you'd open up and tell me what services you did for Mrs. Manning."

"Well, I'll be damned," said Chase. "You don't tell me. Much money?"

"A bundle. In seven figures and on up."

"I will be good and damned," said Chase. "You'd better come in here." The inner office was bigger, with a battered golden oak desk, more filing cabinets, two chairs and a view out the rear of the building to an alley and the top of another old building on the next block. "Sit down," said Chase, taking the desk chair; it squeaked and rattled under his weight. "That one. I thought there was something a little funny about it, but I don't get paid to pry into a client's private business. Just other people's." He grinned. "I have a small hunch that I may have contributed to that unexpected will, Mr. Falkenstein. What do you want to know?"

"What did she want to know? This was back in November?"

"About the tenth, around there. I'd better get you the report. I keep copies around for a year or so—not much space." He rummaged in a file cabinet, took out a thin sheaf of stapled legal-size paper. "I wouldn't have remembered the names anyway. She came in here, no appointment, and asked if I could find out about some people back East. When she went on to explain—" He cocked his head at Jesse. "I like money as well as the next man, but I've also got a conscience. She was a dowdy little old girl, and she sure as hell didn't look like money. Black coat, no fur, gray dress, no makeup—looked like anybody's dear old grandmother in from the farm."

"Oh, if you only knew," said Jesse. "And?"

"I told her it might run into some money. I'd have to get hold of a private operative back there, pay him. She said it didn't matter what it cost. I said, just to warn her, it might run over a thousand—anything, if it was a long hunt. She never blinked an eye. She just wanted the information. So"—he shrugged—"I took the job. She gave me a retainer of three hundred."

"And what was she after?"

"She wanted to know if there were any relatives of one George Tilton still alive, and who they were and where. She said Tilton was her father, and she'd lost touch with all that family—there might be cousins—and she wanted to contact them again. Tilton had lived in Passaic, New Jersey. She didn't know if the cousins or whatever might still be there."

"And were they? You found out?"

Chase looked at the report in his hand. "We can make you a copy of this on the Xerox in the lobby. Yep. As a matter of fact, it turned out to be a fairly simple job, which I didn't expect, seeing she'd been out of touch with the family since 1928, she said. The nearest operative I could locate was in Newark—the Howard Phillips Agency. They sent a man over to Passaic and some records showed up right off. The local newspaper had a pretty complete morgue. Tilton died in 1928, and the obit turned up some names to look for, so the operative had a look at Vital Statistics at the city hall. It's all here." He waggled the report.

"What it boils down to, apparently Tilton married late and only had the one child, girl. Your Mrs. Manning. But he had a sister who'd married years before, and her son was a Raymond Pollock, who got married in 1900 and had four kids, son and three daughters. William, born 1901, Mary, born 1902, Susan, born 1905, Rose, born 1906. He couldn't find anything else on the girls—the family might have moved away later on—but there was a bit more on William in the newspaper. He got married in Passaic in 1927—evidently came back to the hometown for a bride, wherever he'd been since. There was a story on the society page about the wedding, and the happy couple was to live in New York. So our man had a look there in the official records, and traced them through half a dozen addresses between 1927 and 1975. There was a son born in 1930 at a Queens hospital— Adam Pollock. Last listing for William was 1975. After that, just Mrs. At a very classy apartment house. He asked some questions there and heard that she doesn't live there all the time, spends summers at her son's place in Highland Park, New Jersey. He was easy to find—a big place outside of town, looking like money. End of hunt."

"So you called her and said you had the information."

"She called me. She never gave me an address or phone."

"No, of course not. And?"

"She came in and I gave her the report. I asked if she wanted to follow it up any further, and she said this was all she needed, and thanked me. Wait a minute," said Chase. "I just remembered something. When she read over the report, all of a sudden she said, 'That's queer, he's just about John's age.' That mean anything?"

"No," said Jesse. Just a coincidence, that the unknown third cousin was about the same age as her own son she'd decided to disinherit.

"I told her the tab, and she wrote out a check without turning a hair. And that's all I can tell you."

"It's enough," said Jesse. "You'll be testifying at the hearing, Mr. Chase. What you tell us is that she'd been completely out of touch with this side of the family for"—he calculated—"nearly fifty-two years, and knew so little about them that she had to hire a private eye to find out their names and addresses. That'll be very helpful on the Unnatural Provisions ground. And I've got no idea when it might come up—you know the backlog in the courts. Just bear all this in mind."

"Will do," said Chase. "Good luck on it. I suppose the old girl had a bee in her bonnet about auld lang syne and family feeling —or had she just had a fight with the son?"

"No, oddly enough. And I wish to God I had any idea what bee she had in her bonnet," said Jesse querulously.

As he had expected, he found Peter J. Kellogg, attorney-at-law, unoccupied in a cubbyhole of an office with one very young eager-eyed receptionist. At a guess Kellogg was about a year out of law school, trying to build a practice and finding it uphill work. He was a long, thin young fellow with friendly brown eyes and reddish hair.

"I understand you want to make a will—"

"No," said Jesse, and handed him a card and the copy of Claire Elizabeth's will.

Kellogg looked at them blankly. "Well—is there anything wrong with it? What's your interest?"

"It's a perfectly good will. Too damned good. Drawn all according to Hoyle, Mr. Kellogg, just the way I'd have drawn it myself. Only it's going to be contested."

"My God, why?" Jesse told him and Kellogg said he'd be damned.

"I could wish you hadn't drawn the damned thing by the book. If you'd forgotten a few legal phrases, or gotten the date wrong or something, we could get it thrown out on a technicality."

"And maybe it's a shame I didn't, for your client's sake," said Kellogg interestedly. "What a mess. But now I know—that was a very cute old lady, Mr. Falkenstein."

"That I know. What way do you mean?"

"Well, she walked in out of the blue and said she wanted to make a will. I was glad to make the forty bucks. She had it all written out, how she wanted everything to go. The money to son and grandson—"

"You curious about the odd specified amounts?"

"You bet I was. We usually deal in round figures, don't we? I asked her about that, and she said that wasn't any of my business, all I had to do was put it in legal language. Of course she was right. I decided—she had a funny, precise sort of way of speaking—that that's exactly how much money she had, maybe stashed in a safe-deposit somewhere, and she was just splitting it between them."

"Logical. Did you ask any questions about the residue?"

"I did, and got snubbed again. It wasn't any of my business what it consisted of. Which, strictly speaking, it wasn't, but—" Kellogg paused and said, "I can't say I'm awfully surprised about this, Mr. Falkenstein. I'm not going to claim I've got ESP, and suspected she was pulling a fast one, and that's why I asked. I didn't. She certainly didn't look as if she had much money, and coming to me—" He glanced around the shabby office and laughed. "But there was something about her—if I can think of a word for it—"

"Furtive?" suggested Jesse. "Guilty?"

"No," said Kellogg doubtfully. "No. She was in a hurry to get it done—wanted it typed up right away. She sat and waited while Emily typed it up. And when she read it over and signed it, it was as if she was terribly relieved," said Kellogg. "That was it. She sort of let out a big sigh and leaned back in the chair. I'd got Emily in to witness it, of course, and while we were signing the rest of it, she just sagged in the chair and looked as if she'd lost all her worries."

"You don't tell me," said Jesse. "I wonder if that's surprising. Well, God knows when this will come up, but you've contributed a little—"

"Oh, and something else," said Kellogg. "All the finicky bits we have to put in—I had to know the county this Pollock lives in, and she didn't know. All she had was the town, Highland Park. I had to look it up in the atlas."

"Now that," said Jesse, "really is a contribution. Thanks very much. She was that far out of touch. Very helpful."

He finished the day at the offices of C.M.R. Management. It was a high-rise office building far out on Sunset, glittering and expensive, but when he got there he was surprised at the modesty of staff and space. Manning had a small private office with a secretary's cubicle off it. There was a larger office labeled Accounting with five men in it, another labeled Investments with two men, and one brisk blond secretary. Obviously everyone had been briefed to expect him.

The head accountant was Harry Fowler, a spare gray man who apologized for Manning's absence. "John ought to be back soon, he just went out to Bel Air on that condo deal— But we all know about this damned impossible thing, and anything we can do—"

Jesse was interested to meet young Jim Manning, who must take after his mother: more blond than dark, not as tall as his father, a good-looking young man with an easy smile; but his eyes were anxious. Just engaged, Jesse remembered, and seeing all this suddenly whisked out from under—he'd *be* anxious.

Five of the staff had been with the firm for twenty years or more. Only two of the accountants had not known Mrs. Manning, had been hired after she left five years ago. Jesse was mildly surprised to hear that the sleek blonde, Rita West, had been there fifteen years; she looked about thirty and might be ten years older. Fowler was the senior employee, there since 1945.

Fowler, two of the other accountants, and Rita West could testify that they had heard Mrs. Manning say this and that, to Manning, to other people, which clearly indicated that she regarded Manning as her natural heir and intended the business to pass to him on her death. They would all be eager and willing to stand up in court and say so, but unfortunately all of the incidents had taken place some while ago; Claire Elizabeth hadn't been coming into the office regularly for five years.

"She was a remarkable woman," said Fowler. "You've got to say that, Mr. Falkenstein. All I can think is that her mind was going—if she'd been herself she'd never have done such a thing. John is just wild. Besides everything else, it's terrible to think of her going like that—insane, really. All the time I knew her she was a very shrewd woman."

He'd taken Jesse into Manning's office. Rita West came in with two mugs of coffee, sugar, and dairy creamer on a tray. "I know she was the little tin goddess on a pedestal around here," she said dryly, "and of course she was quite a gal, Mr. Fowler—quite a character, all right. But I'll tell you one thing, if she hadn't retired when she did, I'd have quit before I got driven batty with the humming."

"Rita," said Fowler repressively, and then laughed. "Oh, well, I know what you mean at that. You got so you closed your ears to it automatically. I don't think she realized she was doing it—an odd habit."

"She hummed," said Rita to Jesse, "all the while. And usually the same thing over and over. Mostly the same tune—that old thing from the twenties, isn't it, 'Me and My Shadow.' When she switched occasionally to 'Blue Skies' or 'My Blue Heaven' it was such a relief you nearly enjoyed it."

"Just a habit," said Fowler, stirring his coffee. "She had faults and foibles like the rest of us. That house on Edgemont. I said to John, we can get rid of that at last—and now all this comes up. And that reminds me, the damned place is empty again. Rita, when he gets back bring another cup."

She smiled and nodded and went out.

Claire Elizabeth, who used to be a musician herself—that was an oldie, "Me and My Shadow." The twenties. "Faults and foibles is good, Mr. Fowler. Most of us have 'em. What about the house on Edgemont?"

Fowler sipped coffee and grimaced at its heat, put the mug down. "I suppose you could say it was the only piece of sentimentality she ever showed. You know," he added, staring past Jesse out the window, "I wish I'd known Robert Manning. He must have been quite a man, for her to mourn him all those years, so—so steadfastly." And he looked a little embarrassed to have said it. "She was a little fanatic about it—his very name, his memory— Oh, John, there you are."

Manning came in briskly, offered Jesse a quick hand, nodded at Rita who brought him coffee, helped himself to the dairy creamer and sat down in his desk chair. "Have you got anything useful, Falkenstein?"

"This and that. A few ideas," said Jesse, not altogether truthfully. "Mr. Fowler was just telling me—"

"That damned place on Edgemont," said Fowler. "The lease was up on the twelfth."

"Oh, hell," said Manning tiredly. "More trouble than it's worth."

"What about it?" asked Jesse. "Something to do with your mother?"

Manning laughed shortly and ran a hand over his hair. "I said, it was the only way I ever knew her to be sentimental," said Fowler. "And maybe it was on two counts at that."

"Maybe," agreed Manning. "It was the first piece of property they bought, that was all. They'd been living there, back in 1928, when the money came in. It's just a ramshackle bungalow, but she never would sell it. I don't know, sentimentality or superstition—the first investment. It's a damned nuisance. Brings in a bare couple of hundred a month when it's rented. But she wouldn't hear of selling."

Fowler said, "Do you remember the fuss about the freeway? You were just a youngster, of course—" He would be in his late sixties at least, a fixture here that long.

"Oh God, yes," said Manning. He leaned back and yawned. "Vaguely. When did it go through? After the war—I was in high school—"

"Just after. The Planning Commission," Fowler told Jesse, "was considering alternate routes, and one would have cut across Fountain and taken six blocks or so out of Edgemont and six or eight side streets— She was terribly worried about it." He drank coffee and smiled reminiscently. "I remember saying to her, what did it matter, and old Hansie—she wasn't old then, God, how time goes—just yelled at me, 'It was their first home together, you idiot!'"

"I've been thinking, we can get rid of it now," said Manning. "But we can't do anything until—" He looked at Jesse. "What do you think?"

"Oh, we'll have a case, Mr. Manning. Remains to be seen what a judge and jury think." At the moment Jesse was pinning more faith to Arnold Chase and Peter J. Kellogg than the staff of C.M.R. Management. But he would like to know a lot more about what had been in Claire Elizabeth's mind.

He got home at six-fifteen and suffered Athelstane's exuberant welcome. Nell was on the phone, and presently came in to report that the painters were at last due to start work tomorrow. She had finally decided on the carpet—tri-tone loop for all the downstairs rooms, sculptured beige for upstairs, and the new curtains were ordered. "Don't tell me what it's going to cost," said Jesse, relaxing over a drink.

Nell said dinner was in the oven and ready when he was. David Andrew had suddenly decided last week that it was time he began to walk, and was assiduously practicing the art, hanging grimly to Athelstane's collar for support. "He ought to be in bed," said Nell. "Nice party last night. I do like Mr. DeWitt."

Jesse rattled ice cubes in his glass. "And I might consult his tame psychometrist about Claire Elizabeth. That damned female, making all this trouble—"

"Who is she?" asked Nell lazily.

She was safe to talk to; he told her. "But fifty-two years," said Nell, going accurately to the heart of the thing. "Really, Jesse, even if she'd been sentimentally reminiscing about dear old days of youth and dear old friends—and she never did, apparently."

"Yes," said Jesse. "Whatever sentimentality she had was all for the unfairly departed husband. I haven't the least clue as to what was in her mind—could it conceivably go back all that way, to sometime before she was married? Damnit, I'd better go through that desk, all her things—secretive old soul, there might be something tucked away."

Nell was sipping sherry thoughtfully. "She wasn't really a cold woman, Jesse. She must have had a lot of fire and passion and what-all, to have done what she did—sublimating it all in the scramble for money, do you see? And all she had left at the end was just nothing, really. She was lonely and all alone—she'd pushed everybody away from her."

"Where does that send me?"

"I don't know," said Nell. "I'm sorry for her. I do hope she found him and everything's all right with them."

THREE

He had a nine-thirty appointment, and Nell prodded him awake half an hour early; he was never operating on all cylinders before noon, and swore at his razor and later at the scalding coffee. He got to the office at nine-fifteen and regarded the Gordons' serene morning faces grumpily; except for the certificate on the wall, the Gordons could run the office without him.

Jean brought him another cup of coffee and was tactfully silent. Jesse felt slightly more alive as the minutes passed. He didn't know what this client had in mind; he had only one other appointment today, at two-thirty, but there was the Ludendorf divorce hearing on Monday morning, and Mrs. Cliff's suit against Robinsons' was called for Tuesday. He had other things to do than play amateur psychiatrist for Claire Elizabeth.

At nine forty-five the new client called and told Jimmy vaguely that he wanted to think it over before talking to a lawyer.

"So I do some work on something else," said Jesse resignedly. "Don't take any appointments for next week, girls—I'll bet that damned suit is going to run at least three days and if the bench gets bored maybe four."

At ten-thirty he was cruising up Los Feliz Boulevard looking for the Trocadero Arms. Along here Los Feliz was all top-class apartments; in the thirties it had been a newly fashionable area, new residential streets opened up north of it. Since then a good many of the apartments had been rebuilt, enlarged, or refaced. The Trocadero Arms was a bare rectangle down toward Riverside Drive, ten stories high, its front fussy with square balconies, one to each four windows.

Wilma Hansen lived on the ninth floor. The elevator was

smooth and quiet, the carpeting in the halls plush. He couldn't hear the chime sound; the place was well built.

He waited two minutes, and was reaching for the bell again when the door opened halfway. "Who is it?"

"Miss Hansen?" He offered a card.

"Oh," she said. The door opened. "Oh, John said you'd want to see me. There's nothing I could tell you at all, but I suppose you'd better come in if you want to."

And here, of course, was someone who must have known Claire Elizabeth very well indeed. Jesse looked at her with interest. The first thing he noticed was that Wilma Hansen, unlike her late employer, was clothes conscious. She was smartly and neatly dressed in a black sheath, with a gold necklace and earrings. She was a tall, thin old lady and she'd never been especially good-looking; she had a long face with a long nose, and many wrinkles; but her gray hair was recently and smartly waved, and she wore a little too much makeup, a garish shade of lipstick. Her wrinkled, veined old hands were manicured, the polish a deep mauve.

She turned rather ungraciously to lead him into the living room, letting him shut the door. "John told me about it last night. It's a terrible thing for him, but I don't know what anybody can do about it. Claire always went her own way."

"You'd known her for a long time, Miss Hansen. You'd worked with her a long time. Did she tell you anything about it?"

She turned to face him, lowering herself into one of a pair of armchairs by the window. This was an expensive apartment, well and impersonally furnished. She sat down and crossed one knee over the other, composedly; she was wearing sheer silk stockings and stilt-heeled black patent leather pumps. No, she'd never been a beauty, but she'd learned to make up for it in smartness and grooming. Her pale blue eyes were protuberant, a little thoughtful. "So you're John's lawyer. I suppose you'd better sit down."

He took the chair opposite her. "Did Mrs. Manning tell you anything about it?"

"I wasn't expecting you so soon. I don't know why it all has to go on and on—it's bad enough that she's gone." Under the makeup some very real emotion was in the working of her mouth, the wretchedness in her eyes. "It was so queer—so queer she should go first—she was a couple of years younger than me, you know. I was her closest friend—it had been so long—it's not the same world with Claire gone."

"I can see you might feel that way," said Jesse gently. "How long were you with her?"

"It was nearly fifty years," said Wilma Hansen. "That's a long time. I didn't really want to retire when I did, but my arthritis was getting worse and of course I didn't have to worry about money. Claire was so good, so clever, she'd let me in on some very profitable things—I have a good annuity, and a pension besides. A long time. It was 1930 when I first knew her."

"Yes, a long time. You were her secretary—"

"Oh, not then. Not then. We were all just in real estate." Her eyes glazed a little. "It was when they had the first realty office out on Santa Monica—I was one of the saleswomen—it was all just commission then, and everything awfully slow, the first year of the Depression, you know. They'd just come back from San Diego and—"

"I didn't know about that. They'd been in San Diego?"

"Yes, Bob thought there might be some good opportunities down there. They were there for nearly two years, John was born there, but once the Depression got underway Bob thought this area would be bound to develop faster, on account of the studios. And of course he was right."

"And you'd worked with her all those years, she must have had confidence in you—" He led up to asking the question again. She was fiddling with her necklace, and she gave him a sudden absent smile.

"It's queer how clear it all is, looking back—a lot clearer than things that happened last year. When we were all young and happy together—we were, you know. It was supposed to be a bad time, people out of work and money so tight, the worst Depression there'd ever been, everybody said—but we had good times. Maybe because we were all young—but people were happy then, funny as it might sound to you. We used to go dancing a lot—Claire and Bob loved to dance, and they were good together. And you needn't think I couldn't have got married if I'd wanted to, I had boyfriends—there was Harry Schultz, he was in the office too, and Dick Ledyard—we used to go to the dance pavilion out on the pier, they didn't have the big bands like Russ Colombo or Whiteman, but good ones. I've been looking back a lot just since Claire died—it seems it was all music, that time. We used to sing—she had a really nice voice, I used to think she and Bob were good enough to be on radio. We'd be out dancing or somewhere nearly every night—"

"But then Manning was killed," said Jesse.

Wilma Hansen gave herself a little shake and her eyes focused on him more sharply. "It nearly killed Claire. And I couldn't leave her. It was about then Harry asked me to marry him, but I couldn't leave her. She—they loved each other so much. She was a wonderful woman, you know. When you think what she accomplished." Her gaze was purposeful now. "I don't know how much you know about her, but she had such—such willpower. She used to laugh and say she'd been a regular spoiled, lazy kid —her father was in his fifties when she was born and she always had everything she wanted, never had to turn a hand, everything just handed her. It was different for me, I grew up in an orphanage—the Ada M. Hershey Home for Girls—I was already tough, but Claire had it all to learn." The pale eyes were wandering again. "It was sort of exciting, especially at first—guessing and taking chances and figuring what areas might be growing fastest— And then she went into management instead of speculation, it was safer money and easier. I couldn't have left her, at first, and then—somehow it all went by so fast, and all of a sudden we were both old. It went so fast—"

"But after you'd both retired, you used to see each other. To play cards—talk."

"Yes, but I hadn't seen her for three weeks before—I was so sorry about that, the weather had my arthritis flaring right up and I couldn't get out." She looked distressed, her painted face pinched. "She was my dearest friend, all our lives. Such a wonderful woman."

"She made that will three months ago. Had she said anything about it to you?" he asked directly.

"Not a word. But that was Claire. She was close as an oyster about her own affairs. And she usually knew what she was doing. Only it's terrible for John. I don't know what he'll do." She raised a veined hand to her mouth. "He's always so good about coming, to make sure I'm all right—always a good boy."

"Do you have any idea why she did it?" asked Jesse. "Did she ever mention this cousin to you?"

"I never heard of any cousin. I think I knew sort of vaguely, that there were some relatives back East, but she never talked about them."

"She and Manning had met back there—New Jersey?"

"I think it was New Jersey, yes. Bob had worked his way through college—New York University—and he wanted to come out here and get into real estate, he thought it was the coming place, going to develop fast. He'd gone to college with a man who lived in New Jersey somewhere, I don't remember the town, he went to see him, and that's how he met Claire. Her father was all against the marriage—they had to elope."

Jesse sat and looked at her in silence, summing her up in his mind. A woman of superficial intelligence; faithful dogsbody to Claire Elizabeth. She had probably been a very efficient secretary, no imagination called for. Fanatically loyal and trustworthy on the company's business, but would Claire Elizabeth have confided more deeply in her? Very likely not. He thought about them, two women grown old together, sharing memories, sitting over a game of five hundred or rummy, companionable on the surface. Wilma Hansen had adored Claire Elizabeth, that was obvious, but he doubted if the feeling had been mutual. Claire Elizabeth using the devotion to her own advantage? Repaying it in her own way, with money.

"Why do you want to know all that, donkeys' years ago, anyway?"

"Just background," said Jesse. "As long as she never told you about the will—"

"I don't know anything about it. Not a thing," she said definitely. "It's awful for John. I can't imagine what he'll do."

"Well, thanks very much," said Jesse, and stood up.

As he pulled up in front of the big brick house Winifred Lightner was backing a bright red Honda down the drive. She stopped at the curb and got out. "You again. Some more prying to do? I'm just going out to the market—for the last time. Mrs. Hawes will be house-sitting until something's settled."

"I'll want your address, to let you know about the hearing."

"Oh, yes, Mr. Manning's got it. I'll be at my daughter's place in Pasadena. Mrs. Hawes is here, she can let you in."

Mrs. Hawes was a cheerful ragbag of an old woman who gave him a knowing leer when he introduced himself. "Ho, so that's who you are. We got orders to let you in, all right. Ask me, the missus wasn't near so smart as everybody thought—s'posed to be a regular know-it-all, come to business and makin' money. She ought to've known, leave everything in a mess like she did over that will, now you lawyers'll end up with most o' the money. Well, it's no skin off my nose. She paid me good for over twenty years, and give me clothes and such, and whatever happens about the money the Mannings'll be getting shut of this house. Not that that'll be easy to do, who'd want the place, I ask you. All them stairs, and so dark you got to turn a light on in broad daylight. I s'pose you can go where you want. Know your way around?"

Irrelevantly, remembering those sheeted rooms upstairs, Jesse wondered where Mrs. Lightner had slept, and asked. "Both of us like our comfort," said Mrs. Hawes. "Right where I'll be sleeping —maid's room and bath off the kitchen. They rigged up a bell the missus could ring if she needed her at night. My, wouldn't half give me the willies if it went to ringing some night." She chuckled richly.

Jesse went into the den and began to investigate the drawers in the rolltop desk. It took him ten minutes. He found in the top drawer a letter addressed to Robert Manning dated June 12, 1934. In the others, a folded page of classified real estate ads from the *Citizen-News* (when had that folded? before the war or after?); a few more business letters, the latest dated February 1935; a broken comb; a screwdriver; a long-defunct, tarnished cigarette lighter. In the right-hand top drawer was a box of stationery with her letterhead on it, this address. And that was all.

Bob's desk, maybe a new desk hardly used, moved here when the house was ready for occupancy, and seldom touched or looked at since? Left the way Bob had left it? Or had she sometimes sat here, in Bob's chair, remembering and—keeping the wound open? In a sense, he wondered whether you could say Claire Elizabeth had been an entirely sane woman all these years, hugging the hurt to her so fiercely, building a monument to him with C.M.R. Management. And then, thinking of what Wilma Hansen had said, suddenly he understood more clearly just how it must have been for her. She had done the only thing before her to do—carried on Bob's business just as he would have, teaching herself to do it well, getting interested as the profits began to come; and the time had slid by, the years going down into limbo faster and faster, until suddenly she was an old woman. And in that time, living and planning and working alone, she had learned to keep her own counsel. It had been a long time since she'd had to explain herself to anybody; and she had left no explanations behind.

He wandered through the dining room back to that dreadful gloomy living room. The baby grand sat silently in the dark corner, the Victrola beside it. He'd never seen one of those antiques close, come to think of it; he raised the lid and it creaked protestingly. He compared its inner arrangements with his new stereo. He raised the piano lid and looked at long-yellowed keys, tapped out a scale with one finger and winced. The piano hadn't been tuned in years.

Turning, he stumbled against the piano bench and its lid rose and fell with a little sharp thud. He shoved it up and then stared at the contents.

"Oh, it's you," said Mrs. Hawes. "Thought we had a ghost for a minute."

"At the piano? But she never played it, did she?"

"Never touched it. Used to, I s'pose. She did tell me once her father'd given it to her on her eighteenth birthday." She went back down the hall.

The piano bench was stuffed full of old sheet music. He began to go through it curiously, and he reflected that it might possibly be worth something—there were collectors, and most sheet music of this vintage would be long gone with the wind. Long before his time, but history was frozen to look at in books, old movies, old memories. A piano player in every dime store, and the sheet music for sale—*price 10¢*— And most of this was in mint condition.

There was "Moonlight Bay" and "Sunbonnet Sue" and "Oh, You Beautiful Doll"—"Carolina in the Morning" and "The Sheik of Araby" and "I'll See You in My Dreams"—"Japanese Sandman" and "Chicago" and "Who's Sorry Now"—and then sandwiched in, going even farther back, "Over There" and "There's a Long, Long Trail A-Winding" and "Bugle Call Rag" and "Keep the Home Fires Burning."

"Whispering" and "Kitten on the Keys" and "Nola"—"Linger Awhile" and "Sweet Georgia Brown" and "Runnin' Wild"—"Blue Skies," "When Day Is Done," "Me and My Shadow," "I'm Forever Blowing Bubbles," "The Man I Love," "When Francis Dances with Me," "I Wonder What's Become of Sally," "All By Myself," "Somebody Stole My Gal"—

He was holding Claire Elizabeth's youth in his hands, he thought. The gay and happy times, because they'd all been young whatever the times. Out of books of old nostalgia the decade swam into his mind, what the world had been like when Claire Elizabeth and Bob Manning had been young and happy and hopeful. An era of nonsense, seen from here, and of naïveté. Flagpole sitters and marathon dancers—Model T flivvers and raccoon coats, ukuleles and speakeasies—and the bootleggers organizing the first gangs. The antiwar novels and the first idols of the silver screen—the talkies and the first national radio hook-up . . .

It was aeons away, another world and time. But it had been part of her time, and she hadn't been phenomenally ancient. Time's wingèd chariot, he thought.

He shut the music back into the piano bench and went up the front stairs. Mrs. Lightner, tactful, wasn't a woman to pry into things, which Claire Elizabeth would have known and appreciated. But had she left any more little secrets buried away somewhere? The receipt from Chase hadn't really been a secret, at that.

He started with the closet. Only her clothes, and on the shelf stacks and stacks of cardboard boxes. He took the top one down; it was filled with envelopes of canceled checks, the dates fairly recent. He tried the bottom one in the first stack, and found checks dating back to 1950. He put the boxes back and started a systematic search through drawers.

Nothing but underclothes in the long dresser: scarves, stockings, gloves, handkerchiefs in the smaller top drawers. In the vanity table's two shallow drawers, hairpins, a box of powder, a miscellany of old lipsticks, a brush and a comb, a package of new powder puffs. In the left-hand bedside chest, neatly folded nightgowns. In the other, a box of tissues in the top drawer. In the second drawer, there was only an old-fashioned embroidered handkerchief case. He picked it up and felt it, and there was something stiffer than handkerchiefs inside. He drew out the contents and spread them on the bed. Eight colored handkerchiefs, looking brand new, and a letter in an envelope.

There was a canceled three-cent stamp on the envelope, which bore no return address; the postmark was smudged and illegible. It was addressed in a neat small hand, in green ink, to Mrs. Robert Manning, 1209 Edgemont St., Hollywood, Calif. The address had been crossed out and another hand had scrawled below it: *Manning Realty, 1960 Santa Monica Blvd.*

Jesse took out a twice-folded sheet; it was cheap stationery, a plain white six-by-eight sheet. The writing in green ink was plain as print.

247 West 67th St.
New York, N.Y.

July 1, 1931

Dear Claire,

I expect you'll be surprised to hear from me, and not very pleased. But I never felt right about what happened. I know you must be feeling angry at all of us, not writing to you and feeling as we did, but that is water under the bridge and best forgotten.

I don't have to tell you that this has been a bad time for us. Bill has been out of work since last year and while he hopes to be taken on at Bradley and Forbes soon, it isn't at all certain. Claire, I know that you cannot be in quite such straits as the rest of us, and if you could possibly lend us a hundred dollars it would be a godsend. You know that Bill will repay you as soon as he gets steady work. I'm ashamed to ask you, but I just don't know where else to turn.

Perhaps you'd be interested to know that we have a little son, born last year.

I'll hope to hear from you as soon as possible, and hope you will be glad to feel I am

Always your friend,
Anne

"Well, well," said Jesse to himself. And this hadn't lain in that handkerchief case since 1931, or had it? Conceivably it could have. Or it could have been brought out from some other hiding place recently—but why? And why had she kept it?

He wondered if Claire Elizabeth had answered that letter, whether she had sent the hundred dollars to her friend Anne. Or whether she hadn't, and coming across that letter just recently (in Bob's desk?) had reread it and felt remorse at ignoring it back then.

Anne who? Bill. And a son born last year—1930. Could that be Adam Pollock? And there'd been some quarrel, but not on Claire Elizabeth's part—they had been angry at her. Why? Still over her marriage?

He put it back into its envelope and tucked it in his breast pocket. Going downstairs, he encountered Mrs. Lightner in the hall. "Did she," he asked abruptly, "keep any household accounts?"

"Oh, dear, yes, she was most particular about keeping accounts of everything—I suppose it was her business training. She didn't use the den, she'd sit in her own chair in the living room working on them, and she kept everything in the little chest by the door to the hall. The current canceled checks and the account book."

He pulled out the top drawer. An ordinary dime-store account book: he glanced at the first page. Her neat sloping backhand was firm; the page was headed 1979 and the list below, line by line, was mundane. *Gardener $25. Mrs. Lightner $500. Groceries $77.24. Electric bill $92.54.*

There wouldn't be anything secret in that. And he had an appointment at two-thirty.

The new client was prompt; Jesse came in to find him waiting, and asked Jean to get hold of Dr. Whymant and ask if he could see him and when. The client wanted advice about a rather complicated land-lease on property about to be condemned by eminent domain, and Jesse had to look up a few new statutes.

That took an hour or so, and as he ushered the client out Jean said, "Dr. Whymant says he can see you at five, at his office. And Mr. Grossman called about that insurance claim, it hasn't come through yet and he wants you to write a nasty letter and scare them."

"You can do that," said Jesse. "I'll bet you can write a nastier letter than I can."

She widened her big brown eyes at him. "Oh, Mr. Falkenstein, you say the nicest things."

Jesse supposed that some sad day a couple of personable young men would carry off his Gordon twins; but hopefully not soon, and not both together.

"Manning called, but I didn't have time to talk to him," said Dr. Edward Whymant. "A lawyer? What's it all about?"

Jesse explained. Dr. Whymant, at the end of office hours, looked tired; he was a short, ruddy elderly man with a bald head and a jutting little gray goatee. He listened noncommittally and said, "Funny business. I can see it would be a shock to Manning. I understand there's a lot of valuable property. Wonder what the old lady got into her head."

"You knew her fairly well?"

Whymant shrugged. "None of them are the kind of patients a doctor gets rich from." He wouldn't have much bedside manner; his tone was blunt, offhand. "I delivered both of John and Ruth Manning's youngsters. The old lady came to me on their recommendation about twenty years ago. She said then she hadn't seen a doctor since her son was born. She was just beginning to feel her age a little, pulled down with a case of flu. I didn't see her often—once a year she'd come in for a flu shot, simple checkup.

She just had the debilities of old age—little arthritis, and she was on medication to keep her blood pressure down."

"Would you say she was completely sane—always seemed rational? When was the last time you saw her?"

"The night she died."

"Before then—when she was in the hospital in August?"

Whymant polished his bald head with one hand. "You're not going to pin me down, Mr. Falkenstein, because I don't know—I couldn't give a definite opinion. She seemed perfectly rational and mentally competent, but I didn't have occasion to talk with her all that much. What we know these days about the brain—certain areas responsible for memory, sensations, various emotions, that can be activated separately by some purely physical cause—and particularly in aged people—for all I know she might have been quite sane on ninety-nine subjects and psychotic on the hundredth. You get that kind of thing, even in younger people."

"Faults and foibles," said Jesse. "Yes. But if you had to give an opinion, would you say that she seemed rational, in control of her faculties, say during that illness in August and later on?"

Whymant pursed his lips. "The few minutes here and there I saw her, yes," he said cautiously. "But I'd be a long way from swearing she was completely sane. I wasn't conversing with her —I was listening to her heart, taking her blood pressure, asking questions—elimination normal, much pain in that hip, and so on."

Jesse looked at him. No, he wouldn't be pinned down, which was a nuisance.

Whymant grinned at him. "Sorry if that annoys you, but I'll give you an example. Old lady I've got in a convalescent hospital right now. Strikes you as a really delightful old lady, mentally sharp and nothing wrong with her at all except for the rheumatoid arthritis. She's got just one quirk—she's convinced that television sets emit death rays, and won't stay in the same room with one. Talk to her all day long on any other subject, you'd swear she was as sane as you or me."

"Yes," said Jesse, "but—"

"I should think, if Mrs. Manning had any quirks, the family or that nurse she had with her would be likelier to know."

The only snag there was, of course, that secretive nature. Suppose—to reach way out into the blue—she had convinced herself
that because she'd ignored Anne's letter forty-nine years ago she
owed Anne's son all of her money—which was a ridiculous assumption but *possible*—she had kept it to herself and nobody
could know. "I'd also like," said Jesse, "to talk to the nurses at the
hospital."

Whymant said agreeably, "Why not? Doubt if they can tell
you anything. I don't know which ones were on her case—last
August or when she died—but the hospital will. I'd better give
you a note—hospitals don't like to gossip about patients."

Jesse thanked him. If he wanted to see the nurses who had
been with her when she was admitted to emergency, or with her
when she died, he'd have to wait until the three-to-midnight shift
was on; and he didn't feel like talking to nurses right now. It
was five-forty.

What he did do, on his way home from Whymant's office on
Third Street, was to make a detour up Fountain Avenue to where
Edgemont crossed it, one of the humdrum narrow little residen-
tial streets of mid-Hollywood.

It wouldn't be dark for nearly an hour; the sun was westering.
Its toward-twilight rays softened the ugliness of the streets, the
tired old buildings. All of this had been here a long time, and not
much face-lifting had been done over the years. Fountain was
narrow, lined with blocks of small businesses, little neighborhood
markets, liquor stores, shoe-repair shops and beauty parlors, interspersed with courts and apartments. At the corner where
Edgemont crossed there was a drugstore, a cleaners', a snack
shop and a gas station on the four corners; a block and a half up
loomed the pile of the Cedars of Lebanon Hospital. Down Edgemont were single houses on fifty-foot lots, some with smaller
houses in the rear, two six-story apartments, and an eight-unit
court.

The curb was clear in front of 1209, and he drew in and
looked at it. A shabby little old California bungalow, painted
white with green trim and needing a new coat of paint. This vintage, he could almost visualize its inside: a combination living
and dining room, kitchen and service porch one side, two small
bedrooms and bath the other side. There was a single garage at

the end of a driveway composed of twin cement strips with grass between. The little lawn in front of the house was still green—they'd had a wet winter—but in need of cutting.

The house hadn't been new when Claire Elizabeth and Bob Manning had rented it—later bought it. It probably dated from the teens. At one time, and about the time they lived here, this would have been a settled, permanent neighborhood—most of the single houses occupied by owners, at least. Now, with a more transient population taking over the older parts of town, the elderly retiring into the suburbs to live with younger families, or to senior-citizen complexes or nursing homes—and the fairly affluent fleeing the middle city for the valley or the beach—very likely renters accounted for most of the residents along here.

He wondered, looking along the block where a scattering of boys chased a ball down the sidewalk, whether it was possible that there was anybody still around here who had known Claire Elizabeth and Bob Manning then. He only knew they'd been living in this house in 1928, and they might have lived here longer ago—he seemed to recall that Manning had said they'd been married in 1925. Fifty-five years.

Too long a time.

But there could be people around who remembered them. She hadn't been ancient; plenty of people lived into their eighties. Somebody, perhaps, who had been friends back then? People, young women, she had talked to? Had Claire Elizabeth, all that while ago, been as close-mouthed and stern and secretive as she was as an old lady?

Somebody who, memory prodded, could say, "Oh, yes, I remember Claire telling me about that family quarrel—"

It was probably a very vain hope. Jesse turned the key in the ignition.

At least on Saturday there weren't any office hours to keep. Nell departed with the baby to oversee the painters, and Jesse consulted the County Guide and drove down to the public library on Hillhurst, which was the nearest one to Valle Vista Place.

The several librarians he talked to were cooperative, but at a loss. They had, they told him, a lot of people coming in, and regular patrons they could identify, but they didn't remember her name. They shook their heads. Records? All the records were on microfilm, and filed by dates, not card-holders' names or titles; it would take a month to go through those checking for what books Mrs. Manning had taken out. In any case only authorized personnel had access to the records.

"She wasn't familiar with libraries," said Jesse. "It's possible she asked for some help in locating books."

The head librarian, a woman named Thompson with an ample bosom and suspiciously black hair, said at once, "Then she probably went to the Readers' Assistant desk, to Mrs. Catchpole. That's her desk over there, but she isn't in until noon on Saturdays."

Frustrated, Jesse withdrew; but he'd had another idea overnight, and sought out the Hollywood dispatching office of the Yellow Cab Company, on La Brea. Eventually he penetrated into an inner office and talked to one of the dispatchers, a friendly redhead named Marge.

"Oh, yeah, Mrs. Manning," she said. "One of the regulars. We don't really get all that much business, you know. I sometimes wonder how it pays, keep the cabs on the streets. It's not like New York, anywhere back East—practically everybody's got cars here. We've only got two dispatchers on this station."

"You remember Mrs. Manning? You'll have a record of where she was driven when?"

"Sure, but I guess it'd quicker for you to talk to Joe or Freddy. She'd been calling a cab a couple of times a week, sometimes oftener, for about the last five years, and it was always in the afternoon when they're both on. She likes Joe, she'd ask for him if he wasn't on a run, or Freddy. Joe Bolsa, Freddy Knight. I could get hold of Joe, he's just cruising the last I heard, and call him in. Should I?"

"I'd make it worth his while, thanks."

She came to him in three minutes and said Joe was coming in. "He was only over on Sunset."

Jesse waited in front of the building, and presently a cab drew into the private lot alongside it and a short, stocky, dark fellow got out of it. Jesse went to meet him. "Mr. Bolsa?"

"That's me. What's it all about?"

"Is there somewhere we can talk?" Jesse nodded at a coffee shop across the street. "I'll buy you a cup of coffee."

"Okay," said Bolsa amiably. They waited for the light and crossed; there were empty booths at this time of day.

Jesse told the story succinctly; he was getting bored with explanations, but Bolsa was quick to pick up implications. "Well, God, I'm sorry to hear she's dead," he said. "She was a nice old lady. That's crazy, her leaving all her money to a stranger. I knew she had money, all right. She sure as hell didn't look it, but you can always tell. She didn't care what the fare was, kept me waiting with the meter ticking over lots of times, and she was a good tipper—which the money people aren't always," and he grinned, stirred sugar into his coffee.

"I'd like to know," said Jesse, "about places you took her—say the last six months. If she went to different places than she used to before that."

Bolsa put his spoon down and said, "You got ESP or what, Mr. Falkenstein? Different places is right."

"So tell me," said Jesse softly.

"Well—" Bolsa scratched his ear reflectively. "There's a sort of rough date on it, see. You know that she was pretty sick, in the hospital, last fall?"

"August."

"I guess so. There was about a month she didn't call a cab to go anywhere, far as I know. Then when I got sent to pick her up —starting sometime in September—well, she went to different places. Before that, it was pretty regular times and places. Thursdays I took her to this beauty parlor, the Silver Comb on Hollywood Boulevard, let her off at one and pick her up at two-thirty. And she'd go to the shopping mall where that big Robinsons' is, in Beverly Hills. I'd wait for her maybe a couple of hours while she shopped or just looked around or had lunch there sometimes. That was about it. After she'd been sick, it was different. She had me take her to the old Hollywood Cemetery a few times, and I waited maybe an hour. And she started going to the library—the one on Hillhurst. She went there about once every couple of weeks, and took out books. And, if you'll believe me, she wanted to go down to Venice. She asked me to park where she could look at the old pier. She said there used to be a big dance hall out at the end of it, where she and her husband went to dances." He shook his head, sipped coffee. "And once she went down to Exposition Park. She had me park and wait, and when she came back to the cab she was crying. I felt sorry, and helped her in, and she said she was just being silly, they used to go to dances at one of the park buildings, old-fashioned dances with quadrilles and polkas and all, and now it was just a storage place for the museum."

Lonely and all alone, Nell had said. Claire Elizabeth revisiting her youth.

"It was kind of pathetic," said Bolsa thoughtfully. "I got the idea she was awful lonely, even though she had a family. A lot of people don't figure—you know—the old people have any feelings left."

"Where else did she go?"

Bolsa didn't answer directly. "There was another time, she told me to drive down to Venice, to the pier, and she didn't like freeways, wanted to go surface streets. I was out on Santa Monica, and caught a light, and all of a sudden she said to turn left there —it was Curson, far as I remember—she said some dear old friends of theirs used to live there, pointed out a house—oh, hell, I couldn't tell you which one now, but she said the name—" Bolsa stared out the window past Jesse's shoulder. "I was sorry for her."

"You don't remember the name?"

"It was a funny one. I don't. I went on up to Sunset, round the block to get back onto—my God, *Bakewell!*" said Bolsa, his eyes rapt on the window. "It just came back to me, that Van De Kamp bakery truck catching the light—she said Virgil and Wanda Bakewell. That's funny, it coming back to me— And I took her down on Edgemont Street a few times, she just sat and looked at a house, an ordinary little house."

"That's about it?" asked Jesse.

"All I could tell you. I don't know what it could say. She was a nice woman—I felt kind of sorry for her," said Bolsa. "Lonely." He finished his coffee. "Will I have to testify in court or something? It doesn't seem to add up to much."

"I don't know—probably not," said Jesse. "But thanks very much, anyway." He handed over a ten.

"I don't figure it's worth that," said Bolsa. "But I'm glad I could help you. If all that means anything."

And he'd talk to the other cabdriver just to see if anything else interesting showed. But what that said—she'd been going back to all the places she used to go with Bob, reliving old days? Visiting Bob's grave?

It didn't point in any direction, to say what had been going on in her mind.

It was twelve-thirty. He swallowed a milkshake at a fast-food shop on Sunset and went back to the library.

The Readers' Assistant, Mrs. Constance Catchpole, was there, and Jesse couldn't think of a plausible excuse to ask questions about Claire Elizabeth's choice of reading matter.

She was a slender blond woman about forty, and she remembered Mrs. Manning without difficulty. "I showed her how to make out her library card, she said she'd never had one before. What exactly do you want to know, and why?"

"Did you help her to find the books she wanted?"

"Yes, that's right. Why do you want to know?"

"You can take it that it's an official inquiry," said Jesse brusquely. "Mrs. Manning is dead, and there's some irregularity about her will. And anything which may have influenced her before she died—there'll be a legal investigation," and he handed over a card.

"Oh, I *see*." She didn't, exactly, but capitulated. "That's rather queer. You wanted to know about the books she checked out. They were all the same kind—she asked me where to find them, at first, and after that she knew where to look. They were all books about death. Death, and dying, and ghosts, and mediums —all the books like that."

FOUR

Jesse stared at her. "Oh. Like that."

"The first time I saw her, she wanted a copy of Dr. Raymond Moody's *Life After Life*. It's about people who have clinically died and then come back, and what happened to them. It's quite an interesting book—"

"I know it, yes."

"There was a copy in, and that's when she took out a library card. The next time she came in, she asked me if there were other books like that. I don't think she'd ever been a reader—she said she'd seen Dr. Moody's book mentioned in a magazine article somewhere. I showed her where everything in that field would be—psychic research and spiritualism and so on—the 130's to 133's," said Mrs. Catchpole. "I couldn't say how often she came in after that or what else she checked out, but the couple of times I noticed her here, she was always at that stack—the 130's."

"Thanks so much, that's enlightening," said Jesse. It was. That excellent nurse Winifred Lightner going straight to the truth? Claire Elizabeth realizing she hadn't much time left, and—no religious background?—or having turned away from some orthodoxy, open-mindedly curious or seeking desperately for some hope?—solemnly studying the various researches on death, and survival, and communication.

He found the stack in one corner of the big room and looked to see what they had. He wondered exactly what she had read. Besides the Moody book, there were a good many of the classics —William James, Gardner Murphy, Lodge and Doyle; *The History of Spiritualism*, a battered copy of *Raymond*, *The ESP Reader*, *The Mystery of the Human Aura*, *Nothing So Strange*, *Between Two Worlds*, *The Mediumship of Mrs. Gladys Osborne*

Leonard, This Is Spiritualism, Ghosts and Hauntings, a hodge-podge of popular miscellaneous stuff, Steiger and Tralins, Susy Smith, other standard moderns. There was a row of Cayce miscellany after *Venture Inward,* and further on was Rhine—*Hidden Channels of the Mind, ESP in Life and Lab.* There was all of Cerminara, *Many Mansions, The World Within, Many Lives, Many Loves.* He wondered very much what she had read and what she made of it—possibly the first books she'd read since she left school, except the real estate texts. The mounds of evidence, so much significant and suggestive but unprovable; the tiny gold residue of unassailable evidence not to be shaken by the hardest-nosed skeptic; the majority of the evidence not to be proven but emotionally convincing.

What she had said to Mrs. Lightner—had she been looking for hope, that she'd find Bob again?—or to prove to herself it was all nonsense and hope for oblivion? Again she left him at a standstill; she was an enigma; he didn't know.

When he left the library he went to find the other cabdriver, being thorough. Freddy Knight had called in sick, but the dispatcher Marge had given Jesse his home address. It was Palm Grove just above Jefferson Boulevard, a middle-class black area. The address was a single house, a modest frame newly painted pale yellow, with a neat patch of lawn in front.

Knight answered the door. He was a tall, thin fellow, medium brown, in his early thirties. He was in pajamas and an old bathrobe, and obviously miserable, with a hacking cough and looking feverish, but he overrode his pretty wife's protests and let Jesse in.

"Take less time to oblige the man than for you to cuss him out, hon. If you're not afraid of my germs," he added to Jesse. It was a shabby but comfortable little living room. "You said you're from the company? What can I do for you, sir?"

Jesse told the little story again. "Mr. Bolsa gave me some information, but I understand you drove her sometimes too."

"That I did," said Knight. "Mrs. Manning. Yeah, she was a nice old lady. I probably didn't drive her as often as Joe, but if he wasn't available she'd ask for me. That's right what Joe told you, the last five or six months she'd taken to going different places."

"Can you remember some places you took her?"

Knight started coughing again, got out a handkerchief, blew his nose. "First damn cold I've had in five years. Yeah, I could tell you. Not exact dates, but the company'd have a record. Once I took her up into Griffith Park, all around by the Greek Theatre and up to the top of the hill. She was telling me how she and her husband and their friends used to have picnics there on Sundays, years ago. And how she remembered when the observatory was built up there." He started coughing again. "Another time," he went on thickly, "I took her—that was funny—to Manchester High School."

"She say why?"

"I guess she saw I was wondering about it, just an old school, and she said a way back they used to hold dances in the gym there on Saturday nights—public dances—way back in the Depression. The last time I drove her anywhere—" The cough silenced him for a good three minutes, he wheezed and blew his nose, sat up and swore mildly. "Damn it, I thought I felt better this morning, but this damn cough hangs on— It was about a month back, and she wanted to go to Forest Lawn."

"Forest Lawn. What did she look at there?"

"A grave," said Knight.

"And you couldn't tell me whose," said Jesse.

"Well, I can, then. It wasn't that long ago. She didn't know where it was, she stopped at the office to ask, and a fellow came out and gave me directions how to find it. You know all those steep hills and curving streets and slopes down from the road with all the graves—when we got where it ought to be, I parked and found it for her. It was a damn steep hill, I had to help her down to it. It was just one of those flat plate things, you know how they do, and it said Louis V. Domino on it."

Jesse contemplated him with interest. "You're sure of the name?"

"Swear on the Bible. She never said a word, about whether he was a friend or relative or what. She just stood there about five minutes looking at it, and the view down the hill over Glendale, and then she turned and started up the hill again to the cab, told me to take her home."

"I'll be damned," said Jesse. "That's something new." Slowly he brought out his billfold, handed over a ten.

"You didn't need to pay me to answer a few questions," said Knight. "She was kind of a funny old lady, some ways."

Back in the Mercedes, Jesse thought about that; it was, at the moment, just another mystery.

But interesting.

Three-thirty found him at the old Hollywood Presbyterian Hospital on Vermont, talking to two nurses. They had both nursed Mrs. Manning when she was here in August and later when she died here. There'd have been others, but these would have been on duty during visiting hours.

"Well, yes," said the older one, Mrs. Currier, to that question, "but we're not supposed to go in when there are visitors unless it's necessary. Medication or something. Of course she was in a private room, both times."

"What exactly did you want to know?" asked the other one, Miss Nathan. The doctor's note had produced cooperation, but they were puzzled.

"Did either of you happen to notice what her feelings seemed to be toward the family—toward her son? Were they affectionate? He come to see her often? How did she—"

"Oh, I see," said Miss Nathan. "Yes, he was here every day— that was both times she was in. The rest of the family, not so often. The way Meg says, we don't go in when there are visitors unless we have to, but especially the last time when she was so bad, I was in and out a lot and so was Meg. There was the I.V. and catheter to check and she was wired to the monitor, if there was any little change we had to check her—"

"And one thing I will say," said Mrs. Currier half humorously. "The old saying is, *in vino veritas,* but in my experience serious illness tells you just as much about a person. They're past covering up, if you see what I mean. And Mrs. Manning—she was a nice woman. As weak as she was, she'd try to say please and thank you. And you could tell she was awfully fond of Mr. Manning—just the look in her eyes."

"He was here the night she died," said Miss Nathan. "Just him, not the rest of them. I noticed a change in her cardiac rhythm and went in to look. She was trying to sit up, and she was hanging onto his hand for dear life and saying to him, 'You're all that's left of Bob, all that's left to me.' You can see—"

Jesse could see. They would be two more witnesses on Manning's side. But riding down in the elevator, he wasn't feeling optimistic. If he produced a hundred witnesses to swear to her affection for Manning, her intentions (too far back) of leaving him everything, against that was that damned tightly drawn will, and Chase to tell how she'd gone to some expense locating the cousin, Kellogg to tell how rational she sounded, instructing him what to put in the will. True, she'd been evasive with Kellogg. True, so far out of touch with the family she'd had to pay Chase to find out about them. Nitpicking.

If he had some sure idea about her reason—why her mind had groped back that far— He found he was coming around to accepting Tregarron's sweeping generalities. One of those little areas in the brain must have been triggered off by a wrong stimulant, something like that. She'd been fond of Manning; damnit, one of the reasons she'd labored at piling up all the money was for Manning—for Bob's son. Only a brainstorm of some kind could have changed her intentions—and her secretiveness and habitual silence keeping any suspicion at bay until she was dead and the will turned up.

With his hand on the car door, he stiffened and stared at the bunch of keys in his hand. The safe-deposit vault, he thought. Where did she bank? Mrs. Lightner had said that Manning paid his mother's income in to the bank and she wrote checks. Neither cabdriver had mentioned taking her to a bank. But she'd had a safe-deposit box—that was where the will turned up.

For God's sake, he thought, how wild could he get? Just for a flash wondering if that had been Claire Elizabeth who made that will? Some deep-laid plot, with a similar little old lady impersonating her, forging her signature—not only to the will, but to get into the safe-deposit box . . .

Ridiculous, of course.

And Saturday was supposed to be a day off, but there was going to be a lot more looking and thinking to do about Claire Elizabeth. It was a damned good thing the case wouldn't be coming up for a while; all he had to offer a jury was the Unnatural Provisions line and a few witnesses, and he was feeling pessimistic about it.

He drove down Vermont, turned on Santa Monica, ambled slowly up to Van Ness. The old Hollywood Cemetery occupied a couple of square blocks to his left there, behind high cement walls. He found a public lot a block away and walked back.

There was a small office and maintenance building just past the entrance gate. Inside, a youngish man in a tan jump suit was sitting at a desk, reading a paperback copy of *Gone With the Wind*. He looked up vaguely when Jesse rapped on the open door.

"Well, I don't know, but we can look it up in the records. There's a list of everybody here." He had to hunt for it, but found it at last and looked. "Yeah, here he is, way out in back. I'd better show you, it's over in the old part." They walked gravel paths beside green lawn and old-fashioned grave markers, and just inside the cement wall at the far end of the cemetery the attendant pointed it out: an unpretentious square headstone.

Robert Wilson Manning 1900–1935. And that was all.

The rest, thought Jesse, is silence. Or is it?

"Many people come in to visit graves?"

"Hardly any," said the attendant. "This is an old cemetery. I guess most of the people had somebody buried here'd be dead themselves now. Years ago, they tell me, we used to get crowds —there are some old movie stars buried here—we've got Valentino, you know. Years ago there used to be crowds of dames come to visit the grave. I saw one of his pictures once at that Silent Movie House, it was real corn—terrible. But I guess everybody's forgot him now."

She hadn't come here regularly, at least in the last five years, until she came four or five months ago. Up until five years back she'd been driving; but also she'd still been going into the office, living a busier life. And very possibly, until she started reading all the books she hadn't given any thought to the grave or a possible life beyond it.

Sometime, he thought, he must talk to Ruth Manning. But not when Manning was around. She'd be inclined to more frankness with him out of earshot. Try to find her home sometime on Monday.

He got back to Vermont, went up to Los Feliz and drove over to Glendale, to Forest Lawn Memorial Park. Past the tall iron gates he stopped at the office. Here all was efficiency and courtesy; he was given precise directions, and drove up the steep winding little narrow streets to the area called Sunset Slope. It was a slope all right, a precipitate one; down there about forty feet from the road he found it. A flat bronze plaque—headstones were *verboten* here—with the bare information. *Louis V. Domino 1899–1973.*

And what the hell did he have to do with Claire Elizabeth?

Echo answers, he thought. He got back into the car and drove home.

Nell's Mercedes was still gone, and Athelstane was huddled lonesomely on the back porch. He whuffled at Jesse and rose on hind legs to greet him, nearly knocking him over, and followed him in happily.

Jesse made himself a mild drink and carried it down the hall to the phone. Athelstane was fascinated by the voices in the black box, and planted himself on Jesse's feet, prepared to eavesdrop. "Monster," said Jesse.

The Mannings lived, expectably, on an expensive street off Beverly Glen Boulevard in Bel Air. He dialed the number and after four rings Manning answered.

"Where did your mother bank?" asked Jesse.

"Security Pacific. The branch in that big shopping mall in Beverly Hills," said Manning.

So that answered that. The cabdrivers had taken her there rather frequently. "Did you ever hear her mention anyone named Bakewell—Virgil and Wanda Bakewell—or a Louis Domino?"

"Never heard of either of them," said Manning blankly. "Why?"

"I don't know anything about the Bakewells, but she visited Domino's grave recently."

"The hell you say. I never heard of the man."

"I suppose," said Jesse, "it'd be impossible to locate any of them, but I'd like to find somebody who knew your parents way back then. Could you offer any suggestions?"

"Knew them before my father was killed—hell, I wouldn't know—"

"Before that, say back to when they were first married."

"My God, Falkenstein—fifty-five years— Anybody they knew then would be dead by now."

"Not so necessarily."

"Well, all I can tell you," said Manning, "is that by the time I was of an age to notice anything like that, Mother was immersed in the business, hadn't any social life at all. When I was in high school, college. While I was at military school, in the thirties and early forties, I couldn't say, but when I was living at home I never knew her to go out evenings—sometimes she'd be at the office late, just come home and go to bed. She didn't have any friends, calling or asking her out." He paused, and after a moment added, "Looking back at it, she didn't have much of a life really, did she?"

"You could look at it that way," said Jesse. "Maybe she felt different." He heard Nell driving in. "I'll be in touch."

On Sunday morning Nell dragged him up to the house at the end of Coldwater Canyon to admire the first of the refurbishing. The painters had finished the living and dining rooms in a light cream color. Jesse's den was to be paneled to match the three walls of bookshelves.

"And Fran was absolutely right about curtains, better stick to solid colors—wait until you see, a nice rich shade of chestnut for our bedroom, and green for the guest room, that's on the east so it won't fade." Nell was excited about the house; it would be so much nicer for Athelstane, a whole fenced acre, and it was so quiet and private up here, space for the baby to play as he grew.

Jesse followed her around, smiling at her enthusiasm, visualizing what was going here and there. He didn't look forward to moving all the books, but he hoped it would be the last time.

"I saw some perfect wallpaper for the nursery," said Nell, coming to the top of the stairs, "and I thought—" She let out a sudden shriek and he jumped. "My heavens, I never *told* you! And you're not to say a word to anybody until we're sure—"

"Sure about what?"

"Fran thinks she's started a baby, but she can't get in to see the doctor until next week—"

"Well, that'll learn her," said Jesse. "Keep her occupied at home instead of leading you astray spending my money."

Nell laughed, hanging onto his arm and looking around the room that would be the nursery. David Andrew was busily pursuing a spider across the dusty floor. "It's going to be a lovely house, isn't it? Jesse, it isn't costing too much, is it?"

He kissed her lightly. "It's only money. The old boy wanted us to have fun with it, Nell."

"Yes, I know. I hope he knows about it," said Nell seriously.

He left her there—they'd driven up separately—taking measurements and looking at paint samples, and drove home. He ought to have a look at the various depositions on Mrs. Cliff's damage suit, but he'd just gotten out the brief when the phone rang. It was Manning.

"I've probably just got a simple mind," he said, "but do you know that that Bakewell you were asking about is in the phone book?"

"What?"

"I just thought I'd look. It's an address in Burbank. I thought I'd better tell you."

"Thanks so much." Jesse looked for himself. There were only four Bakewells listed in the Los Angeles area, and only one Virgil. He lit a thoughtful cigarette, pushed Athelstane off his feet, and dialed the number.

A man's voice answered unhurriedly. "Mr. Bakewell?"

"Yes?"

"You won't know my name, but are you by any chance the Virgil Bakewell who used to know a Robert and Claire Manning back in the thirties, in Hollywood?"

There was a long moment of silence, and then Bakewell said, "Good God a-mighty, sir, you just took me back forty years and more. I hadn't thought of the Mannings in—who is this?"

Jesse told him. "I'd like to talk to you, if it's convenient. I'll explain when I see you. Now?"

"Don't know why not. We're just sitting here passing the time. What did you say your name is? Know how to get here?"

"I'll be there in twenty minutes."

It was a snug and pretty little green stucco house on a quiet residential street. Virgil Bakewell was a big, fat man with a lot of snow-white hair and apple-red cheeks; his wife was a thin, little woman with merry brown eyes. They welcomed Jesse in with childish curiosity.

"I had to stop and think when you said the name," said Bakewell. "Lord, that does take us right back! Claire and Bob Manning—it beats all how you drift away from friends—"

"It was the Depression," she said. "Sit down, Mr. Falkenstein. What on earth's your interest in Claire and Bob?"

Tediously, he told them. They listened interestedly. "So Claire's gone," said Wanda Bakewell with a sigh. "She was just my age. She was such a pretty girl. We were good friends, way back there—had some good times together. It seems queer, but we did, even in the middle of the Depression. Bob was in real estate—you know that, of course—things moving slow, he'd say, but they were a bit better off than most people. And so Claire made a lot of money, did she? Well, she was a smart girl. But it seems peculiar she'd cut off her own boy—she was crazy about Johnny, a real good mother. My heavens, Virg, do you realize little Johnny'll be older than our two? The years go by so quick—"

He smiled and patted her arm. "It was the Depression, you see. I lost my job in 1933—I was in hardware at the Sears store on Santa Monica. Up to then we'd scraped along, even with a salary cut, and like Wanda says, we had some good friends and good times. Claire and Bob, and the Newsomes, and Betty and Jim Franks—we used to have potluck suppers with everybody bringing something, and picnics in the summer—we never went in for dancing much, but Claire and Bob were hot on it. But, time I lost my job, we had to go up to my brother's in San Jose. He was doing pretty good, getting by anyway, he had a short-order restaurant downtown. Wanda was expecting our first, and we hated like the devil to impose on Ted and June, but there wasn't anything else to do."

"I never was much of a one for writing letters," she added to that. "It was a busy time. I heard from Claire a few times, and then the next year she wrote me how Bob had been killed—that was terrible, I know how it must have been for her, they were just crazy about each other. But after I wrote her back then, I didn't hear, and time just went—I never heard from her again, I suppose she was busy too. We were in San Jose until 1965—"

"I got a good job at Sears again, the year after we landed there, and put in twenty-five years, ended up head of the men's department. But by then Ted and June were both gone, and our boy Don and our daughter Edna were both down here. Don's with an engineering company in Pasadena and Edna's married to a doctor, they wanted us to live nearer, so we sold the place in San Jose and came down."

"Now don't ramble on, Virg, Mr. Falkenstein said he had some questions."

"You might not remember," said Jesse. "Did Claire Manning ever mention her family back East?"

They consulted each other mutely. "I don't recall that she ever did," said Wanda Bakewell slowly. "I knew her folks were dead, she'd come in for some money when her father died, that was three or four years before we knew them. They had their own realty company, they were doing pretty well compared to most people, I guess they'd been able to start it on that money. But I don't remember her ever talking about any relatives. I'm sorry."

"Can't be helped," said Jesse.

She looked at her husband. "We can show you something, though. When you phoned, and we were talking about those days and all, I wondered if those snapshots were still around, and we looked them out."

"Of the Mannings?" He was interested.

"Lying around for years," said Bakewell. "Neither of us had looked at the thing in I don't know how long. These funny little old pictures—I had an old Kodak." He produced an ancient black photograph album about ten by six, its edges much frayed. It had thick black pages, and it was filled with the little rectangular black-and-white snapshots of the twenties and thirties, carefully fastened to the pages with triangular black pockets. Some of the snapshots were surprisingly clear.

"There's only a couple," she said. They crowded on either side of him, the album spread on his knees. "I remembered that day so clear when I saw these again. We went down to the beach in the Mannings' car, us and the Franks—Claire and Bob had a spiffy new four-door Chevy. It was along in April and the beach not crowded."

"That's Claire and Bob in the middle, and Betty and Jim either side."

Jesse studied the little snapshot with interest, the first picture he'd seen of Claire Elizabeth. "It really didn't do her justice," said Mrs. Bakewell, "just a candid snapshot. Bright red hair she had, and real white skin."

Bob Manning he recognized; in the formal photograph in her bedroom he'd been wearing a suit, shirt and tie, but here he was clad in one of the ludicrous bathing suits of the thirties, striped above and some dark color below, with pants to the knees. He had a satisfactorily broad chest and good shoulders; he was laughing into the camera. He had his arm around the girl beside him, and she was laughing too. A very pretty girl, Claire Elizabeth, at what?—twenty-eight or so. She had a triangular face with rather high cheekbones, a full mouth over a pointed little chin. Her hair showed dark in the snapshot, cut in the awkward bob of the period, with flat marcelled waves. Her figure was slight but feminine in a one-piece dark bathing suit.

The other snapshot was less clear, taken at the same time, showing two much younger but recognizable Bakewells with Claire and Bob Manning in a similar pose.

"Thanks very much for letting me see them," said Jesse, getting up.

"I'm just sorry we couldn't tell you anything you wanted to know. But you sure have us thinking about those old days. Hadn't thought of the Mannings in years. Life's a funny proposition," said Bakewell profoundly.

On Monday morning, as he'd expected, the Ludendorf divorce hearing went through smoothly and the decree got handed down at eleven-thirty. Aware that that damned damage suit would probably occupy the rest of the week, Jesse was driving up Beverly Glen Boulevard by one o'clock; he had called to make sure she was in.

It was, of course, an expensive house filled with expensive things: quite a contrast to the place on Valle Vista. Ruth Manning looked expensive too, a still good-looking blonde with a pleasant figure and smart clothes. She gave him a chair and accepted a cigarette with a nod.

"But I don't know what you want of me, Mr. Falkenstein. If I had any idea why she did such a thing I'd have told John already."

"Just like your—mmh—unvarnished opinion of her," said Jesse. "People can seldom look at their parents objectively."

"Oh," she said. "But that wouldn't tell you anything about what reason she had—oh, well," and she shrugged. "I didn't like her, nor she me, you know, John knew that—she and I both knew it. We were polite to each other—keep it all smooth on the surface kind of thing. Yes, I know you had to admire her for all she'd done, she was a strong character. But having everything her own way so long—she was rather a petty tyrant." She brooded over her cigarette. "She didn't approve of the way we brought up the children, too big allowances, too much freedom —but give the devil his due, she didn't openly criticize very often. We just knew. John was something else. She kept telling him the business was all for him, she'd created it just for her boy, but she kept the reins in her own hands as long as she could— her and that obnoxious Hansen woman, dragging heels on giving John authority until it all got to be too much for her to oversee herself. He ought to have been general manager ten years before he was." Ruth Manning laughed and leaned back. "Oh, I sound like a jealous wife. Old people get set in their ways, always criticize the younger generation—they get inflexible. I hope I won't, but maybe it's a law of nature."

"Do you ever remember her saying anything about her family?"

"Never. Of course John and I discussed that. He'd never heard her talk about any relatives. I know—we've been over and over it—she sounded as sane as anybody, but I can only think she was starting to get senile. She can't have been in her right mind— everybody knew she meant to leave it all to John. I suppose I shouldn't ask, but do you think—"

"I can rescue it for him? We'll have a damned good try, Mrs. Manning. But I can't promise anything."

"No." She looked around the beautifully furnished room, and her eyes darkened.

Jesse took her evaluation with just the slightest grain of salt; she was a strong character too, and such people seldom admired each other. He thought that Manning must be a strong character too in his own way, to have scraped between Scylla and Charybdis without relinquishing any of his masculinity.

And that small idea his little sister Fran had given him, on another case, had also reoccurred to him. Women, said Fran, talk to their hairdressers the way men talk to bartenders.

When he left Mrs. Manning he drove back to Hollywood and found the Silver Comb close in to downtown on Hollywood Boulevard. He had to park two blocks away. Evidently Monday was a slow day in the beauty business; there was no one waiting in the little square front room, and only a couple of voices sounded from behind a paneled partition past the reception desk. Here, thick red carpeting, a couch and several chairs to match, a round glass table spread with magazines. The woman at the reception desk was sleek and dark and plump, not young; she raised her brows at him.

"I'd like to talk to the operator who used to do Mrs. Claire Manning's hair. I'd make it worth her while." He passed over the inevitable card. "Just a couple of questions—it's to do with settling the estate."

She was curious. "I can't imagine what Ruby could have to do with that, but I suppose you know your own business. She ought to be finished with Mrs. Anderson by now, I'll go see." She vanished behind the partition. In a minute a plump elderly woman in a fur jacket appeared and went out the front door. After her came the receptionist and a rather dumpy woman in a white uniform. "This is Ruby Fisher. I'm due for a coffee break, I guess you can talk here." She went away again.

Ruby was blond, probably not by nature, and had a round good-natured face, a thickened figure in the plain white smock. She sat down on the couch and looked at him curiously. "What's it all about? I took care of Mrs. Manning for over twenty years. I was sorry to hear she'd died—her nurse called in to cancel the appointment and say she had. But what her lawyer wants of me— Did she leave me something?" That had just occurred to her; she looked surprised.

"No, I'm afraid not." He went through the tale again, and she looked shocked.

"Why, that's just terrible, isn't it? And I can't understand it—she thought the world of her son. It wasn't so much what she said as the way she said it—you know. Sure, I could tell anybody that."

Another witness, such as she was. Jesse asked her if she'd ever heard Mrs. Manning say directly that she meant to leave her property to her son; regretfully she said no, not in so many words. "But she would have, naturally. She didn't need to say so."

"Did she talk much to you? Did she ever—"

"Well, sometimes she wanted to talk and sometimes she didn't," said Ruby. "Oh, it'd be different things, just as things came up. She'd talk about her son, how much like his father he was, and the rest of the family—I don't think she liked her daughter-in-law much, but there's nothing unusual about that. She could be sharp, you know, and she was fussy, liked things done just so. I suited her. She'd be real put out, times I was sick or on vacation and Liz or Doris had to take her. Twenty years— When she first came in, she'd been keeping her hair hennaed, but it wasn't long after that she said to me she was tired of taking the trouble, it was probably all gray then anyway, and she let it grow out, and it was. It was really more becoming to her, didn't make her skin look so hard. She stopped using much makeup, too." Ruby thought. "The very last time I saw her, she wasn't looking too good. Sort of tired. That was a month ago last Thursday."

"Did she talk much then?"

"Yes, she did," said Ruby. "She talked about her husband. She didn't very often, but you could read between the lines sort of, when she did. She was the kind of woman—you get some like that—what they call a one-man woman. You take me, I was just crazy about Jim—my first—he was a real good man, and I was all broken up when that truck jackknifed on him, I cried for days and days—but that's life, you got to go on, and I was lucky to meet Ken. You couldn't ask for a better guy, and he's been real good to my first two kids, Jim's I mean, and we got two of our own. But Mrs. Manning was different. I suppose some women would have taken it all out on the boy—she might've wrapped herself all up in him—but she was the kind, a husband'd come first."

"And she talked about him, the last time you saw her?"

"Yes, that's right. When I combed her out, she sat looking in the mirror and she said, I wonder how I'd look to Bob now. And I didn't say anything, and she said like to herself, I wonder if he'd think I did right. She wasn't really talking to me, you know. And then she said, 'You know, Ruby, time's a frightening thing.'"

Jesse felt as exasperated as he'd ever felt in his life.

Ruby added suddenly, "At least I'd cured her of the humming. She didn't know she was doing it, I guess, but she couldn't tell how loud it was under the dryer. I got so I'd just touch her arm and she'd stop. But she hadn't been doing it in a while."

"'Me and My Shadow,'" said Jesse.

"That was her favorite, how'd you know?"

He stood up. Another handful of nothing. If you wanted to go back to the out-of-date popular songs, there was one about a long, long trail.

As he'd foreseen, the damage suit was going to occupy some time, and he could almost predict the outcome. Mrs. Cliff was asking fifty thousand and costs for her fall on a heavily waxed floor in Robinsons' beauty salon, and consequent compound fractures. Court convened at ten on Tuesday and they had only just got a jury when it adjourned at five. Wednesday and Thursday were occupied with the witnesses; Jesse had had hopes that the thing might be handed to the jury by Thursday afternoon. But it was a nice day and possibly the judge wanted to get in a round of golf before dark; he adjourned at four, after the last witness.

Mrs. Cliff delayed him, asking what he thought would happen; he thought he knew, but juries were unpredictable. It was nearly five when he got away and started home, and he was thinking about Claire Elizabeth again.

He went out of his way, down Los Feliz, and landed at Wilma Hansen's door just as it opened; they nearly collided as she swept out.

"Oh!" she said sharply. "I was just leaving—I'm sorry, did you want—something?"

"Sorry to delay you," said Jesse.

"It's all right," she told him ungraciously, "I'm just going out to dinner with Mrs. Kane—in the next apartment. Sometimes we go to the theater, or a movie, but we're just going out to the Tail o' the Cock tonight, so time doesn't matter. What is it?" She didn't ask him in. She was haggard and smart, in a coral wool sheath with matching silk coat, a good deal of costume jewelry, black patent bag and the stilt-heeled pumps.

"I just wanted to ask you if you could tell me anything about a man named Domino—Louis Domino?"

Wilma Hansen dropped her bag. Under the too-light face powder her skin looked gray. "That horrible man!" she spat. "Where—where on earth did you hear of *him*?"

Jesse picked up the bag and handed it to her. "You knew him?"

She said coldly, in control, "Thank you. I'm sorry, you really startled me. I hadn't thought of him in years, Mr. Falkenstein. It wasn't important."

"Who was he?"

"Oh, the company was in a deal with him once—years back, the forties. He was a realtor, and I think into construction too. It was just"—she gave a hard laugh—"he impressed both Claire and me as a completely untrustworthy man, and in fact I think he was indicted for fraud later on and went to prison. We never had any more dealings with him."

"Do you remember when that was exactly, that Mrs. Manning was in a deal with him?"

"Heavens, no. Years ago. How on earth did you come across him?"

"The name came up in some of her papers," said Jesse vaguely. "Thanks so much." He started back for the elevator, and felt her eyes follow him.

Court convened at ten on Friday and the case was handed to the jury. They stayed out an hour and returned the verdict Jesse had expected; they awarded Mrs. Cliff half of what she had asked and the court costs.

It was more than she'd hoped, she confessed pleasedly, and he'd been so good and clever. Jesse was inclined to think so too,

against the slick fellow Robinsons' had hired. He got away to
have a leisurely lunch and was back in his office by one-thirty.

The Gordons had several appointments for him in the coming
week, looking like run-of-the-mill business, wills, two new divorce cases. Ten minutes after he sat down at his desk, he had a
call from Tregarron.

"I have not heard a word from that Pollock, and it seems
strange—he should have had my letter at least by a week ago
today. I have wondered if the address—"

"State of the mails," said Jesse.

"I still think it's strange," said Tregarron fretfully. "May I ask
whether you've got anything useful at all?"

"I don't know," said Jesse. "Some good evidence on her relations with Manning, but we'd be in a lot stronger position if we
could show her reasoning for making that will. Either irrational
reasoning or— Because, why the hell Pollock? If she'd decided to
cut out Manning, she could have left it all to the Humane Society or something. Does that say it goes back—her reason—to
something way in the past, before her marriage?"

"Yes," said Tregarron. "It occurred to me—some girlish attachment—by the dates, this cousin's father possibly. And she'd been
dwelling in the past as old people will—and as I said, a brain
lesion— She was obviously quite incompetent. I trust you'll be
able to demonstrate that without much trouble. I will let you
know when I hear from Pollock."

Jesse got out the will and read it through again. Those odd
amounts of money—he couldn't make head or tail of that.

He called C.M.R. Management and got Fowler. "Domino?"
said Fowler. "Doesn't ring a bell. Have you got a date on it?"

"Just, a while back."

"Well, it'd be before my time, I don't remember the name at
all. There are cartons of old records stashed in the dead files,"
said Fowler. "Ought to've been cleared out long ago." He
laughed. "Hansie'd probably put her hand on the right one in
five minutes. If I had a definite date—what's the interest in it?"

"I don't know," said Jesse. "It'd be the hell of a job to look for
it, I suppose—"

"I don't mind at all if it's important. Glad to do anything to
help. Though how it could have anything to do with that will—"

"I don't know either," said Jesse. "But we don't know what was in her mind. And evidently she'd been thinking of Domino just lately."

"Oh, really?" said Fowler. "Well, I'll have a look and see if I can find anything."

Jesse decided to go home early.

FIVE

Fran walked in about five o'clock with a large brown bag of groceries, handed it to Nell, and sat down on the couch beaming fatuously at them. "It's official," she announced. She was ridiculously pleased with herself. "It's due about the end of December. I called Andrew first and then Father, and all he said was, it was about time—we haven't been married two years after all—and Andrew's coming to dinner to celebrate. I thought—"

"Celebrate indeed," said Nell, investigating the bag, "with New York cut steaks at how much a pound—darling Fran, I'm so glad—we really ought to have champagne—"

"It's at the bottom of the bag," said Fran. "You'd better put it in the refrigerator right away. Of course it doesn't much matter which, though Andrew would like a boy—and I've been thinking about names. Do I remember that you've got a dictionary of names, Jesse?"

"Somewhere around." Jesse grinned at his little sister—svelte, smart Fran, who presently wouldn't be so svelte. "Well, I wonder how you'll do at it. Strikes me, it's a wonder anybody grows up to be a normal adult, considering that all parents start out as amateurs."

Nell came back from putting the food away and said, "I rather liked Daniel, but Jesse wouldn't let me."

"Sort of nice." Fran wrinkled her small nose. "Not first choice. What I did think about was Charles. Except that really, with a short last name, it ought to be two syllables."

"Chauncey," said Jesse. "Ebenezer. Ethelbert. Launcelot."

Fran threw a sofa cushion at him and he fielded it neatly. "Christopher," said Nell.

"Yes, if it didn't turn into Chris."

"You don't," said Jesse, "automatically get what you want. I'll bet you it's a girl."

"I don't mind at all," said Fran. "It'd really be easier if it's a girl, there are so many nice girl's names. Cynthia and Elaine and Jennifer and Felicity and Karen—"

"Not Karen," protested Nell. "Too common. Let me find that book—"

Jesse listened to them arguing about names, when Nell found the book in his study. He checked the liquor supply, opened a new bottle of Bourbon; he didn't see Andrew guzzling champagne.

When Clock arrived, having escaped from his heisters and unidentified bodies a little early, Jesse offered him a hand and congratulations. "Though you'll find it's not an unmixed blessing when it sounds off at two in the morning. And you can blame Nell if you end up with a Gwendolyn or Gervase—she likes unusual names, and of course Fran always has to be different."

Clock gave him a wide fatuous grin. "Doesn't matter at all. But I'll tell you one thing, Jesse," and he massaged his Neanderthal jaw. "I hope to God, if it's a girl, she takes after Fran."

It was a very thin and forlorn hope, but on Saturday morning Jesse parked down from the corner on Fountain and started to ask questions at all the little shops clustered around that intersection. The drugstore wouldn't be open until ten. At the gas station he got mere head-shakes. At the cleaners', the snack shop, a beauty parlor down the block, a hole-in-the-wall thrift shop, a shoddy variety store, everybody looked at him blankly and said, Sorry, they couldn't say.

At ten-thirty he came back to the drugstore, where a white-smocked pharmacist was rearranging a stack of miscellaneous cosmetics labeled Half Price, and put the question again. "Matter of tracing somebody," he explained. "I know it's a while back."

"You can say *that* again," said the pharmacist, who was nondescript, about fifty, a little paunchy. "But let me think. I've been here since 1959. It's a pretty transient area, maybe not as much as some others, but God, that many years— Now I'll tell you. You might ask the Winters. They've got to be in their eighties, and I know they've lived here a long time. They're at 1225. I wouldn't know if they've been here as long as that, but you can ask. He brings in a couple of prescriptions regular, reason I know him."

Jesse thanked him and walked down Edgemont to 1225. It was a single house with a tiny rental unit in the rear, the lawn a little ragged, the cement walk chipped. When the door was opened he looked in some dismay at an old and tottery-looking man with rheumy eyes and a cracked voice, but asked his question anyway, not very hopefully. "I don't know how long you've lived here, Mr. Winter, but the pharmacist up the street thought you might be able to help me."

"Nineteen twenty-nine," said Winter promptly. "Come in and set down. Martha, here's somebody askin' about real old times." The furniture was old and faded, but the room was clean and tidy, and Martha, rosy and fat and bright-eyed, was enthralled by a visitor. They were both easily in their eighties, but they seemed to have their wits about them.

"Tracing somebody? You got to go all that way back? Private detective, like? Well, isn't that interesting. People at 1209—" They looked at him, shook their heads. "Don't think I ever heard of any Mannings along here," said Winter. "And we've been here since 1929. We were married in 1922 but we never got around to buying a house till that year—wouldn't you know, year the crash came and there we was with a mortgage looked like a mountain. But believe it or not, we made it. I was outta work, but I took every odd job I could get, and Martha here did sewing and baby-minding and whatever she could find, and we made it. Hung onto the house and got it paid for in 1949, acourse I was back in steady work then, I got took on by the Board of Education in 1932, maintenance crew at a high school, and I was there till I retired. But Mannings, now—"

"This used to be the kind of neighborhood where people knew each other," she told Jesse. "Where people stayed put. But even then there were renters, people coming and going. 1209, that's fourth from the corner—it's always been rented. When we bought this place, there was a family there, I couldn't tell you the name if my life depended on it, don't think I ever heard it.

They got evicted for getting behind on the rent when he lost his job. My, that's a long time ago—"

"Lot of water under the bridge," agreed Winter. "Kids just small fry—we got three," he informed Jesse, "and six grandkids and would you believe seven great-grandkids—married fifty-eight years next May—maybe you'd like to see some pictures—"

"Do you know of anybody who lived along here before you did?"

"There was the Reveres," she said. "They owned 1211, that is, they were buying it. Hung onto it too, but he was in a steady job, he was with the post office. They had a couple of kids, older than ours. Their boy got killed in the war, but the girl got married along in the thirties—late thirties."

"Would you have any idea where they are now?"

"I couldn't say about Mr. Revere," she twinkled at him. "He died in 1964. She was poorly, with a bad heart, and went to live with the daughter. Some real estate firm owns the house now, rents it out."

"The daughter's name—"

"Dear me now, what was the name of that fellow she married? It was a funny sort of name, I know that. If I could think—" She rocked back and forth, ruminating.

"—All good kids, and done well. Even had two of 'em go to college, what about that? Don't know but what they'd have done as good without, but then you never know. I never graduated from high school, I got along all right, but I suppose times change—"

"Kindly!" she said in a small triumph. "I knew I'd get it once I thought a minute. Fred Kindly, and he worked at the Southern Pacific."

"Thanks very much," said Jesse. "Do you happen to remember where the daughter lived when Mrs. Revere went to live with her?"

"Goodness, I don't recall. I think it was down toward the beach somewhere."

"This is our oldest, Jim, and his wife and kids—Bill and Buddy and Pearl, she's married to a doctor now and they got—"

"Oh, don't bother the man, Fred, he's not interested in our pictures. A private detective'll be a busy man."

Jesse departed hastily, walked back to the snack shop, ordered a milkshake, and started looking through the phone books in the public booth outside. He found a few Kindlys listed in Glendora, San Dimas, and Sherman Oaks, which didn't put them anywhere toward the beach; and a Kathleen Kindly in Hawthorne, which might be more likely. When he finished the milkshake he tried that number, and was answered by a pleasant female voice.

He asked if she'd once lived on Edgemont Street in Hollywood. There was a startled pause. "Well, not for about forty-five years," she said. "Who is this?"

It was easier to be a private detective than a mere lawyer chasing a will-o'-the-wisp. He convinced her that he was respectable, and to agree to talk to him. It was a little drive in traffic, down to Hawthorne.

She was a thin woman in her sixties who had once been pretty. She was slightly dowdy but neat in a navy dress, pearl necklace and earrings. Her gray hair was becomingly curled, her hands a little rough from hard work. Her eyes held a little suspicious caution at first, but she thawed rapidly as he talked.

"Now that's very funny, you wanting to know about the Mannings," she said. "Speak of the devil, like they say—because I was thinking about her just the other day. How it was, my daughter May was showing me what she'd got for Jeanette—that's my granddaughter, she just turned twenty-one—and it was one of those pendant watches, and all of a sudden I thought of Mrs. Manning, and wondered what ever happened to them. She had one of those she wore all the time, it was gold and all engraved, had a cover and you pressed a little lever to open it."

"You lived in the house next door, at 1211? But you wouldn't have been very old. I wonder if your mother would remember—"

"Oh, Mother's been gone for four years. I don't suppose she'd have remembered as much as I do." Mrs. Kindly's face crinkled in a reminiscent smile. "Oh, my, I had a real crush on that girl," she said. "I think they'd lived there a year or two before I took notice, but when I got to be thirteen, fourteen—just the age to have a crush on somebody older, you know how teenage girls do —I thought Claire Manning was the most beautiful girl there ever was, the most wonderful thing ever." She laughed. "I was always telling her she ought to be in the movies—she had that fiery red hair just like Clara Bow, the It Girl, only I thought she was really prettier. Looking back, my goodness, I must have pestered the poor girl, but she was always nice to me. I was forever running over asking to do errands or help her with the housework, just to get to talk to her. Teenage girls are funny."

She might have something for him after all. "Did she talk much to you? About herself?"

"Well, I don't know about that so much. She was nice to me," repeated Mrs. Kindly. "I suppose she was flattered—I was transparent as glass, a kid that age, letting her see how I felt. She was —gay. Happy and gay—they hadn't been married long, you know—and she told me about that, I thought it was the greatest romance I ever heard of. She'd been engaged to somebody else, and then Mr. Manning showed up and they fell madly in love and ran away together. Her father was mad about it. But she'd laugh and say she could always manage him, he'd ranted and raved but he forgave her for it and it was all right."

"When would this have been?"

"Well, let's see, I was about thirteen going on fourteen, that'd make it 1927 and 1928, around there."

"Did she tell you anything about her family back East—the fellow she was engaged to? You remember his name?"

"If she ever told me I've forgotten. I remember she said once her father wanted her to come back for a visit, and sent the money, but she wouldn't leave Bob, she said. It wasn't—looking back—just that she was so pretty, and gay, and they were like lovers in some story—but they had such fun out of life." She laughed again, and sounded rueful, amused, looking down the years. "My folks were a bit straitlaced, and besides we didn't have a lot of money—Dad was a motorman on the trolley—and we hardly ever went to movies, anywhere but church and picnics at the beach sometimes. And next door there, the Mannings had such *fun*—you could hear them. She played the piano just like a professional, she was good—all the old ragtime and jazz—and they had good singing voices too. They used to have parties, a couple of times a week, and they'd all sing around the piano—

summer nights with the windows open you could hear everything. All those silly old songs, 'Yes, We Have No Bananas' and 'Ain't We Got Fun' and 'Margie.' They always seemed so happy, the Mannings. And she was surely a beautiful girl."

Jesse waited. "Anything else come to mind? Some other people were renting the house in 1929—when did the Mannings move away?" But Wilma Hansen had told him that; they'd gone to San Diego, been there a couple of years, come back in 1930.

"Oh, her father died. I remember when I went over once she'd been crying, and told me. But I don't think they went back East to the funeral, it was later on they moved. I know I never got to say good-bye to her. I'd been sick in bed with the flu, or whatever it was called then, and I remember Mother saying they were going somewhere, putting suitcases in the car. And about a week later a truck came for her piano. I forgot all about her after a while—kids!" said Mrs. Kindly, looking back at her teenage self with a chuckle. "But I still think she was the prettiest girl I ever knew."

And that was all. As a period piece, interesting, but not helpful to the immediate problem. Feeling remotely sad, he thought about that gay redhead Claire Elizabeth, what time and life had done to her. Everybody was on the same road, only some a little ahead of the rest. Which was a fine morbid thought.

Resignedly, he realized he was going to have to go through every scrap of paper in that house. No telling where some clue, some suggestive pointer, might show. And the sooner he got at it the better.

Mrs. Hawes let him in. He started in the living room, with the account books, skimming over them rapidly, to get those out of the way. They were meticulously kept; as well as noting running expenses, casual shopping, she had recorded business transactions; evidently she'd been playing around a little in the stock market. There were records of payments to a brokerage, Amberly-Chatham, downtown. The sums weren't astronomical. Notations of birthday presents for the family, and those sums were generous.

Half an hour took him through the two account books from

the little chest: it all looked straightforward, nothing unusual. The box of canceled checks equated with the last accounts, for February; she hadn't gotten around to covering March, of course.

In one corner of the top drawer, nearly invisible against the dark wood, was a bank book. He picked it up and then discovered a second one underneath it. Savings account, probably.

It wasn't. It was a bankbook for a checking account at a Bank of America in Hollywood. The latest balance, filled in in her hand, with no bank-stamp against it, was $22,871. He riffled back through it. All the dates filled in by hand, and they were dates long apart, all recording deposits. The first date in the book, on the first page, was dated by the bank: January 10, 1942, a deposit of seventy-five hundred. The book was filled up to the last page.

Jesse cocked his head at it. Now that was a queer one. Cautious old lady, who had known some anxious times in the Depression, playing both ends against the middle with an account in another bank? But why not a savings account, in that case? He wondered if Manning knew anything about this.

He tucked it into his breast pocket and proceeded upstairs. He knew there wasn't anything in the bedroom drawers but what he'd seen already, but he took down the boxes of canceled checks from the closet shelf; there must have been twenty years' worth of canceled checks there, nothing else in the boxes. He put them back on the shelf.

Hanging neatly on one of the hooks at the front of the closet was a handbag, and it was evidently the one she'd been carrying most recently, a plain black leather envelope bag. In it were the checkbooks for the two bank accounts, her billfold with a little wad of cash in it, an out-of-date driver's license, a powder puff and shell-pink lipstick and another handkerchief. He hung it back on the hook and began looking through all the clothes. Not every garment would have a pocket, but he looked systematically. He found a couple of crumpled handkerchiefs in the pocket of a suit jacket; a pair of wool gloves in the pocket of a worn black coat.

At the far side of the closet, the last item, on a padded hanger, was a navy-blue cardigan jacket. It had patch pockets. The left one was empty, but in the right he felt a piece of paper, and brought it out into the light of the room.

It was a single half sheet of slick paper, cut or torn out of a magazine by the look of it; there was no clue to its origin, for it had been taken from the middle of a page. The only thing on it, in fine italic print, was a poem called "Sonnet" by someone named Nancy Shores Burcham whom he'd never heard of.

> Most excellent heart, strong against time or men,
> Or subtle incantation of the spring,
> Running your cadences in the slow swing
> Of good red tides that ebb and flow again,
> Unaltered by the season or the storm,
> Equivalent always to the moment's need,
> Proof against any weariness of deed,
> Staunch arbiter of sleep, while yet the warm
> Flesh lies along my little, jointed bones—
>
> Remember how your pulses roared and sang
> Against the cobalt night when love was young,
> And life was stored in casual overtones.
> Remember the toccata of your beat
> When life was sweet, when love was very sweet!

Something she had read, cut out to keep. It didn't matter from where. And now, thinking of what Tregarron had said, he wondered if she had been thinking of Bob Manning when she cut this out—or somebody else?

Nothing else here. There'd be nothing downstairs, in the big breakfront in the dining room; no other drawers in the living room apart from the little chest. But as he stood there with the warm lines of the sonnet running through his mind, he suddenly remembered the old wardrobe trunk. The trunk in the basement, which she had mentioned when she was dying.

Galvanized into action, he took the stairs three at a time.

"The basement?" said Mrs. Hawes, looking up from a pan on the stove. "Well, I've never been down there myself, the missus always said never mind, nothing there. That's the door. Horrid dark places, basements—I'll find you a flashlight—I don't know as the light's working. I don't know why the missus wanted such a thing, but then I don't know why anybody'd build a house like this anyway. The switch is by the door, and don't be surprised if there are spiders all over or worse."

The light, a low-wattage overhead bulb in the ceiling, showed steep wooden stairs. It was only a half basement after all, housing an outsize gas furnace. There were empty shelves built in on two walls. And there wasn't another thing there but two old suitcases against the back wall and the wardrobe trunk.

He checked the suitcases first. The leather was cracked with age; the locks fell open at a touch. One was empty; the other held three men's shirts and a suit of old-fashioned one-piece underwear. They were wrapped in a sheet of newspaper which bore the date January 10, 1935. Bob's?

The trunk was a monstrosity out of a leisured age, the kind that opened out in two thick leaves. It was unlocked, but it hadn't been opened in so long that it was stiff, and it took all his strength to shove it apart. There were little drawers and pull-out shelves at the top. In the first drawer he opened were odds and ends of old tarnished costume jewelry. Scarves, handkerchiefs, gloves, more jewelry. In the first deep drawer, clothes—the clothes of the twenties. The dress he pulled out was a shapeless, skimpy tube of faded green silk, half rotted away. Underwear—strange one-piece underwear—what had been called teddies?—he vaguely remembered that. More shapeless dresses, a knife-pleated white skirt with moth holes all over it—sweaters, the remains of stockings, even a couple of pairs of shoes, narrow pointed shoes which surely had never fit any woman's foot—

All bundled carelessly away here and forgotten? The other drawers held more clothes; but the right-hand bottom one, after sticking stubbornly, slid suddenly out to reveal papers, a little mass of papers in a pile. Jesse turned the flashlight on them. Letters in envelopes, a thick sheaf of them, and underneath—he held the flashlight closer—a fat green book with a clasp and lock. On the cover was stamped, in gold that hardly showed now, *My Diary*. He opened it with a grunt and read the inscription inside. *Claire Elizabeth Tilton 1922*.

"O frabjous day," said Jesse. He climbed the stairs to ask if Mrs. Hawes could find him a box.

He came home with his treasure to find Nell in her newest dress spraying cologne lavishly. They were, she reminded him, going to dinner at the Haywards'. "Oh, hell," said Jesse. Neither of them was given to much gadding around, but in a civilized community there had to be some social life. He went to shower again, and put on a clean shirt and tie. Fran arrived to baby-sit.

They didn't get home until after eleven, and socializing being tiring, went to bed after Jesse had walked Fran the block home.

He got up late as usual on Sunday morning, and after waking up over a couple of cups of coffee, had just settled down in the study to look at those letters when the phone rang.

It was Manning. "I've been racking my brains," he said, "ever since you asked me about old friends of Mother's. There was something just on the edge of my mind, but I couldn't pin it down. Finally it halfway came to me. About nine or ten years ago we sold a piece of property to a bank, they were putting up a new branch. And when the papers were drawn up a couple of the bank officers came into the office. One of them asked—when he heard my name—if I was any relation of Bob Manning, and when I said he was my father he greeted me like a long lost pal. He said he and my father had been in business together, worked for the same realty company, way back before the Depression. As I recall, he was a nice old fellow—he just mentioned it, said he was glad to see Bob's son doing so well and so on."

"Remember his name?"

"It was Meiklejohn. But I couldn't think which bank it was to save my life—the lot was somewhere in West Hollywood, I couldn't remember the location either. I did remember it was just before Hansie retired, so I called her, and she said it was Crocker National. But hell, Falkenstein, that was nine or ten years back and he was an old man then, he may be dead."

"No harm in asking," said Jesse. "Did you know your mother had a second checking account with Bank of America? I found the book. There's over twenty thousand in it."

"What?" Manning was astonished. "No, of course I didn't. That's damned queer—why would she want to do that? Wait a minute, now. There was a lot more coming in than she could spend—a lot of it was ploughed back into investments, but since she'd been retired she'd amused herself playing around in stock —nothing big, a few thousand at a crack. She was dealing with a downtown brokerage, she could have set up an account just for that, but why a different bank—"

"No," said Jesse. "Been looking. She paid the brokerage commissions out of the account at Security Pacific, and the price of the stock. And the other one's been going since 1942."

"Since—oh, now, wait a minute," said Manning. "That's crazy."

"Sorry, but there it is. No indication of what withdrawals when, just deposits. I'd like a look at the bank records on it."

"You're damn right we'll have a look at it. Which bank? All right, I'll meet you there when it's open in the morning and we'll go into it."

"Not quite so simple," said Jesse. "Everything's legally tied up until this is settled. Some will admitted to probate. You can talk pretty to the bank manager, but I doubt very much that anybody can see those records without a court order."

"Oh, damn. Can you get one?"

"Sure—pure formality. But with the will in doubt and to be contested, we'd naturally want to go into everything thoroughly. It'll take a few days. We'd probably have it by the end of the week."

"We can try for a shortcut at least. That is the damnedest thing," said Manning. "I can't understand it. I know she was secretive—she'd gotten a lot more so the last few years—by my God, 1942!"

"Preserve the soul in patience," said Jesse. "We can try. I'll see you there at ten."

He settled down to the letters, leaving the diary for later. The letters were a hodgepodge of miscellaneous dates, when they carried dates at all; methodically he sorted them into piles by the handwriting. They were letters from three different girls: Anne's neat sloping green ink, a Rose who wrote in a sloppy sprawl in black ink, and a Mary who wrote in near-print in blue ink. Not all the envelopes were there. Only four letters from Rose, a dozen or so from the other two.

The letters were period pieces too. The first he picked up was from Rose, brief, undated. "Thanks for the nifty teddies, really chic, kid. Jack took me out for my birthday, went to the newest whoopee parlor, oh boy, the cat's meow and too much gin as usual. Have you seen any movie stars yet?"

The next envelope had two letters in it. Another from Rose, evidently an earlier one than the other, and it was dated: July 10, 1925. "Dear Claire, you sure left a goofy situation here, kid. Dont worry we're all on your side, I think it's just swell you had the nerve run off like that. Ron's no good for a sweet sheba like you and anybody could see you and Bob fell like a ton of bricks. He's sure a handsome sheik, kid. I cant get over you going to live in Hollywood where you'll see movie stars every day and all the swell places they go. Write and tell us all about it. Uncle George is just like a raging lion and I guess he'd kill Bob if he could but you know you can always get around him and I dont suppose this time be different. That dumb Ron sulks around like a little kid. Well all for now write and tell us how you like Hollywood."

The other letter with that was short, in a heavy masculine hand. "My dear Curlytop, I suppose I'll have to put up with you throwing your cap over the windmill, you always were head-strong and stubborn which you get from me. I wish you had been content to stay home and marry Ron Elkhart, a good steady young fellow, but I'll have to accept matters as they stand. I will continue your allowance despite what your damned insolent husband desires. I have made the arrangements to have your piano shipped to you. Write and let me know how you are and whether that young man can indeed earn enough to support you. Father."

He read through the letters methodically. Rose was a boisterous youngster, and Mary struck him as a deadly smug prude. "Nobody can control Rose," she had written under a 1926 date, "and she just gets worse going off to speakeasies with Jack Shephard. She sneaked a copy of *Flaming Youth* into the house and dared me to read it, it is awful and have you read it. Anne's going to Europe, imagine, for a whole three months with her family. Mother hasn't been so well and Bill came home from N.Y. last weekend to see her, he says he's making a lot of money at that bond business but I don't think it is true, you know how he jokes." And: "That new Garbo movie opened here this week, the one they say is so awful, *Flesh and the Devil*, Anne and Jim Hobart went to see it and Anne said it is pretty *you know*, but Mother asked me not to go and of course I won't."

He liked Anne the best of the three. The green-ink letters were scattered with the slang of the period, with nifty clothes and cars, with Dumb Doras and cute shebas and sheiks that were the cat's pajamas, but underneath the colloquialisms she showed more common sense and maturity. She mentioned sending post-cards from the European trip; they hadn't survived to end up in the trunk. Under a date in June of 1926: "Rose and Jack Shephard eloped two days ago and got married in New York! Mr. Pollock is furious and you can't blame him, Jack hasn't even got a job and I can't see Rose trying to cook and housekeep! I hope it works out but not every great romance turns out like yours, you know. I can tell from your letters you're still blissfully happy with Bob and I think it's wonderful. But you know your father wants you to come for a visit and I think you should. He looks very old and tired lately."

Mary, in July 1926, in the middle of a long dull account of daily grievances: "Uncle George had a fit or something last Saturday night, the maid got Dr. Forbes and he seems all right again but Mother has been there looking after him. It is hard on me as I have all the housework and planning to do all alone and I don't see why Father can't get in another maid."

The next envelope was thinner and stiffer. Out of it slid a folded slick cardboard with the little slice of onionskin still between the leaves, and the engraving still pristine. "Mr. and Mrs. Alfred Parkinson request the honor of your attendance at the marriage of their daughter Anne Margaret to Mr. William Pollock at the First Presbyterian Church, Passaic. June 12, 1927 at two o'clock P.M. Reception follows."

And three years, four years later Anne was feeling desperate, trying to renew friendship with Claire, begging for a hundred dollars. Anne, with a year-old son who would be Adam Pollock.

The wedding invitation was the last word from Anne, at least the last preserved here. He was already aware that there had been more letters exchanged than were in this collection; references to previous letters—"what I wrote you last month"—"I told

you all about Dora's wedding—." Somebody—Claire?—clearing
out a desk, perhaps when they moved from Edgemont Street,
bundling these at random into the trunk, saying, "Oh, I can't be
bothered with all this," and throwing out the rest?

But Mary went on droning away. July 15, 1927: "Well I had a
letter from Anne and they are settled in the N.Y. apt., I don't
suppose she'll like the city, so crowded and dirty. The only time
I saw N.Y. I just hated it but you know about that and we swore
never to mention it so I'll say no more. It seems funny to think of
Bill and Anne married I hope it works out but you know Anne
has modern ideas and Bill is just like Father, pretty dull. Mother
has been staying with Uncle George again as he has had a cold
and I wish she would come home, we still only have one maid."

Jesse was feeling frustrated again. Rose had dropped out of
the picture, or had she written letters not saved? Not another
word from Anne. How many letters were missing? More than
had gotten into the old trunk. But one thing he could deduce
from these, there hadn't been any family quarrel. Claire—reading between the lines—probably coerced into a reluctant engagement by her father, had fallen like a ton of bricks for handsome stranger Bob Manning, and he for her. Bob Manning,
visiting an old college friend on his way to California. There had
probably been scenes, and they had eloped, and the old man was
furious but eventually relented and forgave her. These girls had
been her close friends, had kept up correspondence with her.
And where, he wondered suddenly, was Susan, born 1905?

Because these were the cousins—third, no, second cousins—
turned up by Chase's operative. The grandchildren of George
Tilton's sister. Perhaps Susan hadn't been a letter writer; she'd
have been the one nearest in age to Claire. At any rate, there
was no sign of her. Not even, which seemed odd, a reference.
Perhaps she had died young.

He picked up the last envelope, and again two letters came
out of it. The postmark over the three-cent stamp was plain: January 4, 1928—but there was no indication as to which letter, if
either, belonged to the envelope. Mary again: "It is nice to hear
you and Bob are doing so well in the real estate business. I think
sometimes I would like a job, I get bored here with nothing but
housework and the movies sometimes. I went out with Jim Burke

last night for something to do but never again, he wanted to go to this speakeasy and you know I don't approve of drinking, after all it's against the law and besides you know there is another reason I need not mention. Anyway there was one of these orchestras everybody raves over but I think they're vulgar and silly. Well, I'm glad to hear you're happy Claire I guess we can't all be so lucky and let me hear from you soon."

The last letter was a single sheet, and it wasn't a letter. In Rose's violent black ink, her writing even more slapdash than usual, there sprawled across the page two crude lines: "You bitch bitch filthy greedy bitch Ill never stop hating you." Not even any punctuation.

Jesse stared at it. And what was that all about?

He shuffled the letters together and laid them in a little pile at one side of the desk. He picked up the diary.

On Monday morning, his prediction proved true. Manning was bluntly persuasive with the bank manager of the Hollywood branch of the Bank of America: settling his mother's estate, and it was imperative that they see all the records. The manager, as bankers had to do, was going by the rules. If they wanted access to the records of that account, they'd have to get a court order.

"I told you so," said Jesse.

Manning departed, fuming, and Jesse went back to the office and set Jimmy onto the paperwork for the court order. He had an appointment at eleven-thirty, another divorce suit.

After he'd talked to the client, he handed his notes to Jean to transcribe, went out and had some lunch. Back at his desk, he called the local headquarters of Crocker National Bank and asked about a Mr. Meiklejohn, once one of their bank officers. Crocker National had never heard of him. Jesse checked back with Manning, who said, "Well, I don't think Hansie was sure. As I remember, it was West Hollywood. Let me look up the lot title and description, if Harry can locate it—he may remember. I'll get back to you."

Taking shortcuts, Jesse found the number of the Crocker bank in West Hollywood and tried there. He talked to the manager, who said blankly, "I've been here for twenty years, sir, and there has never been anyone named Meiklejohn on our staff."

Jean came in and said, "I'm sorry, I had to take a five o'clock appointment, he couldn't make it any other time. It's another divorce."

"Country going to the dogs morally," said Jesse. He sat and thought about that diary. Nothing in it, and yet something—something—reading between the lines? There had evidently been some family fight, later than he had thought, by Anne's 1931 letter—but he hadn't a glimmering of what had brought it about, or whether Rose's little epistle had had anything to do with it. There just wasn't a clue.

Manning called him back just before three o'clock. "We pinned it down for you. Harry remembered the deal and found the records. Hansie got it wrong, for once—it was a United California Bank. On Doheny Drive."

"Okay, thanks. I'll see what turns up there."

He had just time to check it out, if traffic wasn't too thick. He found the bank, the usual sleek and elegant plate glass and plush carpet place, with marble counters and everybody behind protective grilles. He finally got the bank manager, a smooth moustached fellow with a gimlet eye, and said, "I don't know why you have to make such a production out of it. All I want to know is, have you or did you ever have a Mr. Meiklejohn on your staff?" Jesse handed over a card. "He may be able to give me some evidence in a probate case I'm on."

"Oh, I see. I'm sorry, but we have to be careful. And he's a very old gentleman, in not too good health. Yes, sir, Mr. Meiklejohn was one of our directors here for some years—he retired about eight years ago."

"I suppose you have his address."

"It's in the book—Mr. Warner Meiklejohn."

It was four o'clock. Jesse took the chance: set up an appointment at least. The address was Evelyn Place in Trousdale Estates; it was a red-tiled mansion past an expanse of green lawn. The fat woman who answered the door said, "Oh, I'm sorry, sir, Mr. and Mrs. Meiklejohn aren't expected home until tonight. They've been visiting their son in Corona del Mar. Who shall I say called?"

"I'll call back, thanks." And in all probability the elderly Mr.

Meiklejohn would simply regale him with more fatuous reminiscences of the young Claire and Bob Manning, the romantic young lovers, and wouldn't know a damned thing about her relations with those cousins back in New Jersey.

He got back to his office just as the client arrived. His name was Leffingwell, and he had a somewhat complicated problem to present. He wanted to divorce his wife, who was running up bills on him and refusing him conjugal rights, but he wasn't really sure if she was legally divorced from her second husband: it was possible they weren't legally married at all. They had gone through a marriage ceremony in Vegas three years ago. She had told him that she'd divorced the other man in Mexico, but he understood that wasn't always legal, and he wanted to get everything cleared up legally because now he wanted to marry his real sweetheart, who had just divorced her first husband.

And talk about moral decadence—the paperwork was going to be a nuisance. It was six o'clock before Mr. Leffingwell left, and the Gordons were just leaving. Jesse called Nell and put in half an hour's work detailing the letters to be written and records to be examined, before he locked the office and went downstairs.

It was full dark, a mild and pleasant April night. He was starving, but Nell would have dinner waiting. He turned the Mercedes into Rockledge Road, and four houses down into their own driveway. Nell had the back porch light on for him, and the garage was open.

He braked the car beside hers, got out and reached to pull down the garage door. And without warning, they were on him from behind—a vicious blow to his head. He fell hard against the garage door, and they were hitting him, feet shuffling on cement, heavy breathing, two at least and maybe more—something pounding his side and back— He tried to twist around and lever himself up, and a hard blow knocked him down, knocked the breath out of him, and he was sprawling face down in the driveway—

Somebody said, a long way off, in a fading voice, "That's for doing Manning's dirty work! You better leave the whole Manning deal alone, see?"

Something hit his head again and he was drifting away. He heard Athelstane barking furiously, and then nothing.

SIX

He swam back and was dimly conscious of Nell's voice crying his name, and pain; then he was gone again.

An unspecified time later he was muzzily conscious and a couple of white-clad nurses, a man in a white smock, were standing over him. They told him soothingly he was doing fine.

The next time he was all the way back, his mind working just as usual, and aware that he ached all over and felt like hell, when a pretty nurse came in and was pleased to find him awake. "Your wife's right outside, I'll call her. You've got concussion and some stitches, Mr. Falkenstein, but you were lucky—no broken bones or knife cuts. These muggers don't care what they do, I've seen some."

Then Nell was bending over him and saying, "Darling, you had us scared to death. Thank God you'll be all right, but you should see yourself."

It was, it seemed, Tuesday afternoon, and he had five stitches in his scalp, two black eyes, and the right side of his face scraped raw on the driveway cement; he was a mass of bruises and contusions. But by the time everybody showed up for visiting hours that evening—Fran and Clock, Falkenstein senior and Nell—he was sitting up, all there mentally, and feeling indignant and bewildered.

"Nothing showed, of course," said Clock. "It's been dry, no chance of footprints. Nell wasn't sure what they got—how much did you have on you? Your watch is gone."

"Goddamnit, that's a good watch," said Jesse. "About thirty bucks, and all my I.D.—"

"I don't know how many muggings we've had lately, the punks out all over. The hot list—"

"Damn the hot list," said Jesse. "Not ordinary muggers, Andrew. Hired thugs." He quoted what one had said to him. Manning's dirty work. "Now what the hell? And who the hell could be behind it? It doesn't make sense, but there it is." They were incredulous; he must have been wrong. His father said that concussion had curious effects, and Jesse told him to go to hell. "I know what I heard, damnit."

"Well, I've got your watch on the hot list," said Clock. "Whoever they were, just punks doing what comes naturally or whatever, it's possible they'll pawn it."

"Damnit, I like that watch," said Jesse. At least it had his initials engraved on the back. It was a solid gold Longines; the punks would get something for it.

By Wednesday morning he'd had a look at himself, and shuddered. But he was feeling better, and was annoyed when the doctor said he'd better stay another day. "You sustained quite a beating, Mr. Falkenstein, you'll be feeling the effects for a little while. I don't want you gadding around with that concussion."

Clock brought Manning to see him that afternoon; neither of them believed him about the hired thugs. "I know, it's ridiculous," said Jesse. "If they'd murdered me, you'd just get another lawyer. And who the hell thinks you're up to dirty work? I don't blame you for thinking I'm imagining things."

Manning said uneasily that he'd be sorry to think it had been his fault, but he couldn't see how, and he hoped Jesse'd be out of the hospital soon. After he'd taken himself off, Jesse said to Clock, "Listen, do me a favor and look for this Domino in your records. Wilma Hansen thought he was charged with something and served time. I don't know when."

"Will do," said Clock amiably. "You're looking more like yourself, or I should say sounding. You still look like a Neapolitan sunset."

"Thank you," said Jesse bitterly, "and no beauty to start with. I can't hang around here—I've got things to do, and that damned doctor—" Nell came in in time to hear that.

"Now, Jesse, the doctor knows what he's doing. I suppose there isn't any hope of laying hands on them, Andrew? And of course I never tried to get a look at them. I heard you drive in, Jesse, and then Athelstane went crazy, I never heard him make such a fuss, so I opened the back door and saw them murdering you—at least I'm sure there were three of them—and I screamed, and they took off down the drive. I never got a look at the car, all I can say is it sounded old and noisy. It's just a mercy you weren't killed."

"*Whom the Lord loveth He correcteth*," said Jesse irritably. "I don't think anybody intended that. Look, if I have to stay in this place another day I've got to have something to do. You fetch me that diary, Nell. I want to go over it again . . . Manning's dirty work! Poking around a little academic mystery, and then hired thugs mixing in!" He was indignant at the reasonlessness of it.

That damned will—who had any motive to want it probated safely, who wanted to block Manning's contest of it? Nobody. Nobody but, possibly, Pollock. Everybody knew she had meant everything to go to Manning; even Wilma Hansen, old loyalty to Claire fierce, knew that and deplored the will. And Pollock—well, the unknown quantity, but—

He felt increasingly sure that whatever motive lay behind that will, it went way, way back—to before her marriage to Bob Manning. To the family quarrel, whatever and whenever that had been? And that diary—he had thought when he first read it, there was this and that about the diary, innocuous as it seemed on the surface.

Nell brought it to him on Thursday morning, and he spent the day rereading it and thinking about it. The nurse interrupted him now and then with orange juice, or to take his temperature.

Like most diaries, it had been started with good intentions, which rapidly vanished. That kind of book was no kind to keep a diary in, a set number of lines for each day; some days would warrant none, some a lot more. Soon enough she had started ignoring the printed dates and lines.

The first entry was dated April 23, 1922. "My 18th birthday. My dearest wish came true, Father gave me a BABY GRAND PIANO!!! Also this diary, as he says it's a good habit, so I will try to keep it and write something every day. The piano is BEAUTIFUL and I love it. But I have learned all Miss Moore can teach me, I'm a lot better than she is, and so dreadfully tired of all that Debussy and Chopin, I'd rather play ragtime . . ."

She had started out writing at least a few lines each day, but that soon stopped. By June, she was jotting down a few lines once a week or so. "Thank goodness I am now out of school, all that dreary dull stuff no use to anybody." There were current boyfriends, Ron Elkhart, Tom Forbes the doctor's son; innocently, they went to movies together, and Harold Lloyd just slaughtered her in *Safety Last*. "We went to see Four Horsemen of the Apocalypse last night, the third time I saw it and think it's the best movie ever, Rudy is a real dream, nobody ever so handsome." Later on, she was experimenting with the new Coty-tan makeup and her father called her a painted hussy, he was like all old people, against anything new. "I've thought I'd like to get a job, I'm sure I could learn to type in no time, but he says it's *not necessary* and he wants me at home. He's so much older than most fathers, he just doesn't understand."

She began to skip more days, weeks at a time, and then would set down a paragraph or so. The handwriting, in different inks here and there, gave just a suggestion of the sloping backhand, of the firmer hand it would become. August 1922: "Out to speakeasy with Ron! They call them whoopee parlors, and there's a password. We drank gin, must say didn't like it very much and it made me feel *queer* but I didn't say so to Ron, it's supposed to be the smartest place to go." Tom took her to see Chaplin in *Shoulder Arms*—"he really slaughters me, so funny."

A big blank there to February 1923. "Out with Ron, Rose and Jack to Joe's place outside town, an awful time. Rose got drunk, and we had a terrible time to get her sober enough to go home."

Interspersed with such little highlights, she set down the little mundane doings briefly—"shopping with Anne, really nifty' new green chiffon for evening dress, must tell Mrs. Patton to cut neck really low!!—green best for me on account of my hair." "Bill home from college, all stuck up because he's a HARVARD man—can't stand him, he slicks his hair down with some stuff, trying to look like Rudy." There were two maids, Hattie and Eileen, but she had to order the groceries, plan the meals. In those more leisurely days, the grocery would deliver it all, perhaps in a new, high motor-van.

That July there was a family picnic in the country: "Deadly dull, Father acts just like the patriarchs in the Bible and just because Mrs. Pollock is his niece, Mr. Pollock acts so meek when Father orders him around, I expect they think he'll leave some money to them. He has a lot and just seems to get richer, from what he says about the stock market."

Shopping, movies, the ice cream store with Anne, Mary, Rose, other girls Dora and Marion. He hadn't any idea how big Passaic had been then, but not a big city, a little provincial.

"Father has a crystal set and plays with it just like a little boy with a new toy. Ron says radio is the coming thing and he wishes he had some stock in it." It had developed that Ron Elkhart was a teller at the bank where Father was a director. She noted in passing that Bill was in New York selling bonds. Marion got engaged to Greg. The prosaic days were noted in scraps of words: shopping, dates not so naïve now, the speakeasies, the hip flasks, the new car Ron bought—

Then in September of 1923, a cryptic entry. "Will go to N.Y. with Mary and Rose. Am exhausted down to very bones with all worry and the argument about it but the Pollocks *finally* agreed as long as Mary goes. Don't know what I will tell Father about the $100, must think of some plausible story."

Six days later: "Home from N.Y. this afternoon. I feel 10 years older. Have all sworn never to mention this week." Jesse frowned over that.

Nothing more until June of 1924; now she was using the diary only for more important milestones. She had just gotten engaged to Ron "but don't plan to be married for ages. Father is very pleased and gave me a very pretty gold pendant watch." She didn't sound all that excited over the engagement, as a twenty-year-old should have.

That Christmas she noted a family party with the Pollocks. "Ron makes a fool of himself trying to be the life of the party, all those awful old jokes I've heard a hundred times—she was only a doctor's daughter but you ought to see her operate, only a bootlegger's daughter but I love her still—how Father can think he's so funny I can't imagine. The Pollocks were bored, and I'd tried to have everything fixed up so nicely. Hattie broke the best platter, it was just one of those times everything went wrong."

More humdrum jottings; she was losing interest in the diary.

Some of the sheet music dated from this period; she noted buying it, here and there.

Then, in March 1925: "Most wonderful horrible week of my life—last Saturday went with Ron to Joe's place and Greg Lang was there with HIM—Bob Manning. They were in college together and HE is going to California to go into the real estate business, wants Greg to go with him but Greg says it is foolishness and of course he will have his father's store. But ONE LOOK passed between HIM and me and we KNEW. I have never really loved Ron, not real love—I never knew what that was really till now." In a different ink: "HE came to call on Monday, thank God Father was out. I can't write all that has happened. It has been awful but I know fate is taking over our lives. It's all planned. Hattie will be out tomorrow afternoon and I'll send Eileen on an errand. I will have my bags ready and Bob will borrow Greg's car, we will get the 2:20 train to N.Y. It won't matter who sees us at the station, I will leave a note for Father. May not write again until we are MARRIED and in CALIFORNIA!!!"

End of diary. He could see her thrusting it hastily into a suitcase as she packed that night. She wasn't a diary-keeper by nature, and she had gone into a new life—still half naïve, an impetuous, headstrong, sweet girl—and gone into reality too, the realities of marriage and earning a living: a new life busy enough that she forgot the little book. Had it been buried in a desk drawer, those accumulating letters piling up around it, until the next move?—probably.

But there was something faintly interesting about that diary. It gave a picture of the young, rather imperious Claire—as Wilma Hansen said, always getting her own way. Yes, that would have hardened into the boss lady she'd become.

He was still thinking about the diary, about that roaring decade when liberty had begun to turn to license, when the nurse came in and turned out the light.

They let him come home on Friday, with orders to take it easy. He was annoyed to find that his legs were a little unsteady. He called the office, and Jimmy said, "You gave us a scare, Mr. Falkenstein—we thought we were going to be out of a job. I

canceled all the appointments. Shall we take any for next week?"
Jesse said yes, of course, he'd be in on Monday.

But he was just as thankful when Nell insisted that he stretch
out on the couch and have one of the pills they'd sent home with
him. "I never did believe in those heroes who get beat up and
get up to fight a duel an hour later," he grumbled.

Over the weekend the bruises faded and his face healed, but
he was still feeling indignant about the whole thing, and very
curious. It just made no sense. And he missed his watch.

He went in to the office rather late on Monday morning. The
court order was in, to allow him access to that account at Bank
of America. It might be just as well to look at it without Manning; he called the bank to set up an appointment.

The manager, Carter, was ready to be endlessly helpful with
the court order in his hands. All the records were on microfilm
except the current ones. Carter had the girls who did the posting
lined up in his office to talk to Jesse. "Of course the account is a
long-standing one, all the personnel has changed since it was
opened, many times over. But we can tell you enough that I
think you'll agree there's something fishy about it." Bankers usually had a quick eye for anything fishy. "In all the years the account has been established, at least that's what we can infer—I
haven't seen the microfilm—just one check a month has been
drawn on it."

"I took it for granted it was a pension or annuity of some
kind," said Judy Barlow. She was the one who had most often
posted the checks. "It was a private check, of course, no company name, but—" She had been at this bank longer than the
other girls, nine years. "It gets to be so automatic, you don't really see the information on a check, just run it through, but a
regular one like that showing up all the time, you get to expect
it." All of them had seen the checks from time to time, returned
to the parent bank after being cashed or deposited, for return to
the maker.

All of the checks were made out to the same name. Sandra
Watkins. No Miss or Mrs., just Sandra Watkins. The girls
wouldn't have had occasion to look at the information on the
back. There hadn't, of course, been a check in March, and the

February one would have been returned by now. "I hope," said Jesse, "that you take pictures of both sides."

"Oh, we like to be thorough," said Carter. He had already sent for the record on film, stored away in the vaults under the building. He took Jesse down to a little room near the entrance to the safe-deposit vaults and showed him how to operate the viewer; when a messenger delivered the box of film, he explained the coding system indicating dates. "Thanks, I can manage."

"Just let one of the girls in the vault know when you're finished," said Carter.

He started working backward, and he began not to believe what he was seeing. 1979–1978–1977–all the way back to 1970, on the first of every month a check for $500 made out to Sandra Watkins. A check made out in Claire Elizabeth's neat backhand. Her account with Security-Pacific was under her full name; this one was under C. E. Manning, which was how the checks were signed. All of the checks had been endorsed on the back in a rather unformed careless writing, and marked For Deposit Only in an account at the Bank of America in Pasadena.

In 1970 there had been a change. The amount dropped to $450. Back and back, 1969, 1968, 1967, 1966, 1965. Another drop, to $400. "By God," said Jesse to himself, "she was getting cost-of-living raises." Back to 1955, when the take had been $350 per. He was fascinated at the very regularity of it, turning the lever, looking at that parade of checks; he hadn't yet bothered to total the figures.

In 1950 there was a big change. Before April of that year, the checks were in the amount of $300, and made out to Sandra Wyatt. And they had been deposited at a Security-Pacific bank in Eagle Rock.

"So she got married," said Jesse. He took it right back to 1942, when the checks had been for $200.

And it could all have been done by mail; probably had been. Claire had had to come here only once, the first time, to open the account. The checks would have been sent by mail, and it was possible that Sandra had set up a separate account too, to pay into. None of the staff here in 1942 would be here now, and at the other end, the bank would be incurious as long as the checks didn't bounce.

He found the film showing the statements over the years and looked at those. She had opened the account with seventy-five hundred, built it up to fifteen thousand, eighteen, twenty. In 1946 she had withdrawn nearly all of it briefly, returned most of it the following month. After 1955 it had never fallen below twenty thousand.

"I will be damned," said Jesse to himself. She would, of course, have carefully destroyed those canceled checks as she got them back. Apparently she'd gotten the last one in time to destroy it before she died—it hadn't shown up. He put everything back in the boxes and took a turn or two around the little room. Finally he carried everything out to the desk of the safe-deposit vault, told the girl to thank Mr. Carter, and went out to the parking lot. It was after two, but he wasn't hungry.

He found Manning in his office reading a prospectus for a new shopping mall, without invitation sat down and told him all about it. "I don't need to spell it out for you. It was blackmail. Over an incredible length of time, but that's all it can be."

"My dear God," said Manning. "Mother! Mother—she was known for her absolute integrity—she liked to boast, whoever dealt with us always got a fair shake, no fine print, no under-the-counter deals—I can't believe this! What in hell it could have been—I don't believe it!"

"You wouldn't believe that will at first either," said Jesse, eyes on his cigarette. "I don't need to tell you either that there isn't any chance of a court order to look at Sandra's account. No evidence of any crime committed. She may have set up a separate account and never goes near the bank—or she might have told her fatherly teller, my old granny sends me a present every month."

"My God in heaven!" said Manning. He looked gray. "I can't take this in. But it's nothing to do with—it can't be anything to do with—"

"The will, or the reason for it. I don't see how, no. But it is evidence," Jesse pointed out, "that she was of a secretive nature—"

"Look, they can't have it both ways," said Manning. His good jaw had hardened to stubbornness. "Anybody but a cretin would be secretive about blackmail. If she'd—done something—venal

enough that this damned woman could demand money for silence about it, she wouldn't go talking about it to anybody."

"Granted. I just pointed it out. And in relation to the will, I
couldn't say how a judge might react to this—all her affairs have
to be thrashed out, and the picture of her paying out blackmail
all those years— And if you were thinking of finding the woman,
there are probably dozens of Sandra Watkinses in the greater
Los Angeles area."

"Why the hell should I want to find her?" asked Manning
roughly. He was silent, and then said, "I don't care what it was.
Yes, I do. I'd like to know—if it was something to do with the
company. But it wouldn't have been. It couldn't have been." He
was pacing the office. "Why the hell you had to find that thing—"

"You'd have found it sooner or later."

"True."

"And she may find you, if she doesn't know your mother's dead
—or even if she does. If it was anything to do with the firm—
But I don't think it was," said Jesse, "either. Because on any
crime—if we're considering anything like fraud—except murder,
the statute of limitations would have run out long ago. But
Sandra's had quite a slice out of your intended inheritance,
hasn't she?"

After another silence Manning said wretchedly, "Well, you
can't un-know a thing. I told you I respected her more than anybody I ever knew. I did. She had such integrity. I can't believe
she ever did anything she could have been blackmailed for. But
you can't get away from the evidence, can you?"

"Not very well," said Jesse. He left Manning staring out the
window, the prospectus forgotten on his desk.

And, damnit, he felt nearly the way Manning did. Backtrack-
ing Claire Elizabeth down the years, he'd turned partisan. She'd
had her faults and foibles, but she'd been a gallant old lady. The
naïve, rather spoiled Father's girl, impetuous, headstrong, knowing her own mind—*the prettiest girl I ever knew,* came the echo
of Kathleen Kindly's voice—no, the stodgy Ron Elkhart wouldn't
have done for her; and she'd had her great romance with Bob
Manning. And if she had kept the wound open when he was
gone, at least she'd done something constructive with her grief—

MOTIVE IN SHADOW 103

as a monument to him, an inheritance for his son. Damn it, he'd felt a sneaking admiration for the old girl.

He didn't like to think she'd done something underhanded enough to be blackmailed about it. But you couldn't get away from the evidence.

Quite suddenly he was feeling tired, and his bruises were aching again. It had turned colder and he shivered as he got into the Mercedes. He decided to go home and let Nell cosset him a little.

Clock called that evening. "This Domino," he said. "I asked a pal at the D.A.'s office about him. He was a slick operator, Jesse. Apparently they'd been keeping an eye on him for years, but he didn't get caught up to until 1947, when somebody talked too much and they got the goods on him. He was in construction in a big way, and he'd been handing over under-the-counter money about new sites and low bids. You know the sort of thing. To a few men on the Planning Commission. New shopping mall scheduled for such and such a location, so he'd buy up the land ahead of time and hold up the city, or the investors. Put in the lowest bids for city and county construction. The fellow in the D.A.'s office said a lot of the work he turned out had to be rebuilt, ready to fall down in a year. Anyway, he got charged on three or four counts and drew a five-to-ten at Susanville. Got out in three. Of course he couldn't get his license back, but he'd made a pile and stashed it away."

"I don't suppose you could tell me," said Jesse, "whether he was much of a ladies' man—chaser?"

"What? Well, as a matter of fact," said Clock amusedly, "I can. My pal down there got interested in chasing up the record—he's currently doing some work on similar operators robbing the taxpayers right now. He went into it in detail. He mentioned that aside from his little habits of bribery and corruption, Domino was a sober family man who never strayed off the straight and narrow. Wife stayed by him—they had three or four kids."

"Oh, really," said Jesse. "Thanks for another mystery, Andrew."

And what in hell Claire Elizabeth had had to do with one like that— He believed Manning on that count: the very upright

businesswoman. And her heart in the grave with her Bob, anything along the romantic line was unthinkable. She had left him
with another enigma, was all. He just didn't know what to think.

He went in to the office on Tuesday, though there weren't any
appointments set up. Efficient as usual, the Gordons had gotten
all the paperwork started on Mr. Leffingwell's complex problems.
Another new client wanted a divorce, and Mrs. Gorman was
coming in on Thursday to make a new will. He'd lost count of
the number of wills Mrs. Gorman had made.

As far as Claire Elizabeth's will was concerned—

He stared at Sir Thomas More, that man of such eminent
reason, who stared back at him inscrutably. Those thugs. There
was no sense to be gotten out of it at all. Manning's dirty work.

"Well," he said to himself. Brain just started working again.
The thug who said that didn't know what he was doing for Manning, didn't know anything about the will or what this was all
about. Was that deducible? But it didn't help any in explaining
why anybody wanted Falkenstein off the case. Anybody concerned, everybody he'd talked to, would realize that any fair-to-
middling lawyer would be doing exactly what he had been
doing, and if Falkenstein was out of the case another lawyer
would be in. It had been a piece of stupidity, setting the thugs
on him. Nobody concerned directly in this case was stupid. Quite
the contrary.

In fact, the only person he could think of, aside from Pollock,
who might resent any interference with that will, was Claire
Elizabeth. If she could have found some way to materialize—
But he sobered, thinking that. How she would have resented all
the prying and poking, the uncovering of her secrets big and little—from the blackmailer to the nostalgic little poem she'd cut
out of a magazine.

The phone startled him; he picked it up. "I really cannot understand," said Arthur Tregarron, "why I have not heard a word
from Pollock. It is very strange. He must have had my letter at
least two weeks ago."

"That is a little strange," agreed Jesse. One would have expected that any man, informed out of the blue that an unknown

third cousin had left him a fortune, would come panting across country posthaste to lay claim to it.

"I put through a long-distance call yesterday, and was informed that the number is disconnected."

Jesse's suspicions flared into life: had Pollock been out here, exerting the undue influence? "Wait a minute," he said, scrabbling in the folder on the desk. "That private detective traced him through his mother—I've got her address here," and he read it off.

"Thank you very much," said Tregarron. "That gives us another starting place at least."

Jesse put the phone down and suddenly remembered Mr. Meiklejohn.

Starting places. That diary. If Pollock's name in that will said anything at all, it said that the reason for it, the motive behind that will, went way, way back. To the time that diary was written—to the times those letters had been written?

"I hope Mr. Meiklejohn can see me," he said to the fat woman at the door of the big house on Evelyn Place. "Tell him, please, that I'm John Manning's lawyer and I'd like to ask a few questions."

She took his card and went away, leaving him in a large entrance hall floored in black and white tiles, with an antique brass hall tree and a gold-framed mirror. Three minutes later she was back. "They'll be very glad to see you, sir." She led him to a door halfway down a long hall and opened it.

It was a cozy little den with a corner fireplace, and there was a crackling fire in it. The furniture was large and deep and inviting. The old couple smiling at him made a handsome pair; they must be getting on for eighty, but they had weathered well. Mr. Meiklejohn was middling tall and had kept a lean figure; he had a halo of white hair like a dandelion gone to seed. He was comfortable in ancient slacks and mended sweater. Mrs. Meiklejohn was a small, neat woman with gray poodle curls all over her head; she had a voluminous white apron over her dress, and was knitting rapidly, some soft pink wool.

She intercepted his glance and said calmly, "It's to catch the lint. The apron. Such fine wool, but it does shed. Sit down, Mr. Falkenstein."

Meiklejohn had risen to offer a cordial hand. "So tell me what I can do for Bob Manning's boy, sir."

Jesse felt as if he had come home. He sat opposite them and told them the whole story, leaving out the blackmail. They listened interestedly.

"Now that," said Meiklejohn, "is a very peculiar story, Mr. Falkenstein. I'm blessed if I could guess what's behind it. If I had to guess—not having known Claire recently—I'd go for what that doctor told you. Her mind wasn't working right. She may have acted quite competent to the lawyer, to everybody, but that would be habit—all her business experience. I see you hadn't thought of that."

"It's an idea. The only other idea that keeps nagging me is that if she thought she had some valid reason, it goes away back into the past. Before her marriage."

"Hum," said Meiklejohn. He scratched his nose. "We wouldn't be able to tell you anything about that, I'm afraid."

"What could you tell me?"

Meiklejohn got a cigar out of his breast pocket. "The twenties were a funny time. Decadent, some people said. I don't know. Women had got the vote, all of a sudden things turned upside down—no more long skirts, bobbed hair, ragtime, girls shedding corsets—and Prohibition didn't calm things down any. Girls smoking and drinking for the first time, petting parties, and the whole new idea, do whatever you want so long as you don't harm anybody."

"Hedonistic," said Jesse.

"Yes, but you know, human nature doesn't change overnight. I've got the idea there was a lot more talk than doing," said Meiklejohn dryly. He touched a match to the cigar, emitted blue smoke, "Most people'd rather live a quiet tidy life than go racketing around. I see what you mean about Claire, but as I say, we wouldn't know anything about her family. She had some girl friends back there who used to write to her, and her father, was all. I was glad to meet her boy those years ago—I'm glad he remembered me, to tell you. He looks like his father quite a bit. Bob was a nice fellow."

"You told Manning you knew them in the twenties?"

"That's right." Meiklejohn stretched slippered feet to the fire.

"Bob and I worked for the same realty company in Hollywood. I was there from 1924 on, and Bob came out here with Claire the next year, just after they were married. I wasn't married then, going around with a girl named Sophy who got some bit parts in pictures later—"

"I told you she was a little tramp," said his wife. He laughed.

"Maybe she tended that way. Used to have some good times at Claire and Bob's. Lord, how that girl could play the piano, and sing. We were all doing pretty well for money, even if it was all on commission, those couple of years before the crash. But as a banker, I can tell you that—as we say—the discipline's got to come. You can't run high, wide, and handsome forever. Which is what the twenties did. Moneywise and peoplewise. I liked the look of Bob's boy. Seemed like a fine man."

Jesse assented, puzzled.

Meiklejohn smiled. "You're wondering why I should say so all of a sudden. But it's an example of what I mean about the twenties. People ran a little wild and then they settled down. I expect you could say that Sally and I are responsible for there being a Manning boy."

"Oh?" The fire was enervating; Jesse leaned back.

"People had a lot to keep them busy then—new games, new dances, all the talk about freedom and modernity. There were a lot of divorces and family breakups, just because people didn't use common sense. Claire and Bob nearly came to that."

Jesse stared at him. The great romance? The steadfast Claire? "That's something I hadn't heard before."

"No, you wouldn't have. You see, Bob and I naturally saw a lot of each other, working in the same office. I don't excuse him, because it was his own fault, but he got mixed up with one of the girls we had in the office—one of the clerks. She was a nice girl, too."

"Yes, she was," said his wife. "I always liked Alice. She certainly wasn't wild. And funnily enough, she wasn't nearly as pretty as Claire. But sometimes a man wants something more than just prettiness—though goodness knows Claire wasn't just that. A smart girl, Claire."

"But she wasn't using her brain right then," nodded Meiklejohn. "The way it was, Mr. Falkenstein, Claire was five years younger than Bob, and she'd pretty much had her own way about everything, you could say she was spoiled. And Bob was working long hours, he was thrown together with this girl at the office—Alice Parker—and as Sally says, she wasn't a beautiful girl, I don't think anybody'd paid her much attention before. I was sorry for Alice," he added.

"So was I, but she knew she was doing wrong," said his wife firmly, "whatever was talked about the new freedom and all that."

"Were they—?"

"Well, I don't think there was anything in it," said Meiklejohn. "Bob was just kicking up his heels a little. I don't suppose it went beyond a few kisses, dates on the town. He could always tell Claire he had to work late. Anyway, some kind soul told her about them—"

"Bunny Newsome," said his wife to her knitting.

"Could be. And she reacted without using her brain at all. She was so mad in love with Bob, it was such a shock to her—she was only twenty-three—she came rushing right down to the office and started shouting and crying at them at the top of her voice. Bob was all she had, the most important thing in the world to her, and how could he betray her with this horrible homely girl, taking her dancing at their very own special place, he needn't deny it, they'd been seen—and on and on. Bob, well, you can see how he'd feel. You could hear her all over and the boss had a customer with him. It was damned embarrassing."

"It certainly was," agreed his wife. She smiled at Jesse. "I was the other clerk in the office. Nobody said anything—and Claire was crying and carrying on—Bob and Alice just sat like stones—somebody had to do something, so I just got hold of Claire and got her out of there. I had a little apartment right around on Romaine then, I took her there and just let her get it out of her system in private. And then I talked to her like a Dutch uncle."

"And I talked to Bob," said Meiklejohn. "He was sore about it, her making such a scene in public. All ready to carry the fight back to her. But there wasn't anything in it—they were young and in love, and there wasn't anything wrong with that marriage that a little sense and forgiving wouldn't cure. Bob hadn't meant anything serious, but the way Claire took it—well, she was all set to run out and get a divorce, and both of them regret it all their lives. But Sally talked sense into her."

"I did. I told her not to be silly, over the man flirting a bit. And I said she ought to try and take more interest in Bob's work, not just play around at parties—Claire had a good brain. When she got her senses back, she saw what I was talking about. She grew up some that day—I could see her thinking about what I said."

"Anyway, a couple of days later Bob told me they'd made it up and were going to make a fresh start. To get away from associations, he said. They were going down to San Diego awhile, see how they made out there."

"Claire had the manners to come in and apologize, too," said his wife. "Of course she'd been brought up a real lady. She thanked me for making her use her common sense. She said if she'd lost Bob she'd want to kill herself, she loved him more than her own life. And about then Alice came in and just like the good soldier she was she went right over—Claire, I mean—and said she was sorry for what she'd said and she knew Alice hadn't done anything wrong and hoped she'd forgive her. I was proud of Claire. She was a good girl," said Mrs. Meiklejohn.

"So they patched it up and that's why they went to San Diego," said Jesse thoughtfully. "What happened to Alice Parker?"

"I was sorry for her," said Meiklejohn. "I think she was really in love with Bob—it was a shame. She stayed at the agency for about three more months and then quit. She told Sally there were too many associations there for her, she wanted to get right away and start somewhere new. She got a job with Sullivan-Hartley, I think it was, she wanted to get her own license and get into selling. I wonder if she ever did. But anyway, Claire and Bob got back together and maybe the marriage was all the stronger for that little upset."

"Just exactly when did all this happen, do you remember?"

"Let's see, it was just after New Year's—" He chuckled. "I remember because Claire was so wild, they'd been out at the dance hall on the pier New Year's Eve, and he'd taken Alice there the next night, and she kept on about that. It was around the sixth or seventh of January, 1928."

"You've just restored my faith in human nature," said Jesse. They looked at him inquiringly, and he laughed. "George Tilton died on the fifth of that month, and left her all his money out-right. About two hundred thousand. It occurred to me, if Bob Manning already knew about that, it wouldn't have mattered how he felt about Alice, he'd stick to Claire. But they couldn't have known for another few days."

Meiklejohn looked shocked. "Oh, no, Bob wasn't like that, Mr. Falkenstein. He wanted to make money all right, but he was an honest man—a good man. Anyway, I've always been glad to think that between us we patched that one up."

"She couldn't have known about the money when she called to say good-bye," said his wife. "That was a day or so later, as I recall. We never heard about that."

Meiklejohn was brooding over the stub of his cigar. "We never heard about Bob getting killed like that, until I ran across his boy those few years back. After the crash—Sally and I were just married then—I had to take what I could get for a few years, and then in 1934 I got the job at the bank and we were all right. We never knew Claire and Bob had come back here."

And that, thought Jesse, was understandable; when they had, they wouldn't have contacted Meiklejohn and Sally, who knew how close the romance had been to breaking up. They were busy; their lives had drifted in another direction.

"Funny how things turn out," said Meiklejohn comfortably. "Nobody had much of anything, back then. Sally and I in a one-bedroom apartment on Hobart, I was making thirty bucks a week and glad to have it, and here I retire eight years ago from a bank director's job. And Claire going on to make all that money —I suppose, when I ran into Manning that time back, I should have got in touch with her again, but I didn't. Felt I'd like to remember her the way she was—a damned pretty girl. Well, she took Sally's advice to heart, didn't she? But at least she and Bob had the boy. That is a mighty peculiar thing about her will. I hope you can get it straightened out."

"So do I," said Jesse.

He was learning more of Claire Elizabeth's story, and surely it showed her maturing and growing toward the tired, gallant old lady she had been at the last. The gay redhead, so brave and open on apology to the colorless Alice Parker—that was the woman who tried to say please and thank you in her last extremity. He was absurdly glad to know that the love she and Bob Manning had shared had been saved and strengthened by those two nice people. And that in a way explained all her steadfastness, when she lost him to a greater adversary than another woman. And Bob Manning hadn't been a cynical opportunist; he had loved her. They had just been lucky—for a little while.

And after that—the one-man woman—she had walked with his shadow at her side.

He left the Meiklejohns regretfully. They told him to let them know what happened, or if they could help any other way. They had liked Claire and Bob; they were interested in their boy.

As he went down the brick wall dividing twin lawns, Jesse found the old tune had slid quietly into his mind, and he was humming it under his breath, groping for the words: "Me—and my shadow, strolling down—the avenue— Me and my shadow— No one else to tell our troubles to—"

SEVEN

But, he thought, sitting at his desk staring at Sir Thomas, there was that blackmail—or implied blackmail. There was an implication in that diary, too. Something had happened back in September of 1923, something they had sworn "never to mention." A secret to be kept at all costs. Something she could be blackmailed about nineteen years later?

By that time Bob Manning was dead, and whatever secret there might have been in her past couldn't matter to him—or to her, to keep it from him. And how would a Sandra Watkins out here know about it anyway? How had she been connected to Claire Elizabeth? Manning didn't know the name, but during that period he'd have been away at military school, he wouldn't have known, say, about the domestic help she hired.

A vague picture was forming in his mind, some forerunner of Mrs. Hawes snooping, coming across a letter—a letter giving away the secret? Girls would talk, whatever vows they made. A prying domestic, bringing the pressure to bear. But, for all these years? That deadly and important a secret?

And would it be possible to chase the woman down? In the greater Los Angeles area, how many Sandra Watkinses?—and there was no telling how she used that bank account. It might be her only one, or one she never went near. It would take a year to check out all the available Sandra Watkinses.

But he'd like to know what was behind that. It was always better to get at the truth, bring it out in the open, however ugly it was.

And with all due respect to Arnold Chase, he thought he'd put the thing in the hands of a bigger and more experienced agency. If it was possible to ferret any truth out of this segment of the mystery at all— He had occasion now and then to use the private eyes; he consulted his address book and called Thomas Garrett Associates on La Cienega Boulevard, asked to speak to Mr. Garrett.

"I've got," he said, "what may be an impossible job for you."

"Nothing's impossible to a persistent shamus," said Garrett, who had identified his name instantly after a lapse of two years. "What is it?"

"I want to find a woman named Sandra Watkins. She was probably Sandra Wyatt before 1950. I don't know where she lives or works or what she looks like or anything about her except that she's been taking a nice piece of change in blackmail. She's got a bank account, I don't know what kind, at the Bank of America in Pasadena. For the last nine or ten years she's been depositing a check for five hundred in it every month, possibly by mail. The checks were signed by C. E. Manning and undoubtedly sent by mail, checks on the Hollywood branch of the Bank of America. Can you possibly do anything with that?"

"Don't know until we look," said Garrett. "Shortcuts and contacts. Are you in a hurry?"

"Well, I'd like to know whether it's possible to find out anything soon."

"I'll put somebody on it. Usual retainer?"

"I'll get it in the mail today."

"Okay. I'll get back to you, probably around the end of the week," said Garrett.

Jesse had just put the phone down when it shrilled at him; he jumped and picked it up. "Say, Mr. Falkenstein," said Harry Fowler, "I've been pawing around through a lot of back records, prior to my time because the name didn't ring a bell at all, and I can't find that we were ever in any kind of deal with this Domino. But I've got a vague feeling that the name's connected with some shady doings of some kind—"

"You would have. Back in the late forties he was indicted for bribery and fraud. He owned a construction company."

"Well, we wouldn't have had anything to do with anyone like that," said Fowler definitely, sounding slightly affronted.

"Thanks for looking anyway."

All sorts of little enigmas she had left behind her. And among them, he would especially like to know who had hired the thugs to warn him off. Who didn't want that will challenged? It wasn't to the advantage of anybody in the case that that will be proven. Except, of course, Adam Pollock, who was still very much the unknown quantity. It would be nice to build up Adam Pollock as the villain, spying out Claire Elizabeth's routine, coming to butter her up—when Mrs. Lightner was off duty—and that could have been done in letters too, of course. Even—wait for it—holding that old secret over her? Now wait a minute, he thought. Sandra Watkins lived here. But she needn't have always. They could be in touch.

How wild could imagination get? Those maids, back there—living in the house, one or both of them could have nosed out the secret. And gossiped a little, to somebody who later came out here and looked Claire up—someone in touch with the family back there— But that was nonsense, of course. Whatever had happened, a scandalous secret fifty-seven years old was dead as a doornail. And what might have been scandalous in 1923 probably wouldn't be thought twice about now. And who was left to care?

But, the blackmail. Look at that logically. She would have known about the statute of limitations. Had she been paying out that blackmail money all these years to keep some knowledge from Manning? Manning alone? Something she had done, then, that she was ashamed of—something not necessarily criminal or even very wicked—just something she was ashamed of? And she took the gamble that he wouldn't find out, after she was gone. She could have said to Sandra, All right, you get this for your silence until I die, but be satisfied and leave it, after that. Took the gamble that then, when Tregarron and Manning came across that other account, they might wonder but wouldn't bother to look back into it. In a way, that made sense; if the something had been really venal, really serious, a blackmailer couldn't be trusted to call it quits.

But—but— For the first time, another aspect of the matter occurred to him. When she made that will, she must have known —if she'd been thinking straight—that it would be a shock to Manning, that he'd contest it, wouldn't just tamely step back and see everything handed over to a stranger. She should have foreseen that in a legal attempt to bypass that will, all her affairs would be examined thoroughly. Her mind hadn't been working logically—or only by some irrational logic. Those odd amounts of money left to Manning and his son underlined that. The mind, once so sharp, beginning to crumble, overlooking what she didn't choose to see—in the grip of some strong emotional obsession?

They were all points to bring out to a judge; it could be that the grounds of incompetence would be more telling than the Unnatural Provisions.

The Gordons were leaving, calling good-nights. Jesse got up.

When he came in, Nell had built a fire and was waiting for him. "I have," she announced, "been doing some of your work for you. Get yourself a drink, and I'll have some sherry—I got the baby to bed early, and dinner's in the oven—and I'll tell you about it."

Obediently he fetched the drinks and ensconced himself in the other armchair. "What have you been up to?" She was looking a little smug and pleased with herself. She sipped sherry; he had brought in a bowl of cocktail pretzels and Athelstane crowded up to beg.

"Well, I got interested in your enigma—Claire Elizabeth, as you call her. It *is* a funny sort of thing, Jesse—though it's ridiculous to mix your muggers into it, you just misunderstood something they said—"

"The hell I did."

"Anyway, I've been going over her diary. You said there were a couple of queer entries, that seemed to say something out of the ordinary happened in September of 1923. And I think I can tell you what it was."

"And what was it?"

"She had an abortion."

"How in hell do you make that out?" He was startled.

"You," said Nell, "are a mere man. Though more noticing than most, sometimes even you miss the nuances. And you skipped over something she wrote before that, but it said something to me." She had a bookmark in the fat green diary, and passed it over. "Under July 13."

Jesse read it and said, "Oh. No, I didn't connect it." He read it again. "July 13. Met Rose and Dora to attend sale at Gruber's. Some really nifty bargains and Father can rage about bills all he pleases, I really needed everything I bought. Stopped at Drake's for sodas afterward. The hottest day this summer, I nearly fainted in Gruber's, it was so stuffy. Late again, but never know. Little worried about it. I find on looking over receipts I spent fifty dollars, Father will be annoyed!"

"Well, you *see*," said Nell. "Late again. You can read it plain as print, Jesse. She was just beginning to suspect she was pregnant. Probably very soon after she wrote that, she was sure—and then we get that trip to New York. You can tell there was a row about it—women hadn't been emancipated all that long, and young unmarried girls didn't go gallivanting around alone. You see the Pollocks—and presumably Father—finally agreed, if Mary went along. Mary the prude—oh, I've read the letters too—who was older and more responsible."

"But would she have confided in Mary? Mary'd have been as horrified as Father."

"Yes, but she'd have to. She'd have been desperate. And at least Mary would go along with her there, it had to be covered up—she'd have to get rid of it. They must somehow have had information where to go—maybe the man knew."

"Ron Elkhart?"

Nell shook her head. "I stop guessing there. She was never in love with him—just in love with the idea of love and romance and sex. Father pushed her into the engagement. But something Mary said in a letter, later, about drinking— Suppose there was a crowd of young people out at that speakeasy, and she had a little too much gin. You can imagine it—the noise and crowd, and a ragtime band, and the dancing—sneaking out for a petting party in the back of the car—Ron, or anybody."

"The hundred bucks," said Jesse abstractedly.

"Exactly, darling. She paid for it herself. She made up some excuse to Father. It was probably supposed to be a trip to the big city for shopping, going to the theater. And it could just be that she never told the man, whoever it was."

Jesse contemplated his drink. "All right, it's possible. What does it have to do with here and now?"

"Probably nothing," said Nell, "but you said she'd been harking back to old times and the people she knew then. It was an old secret and nobody would care about it now, except herself. She could have been feeling guilty about it all over again."

"Um," said Jesse. "I have come to the conclusion that her mind had begun to slip. She was covering up, sounding all right and acting all right, but she wasn't thinking straight."

"Well, then," said Nell consideringly, "maybe she was thinking back to that, and feeling grateful to Rose and Mary all over again for helping her, keeping her secret—"

"It wasn't their progeny she left it to— Bill! But, Bill!" said Jesse, setting his glass down on the coffee table with a crash. "It could have been Bill—he was coming home from New York now and then, and he sounds like the city slicker, doesn't he? Young bond salesman with brilliantine on his hair à la Valentino —and living in New York, he might very well have located the abortionist—"

They looked at each other, excited at these plausible deductions. "And that would explain her motive," said Nell, "if you grant that she was irrational, mentally off. She was harking back to that time, and feeling guilty all over again about killing Bill's baby, and so she decided to leave everything to the son he did have."

"I don't know—it makes sense in a way—but was she quite that irrational? And she'd been so wrapped up in Bob Manning. And she wrote that she couldn't stand Bill—"

"That was the year before. And damn Bob Manning, this one would have been the first man in her life—you can recreate the atmosphere, all that talk about free love and do your own thing, even if they put it differently—and then when she found she was pregnant, she was just a scared kid. It'd have been the most important thing that ever happened to her—the first important thing. If she was going right back, she'd have skipped over Bob Manning to that."

"It could be the answer," said Jesse slowly. "But we'd never prove it. I wonder if Mary and Rose are still alive. We know Anne is, but by the diary she didn't know about it. Damn it,

I wish we could get hold of Pollock. At least he'd know which of the family is still alive—and we still don't know anything about Susan. But that's pretty deducing, Nell."

"I like it. I think it's your answer."

"And I wouldn't care to suggest it to Manning," said Jesse.

On Thursday afternoon Clock called Jesse and said, "We've found your watch. I'll have to ask you to come and identify it."

"Well, a step in the right direction."

"Oh, you can't have it—it's evidence."

"I know, I know. Where?"

It was a pawnshop on Fairfax Avenue. As Jesse came up to it, Detective Petrovsky was coming in the other direction, and hailed him cheerfully. "Andrew's spotted a few little things could be loot, he called me to fetch down the serial numbers. Let's see what we've got."

They went in, to a small dirty shop. Clock, massive-shouldered and looming, was standing over a smaller man who was saying aggrievedly, "Listen, I been sick, my brother-in-law's been keeping the store and he don't know the business, never looked at the hot list— I called you as soon as I spotted that, didn't I? Didn't I? Listen, he'll tell you anything he can—"

"He'd better," said Clock. "Hello, Jesse. There's your watch." It was; they checked the initials on the back. "Some other stuff, Pete—that tape recorder and transistor radio and portable TV. Have a look at the numbers."

Petrovsky got out a list and checked serial numbers. "Well, there you are, it's some of the loot from that Thalberg break-in on Yucca on Tuesday night. They didn't get much."

"All I know is, Joe said this was all together in a batch, he give thirty bucks for it."

"So let's see if the lab turned up anything on that," said Clock. "Where does Joe live?"

Jesse was interested, and tagged along to the big new precinct building on Fountain Avenue. Petrovsky went and brought in Joe, and he said all he remembered was, it was two young guys brought that stuff in, just ordinary guys, kind of long hair and maybe leather jackets, he didn't remember if they were dark or light or how tall. Clock played the heavy cop at him, but didn't get anything else.

"People," he said to Jesse, and picked up the phone to talk to the lab. When he put it down he said disgustedly, "If we had twice as many men maybe we'd get somewhere fighting the crime wave. And maybe not too, considering the state of the courts. They picked up some latents at the Thalberg house, but they haven't got around to processing them yet. Maybe tomorrow, they say."

"Yes, well, let me know what you find out. I'm interested in those thugs, Andrew. If you ever pick up these punks, I'd like to talk to them. If they had my watch, they're either the ones who beat me up or they know who did."

"I'll bear it in mind," said Clock. And just then the desk called to say they had a new homicide, and he gathered up Petrovsky and rushed off looking annoyed, and Jesse went back to his office.

He had forgotten all about Mrs. Gorman, who was waiting for him in the outer office. She forgave him the delay amiably. "One of your nice young secretaries said I could wait in here," she told him, pulling one of the client's chairs toward the window, "but after five minutes I got in such a dither I had to go out. That Man, Mr. Falkenstein! It seemed he was staring right through me"—she cast a quick glance over her shoulder at the Holbein print—"and you'll think I'm imagining things, but I felt as if he knew every little thing I'd ever done, from stealing my sister's toy dog when I was three to telling Mother a fib to go out on a date. That Man—who is he?"

Jesse suppressed a grin. "You really don't have to be afraid of him—he's been dead for four hundred and sixty-five years."

"I'll bet he was murdered," said Mrs. Gorman.

"Well, not officially. He refused to compromise his religious principles and Henry the Eighth had him beheaded for treason."

"That's exactly the awkward sort of creature he looks like," said Mrs. Gorman. "All righteous ethics and hair shirts. Not that I ever admired Henry the Eighth, with all those women. Now,"—she turned her back firmly on Sir Thomas—"I really have got a good reason to make a new will, Mr. Falkenstein,

because my sister-in-law's just died and of course I'd left her
all my opal jewelry, it being her favorite jewel. So I'd better
let her daughter have it instead, and as long as we're about it
I think I'll leave another thousand to the Animal League—"

On Friday morning Tregarron called, sounding fretful and
flurried. "I must say, Mr. Falkenstein, that this is quite an un-
precedented situation. I have no idea where these Pollocks are.
I placed a long-distance call to the address you had for Mrs.
Pollock, and reached a switchboard—I take it, at an apartment
hotel—where they told me she was away on a cruise and her
apartment closed. They could not say when she might be re-
turning. But why on earth I haven't had some communication
from Pollock himself—"

Jesse agreed that it was very queer. "But I suppose she'll
come home sometime, and can tell us where he is. Like to put
a hypothetical case to you, Tregarron." He outlined the possible
story as he and Nell had imagined it, and sensed Tregarron's
discomfort over the phone.

"Dear me," said Tregarron. "Dear me. If we agree that Mrs.
Manning was indeed failing mentally—and I must confess that
I myself had not grasped the fact that if she had been herself
she would surely have known that the will would be contested
—if she was irrational, I can only say that your theory is possible. Just possible. But of course it rests upon a very tentative
assumption, which—at this late date—could scarcely be proved."

"I realize that, of course."

"I should hate to lay all that before Mr. Manning, you know.
He—er—respected her very highly. So did I," said Tregarron
mournfully. "Well, well, whatever form the delusion took, it's
a sad thing to see a fine mind deteriorate. I had better report
to you that the probate is going forward. Normally we should
have been able to close it out sometime in August, or at the
least September, but with the notice of contest officially filed,
of course everything is delayed pending the hearing, and I
wouldn't expect that to be called until October, though—"

"Yes, we've got plenty of time," said Jesse.

"I just wish," said Tregarron, "we could locate Pollock. So

much depends on the line he will take—and who will be repre-
senting him. It is all very irregular."

On Saturday morning Nell had just gone out to do her weekly
marketing, leaving Jesse to baby-sit, when Clock called to report
progress. "At least we know who one of them is, the lab made
his prints from the Thalberg house. One Edward Thornton. He
piled up the usual j.d. record, narco, B. and E., assault, even
attempted homicide, and as usual got the probation, hasn't
spent any time inside. He's been known to deal in drugs in a
small way. He's now twenty-two. Known to run with others
much the same kind, with the same kinds of records. He's been
picked up for mugging before."

"He sounds very likely," said Jesse. "And I'm aware that you
all think that crack on the head addled my wits that night, but
I know what I heard. When and if you pick him up, Andrew,
for God's sake ask some pointed questions about who set them
onto me and why."

"Well, all right," said Clock dubiously, "but I don't suppose
we'd get anything. Anyway, there's an A.P.B. out on him, and
we've got Traffic on the lookout for his known pals, to haul
in and question. He's driving an old clunker of a Chevy, which
could very well be the car Nell heard take off. I'll let you know
what turns up."

Jesse went out to pour himself a third cup of coffee, and
sat on the couch drinking it, watching David Andrew practice
walking. He was getting the hang of it better this week, but
was a long way from perfection, and Jesse was vividly reminded
of Mr. Ogden Nash's comparison of babies with drunks. David
Andrew, teetering determinedly across the living room floor,
wore the same owlishly concentrated expression of the suspect
driver attempting to walk a straight line.

But the fact that Thornton had had his watch, and was known
to have been on the break-in on Yucca Street, didn't say he had
been one of the thugs. That was another damned annoyance, it
might be weeks before his case came up, and the watch would
sit there tagged as evidence until it did—but these days too,
knowing they'd likely get nothing but a slap on the wrist, and

that the cops' hands were tied, the punks were never disposed to be cooperative.

And he really would like to know about those thugs. Manning's dirty work. Oh, yes?

There was also the elusive Pollock. It would be very gratifying to read Pollock as the villain. And Jesse thought suddenly that he'd never talked to the nurse, or nurses, who had spelled Mrs. Lightner when she was off duty. Had there been any visitors while she was away?

He hadn't any remote expectation that there was anything in it, but in the interests of being thorough— He had jotted down somewhere the phone number where she'd be and, pursued by Athelstane, went down the hall to ask her about the other nurses.

"Well, it was only one actually," said Mrs. Lightner's calm voice. "Miss Shipley. And she hadn't been coming for some time. I told you Mrs. Manning disliked being fussed over. Miss Shipley had been coming in on Sundays when I was off—it's nearly impossible to get a practical nurse for odd jobs like that, and she was available because—well, she's not a very capable woman. It was only to have someone there, you see. But she did rather fuss, and some time last June Mrs. Manning got fed up with her. She said it was silly to have someone in just for the day, she'd be quite all right alone, it wasn't as if she was bedridden and couldn't do things for herself. When she came home from the hospital in August she still wouldn't have anyone. I was a little anxious about it, she could have fallen—but she insisted. And I'd usually be back by nine or ten. I'd leave a sandwich for her lunch and she could make coffee or tea, and something for her dinner she could warm up. I will say," said Mrs. Lightner, "that was one way she wasn't fussy at all—she hardly noticed what she ate, anything would do. I'd put a couple of frozen entrées into the oven and all she had to do was turn it on."

"Oh," said Jesse. "When was Miss Shipley fired?"

"About the middle or end of July, it was. I can't say I blamed Mrs. Manning, she was an annoying woman, and as it worked out, it was all right—I was there with her when she had the stroke."

"Yes. Where can I get hold of Miss Shipley?"

"The nursing agency can give you the address." She gave him

the number. She wasn't incurious, only tactful, assuming that he'd have enlarged on explanation if he felt it necessary.

The nursing agency was disposed to ask questions about his requirements for a nurse, but perseverance finally got him Miss Ada Shipley's address. It was over in the Atwater section.

As soon as Nell came home he started over there, and had a hunt for the place; it was an old apartment building hidden away down a dead-end street. He had to look at the name slots on all the doors before he found hers at the end of the second-floor hall. He knocked on the door; a TV was on inside, and in a moment the volume cut down.

"Yes?" The door opened.

"Miss Shipley? The nursing agency gave me your address—"

She simpered at him widely. "Oh, I'll be only too happy for a new case, I just love my work and my patients usually take to me— When would you—"

"Excuse me, not a case—I'm the attorney settling Mrs. Claire Manning's estate."

Her coy smile vanished instantly and she drew back a step. She was a large clumsy woman with dyed-looking brown hair and buck teeth. "Oh. She's dead, is she? Well, what do you want of me?"

"We have to go into all sorts of things," said Jesse vaguely. "Getting the accounts square, you know. You were with her on Sundays up to the end of July, around there?"

"That's right, and I don't know what that other woman told you but I'm sure I've always given satisfaction on my other cases, and there was no reason, no reason at all for her to have any complaint about me. She was a very difficult patient. She hadn't any real reason to—to dismiss me, whatever she told Mrs. Lightner."

"Oh, I don't think there was any complaint," said Jesse. "You managed her very tactfully, by what Mrs. Lightner told me, there wasn't any personal reason for letting you go, please don't think that. Mrs. Manning just decided she could manage alone."

"Oh, well, then—I was just afraid something had been *alleged*." She gave him a half simper. "You'd better come in." She took his card. It was a shabby, dirty, untidy room, with a black-and-white TV in one corner; she went to switch it off. "I thought myself she just made an excuse to dismiss me—she really was a very difficult old lady—because she had such a nasty secretive nature and was afraid I'd tell Mrs. Lightner about that woman who came to see her. Because—"

Jesse stared at her, feeling that his mouth must have dropped open. Here he'd been building a wild story about Pollock sniffing around exerting undue influence, and lo, into his lap dropped the strange visitor. Out of the blue. "On Sundays?" he managed to ask.

"Certainly. I don't know why she wanted to be so secretive about it, I suppose there wasn't any reason she shouldn't have had someone call on her, except that she never had before. But I really felt it very much, as if she suspected I'd listen at the door or something nasty like that—it was really an aspersion on my character," said Miss Shipley, indignation reddening her cheeks. "That first time, she gave me a list of things and sent me out to get them, I don't know what all, I had to go to three drugstores and the market, and what with parking it took over two hours— and when I came back, if you please, there's a visitor—this woman with her—and she'd made coffee and cut into the fresh cake Mrs. Lightner had made—and when I looked in, she spoke up sharp and said, that's all right, you just go put those things away and leave us alone. As if I was her *maid* or something—"

"Yes, very annoying," said Jesse soothingly. No trouble getting this kind to talk. "What did the woman look like?"

"Quite an ordinary woman, I only got a glance. Blond I think, and not very big. She really was," said Miss Shipley, obviously reverting to Claire Manning, "a horrid old woman, there was something unnatural about her—she wasn't like any other old lady I'd ever taken care of. Do you know she didn't even have to wear glasses?—never had, even for driving—she had eyes like a —a hawk or something, didn't even wear glasses for reading. Unnatural, I call it. Sitting there so stiff and silent and if you tried to be pleasant and chat a bit, she'd bite your head off, say she didn't feel like talking. Anyway, that day after the woman left she said to me, just as well not mention her to Mrs. Lightner, they thought it would tire her too much to have callers but it hadn't. Well! As if I was one to pry where I'm not welcome—"

"Yes, yes. Did the woman come again?"

"The very next Sunday, and when she rang the doorbell Mrs. Manning told me to go upstairs and start getting her winter clothes out of mothballs. In July! Just to get me out of the way! As if I'd listen at doors!"

"Yes, very annoying," said Jesse. "Do you remember anything else about her?"

"Mrs. Manning closed the living room door. I only saw her back when she left that time. And it was the next week the agency called and said I wasn't to go back on the case, they didn't want me anymore. I didn't know what Mrs. Manning might have said about me, it's a great relief to know there wasn't anything. But I can tell you about that woman's car," said Miss Shipley brightly. "I thought myself she was a confidence woman out to get money from the old lady, and the old lady was afraid her son would find out she was giving her money. For some con game, you know."

"Very possibly. What about her car?"

"Why, the first time—when I came back from all that shopping—I saw the car in front of the house, and thought it was queer because nobody ever parks there except Mr. Manning, and I looked at it as I drove in and I couldn't help noticing. It had those, what do they call them, vanity plates—license plates, you know—and it said GLADYS C. I think she was getting money out of the old lady, and I got the idea it was because I'd seen her I was f—dismissed. She was really a queer old woman, so crabby and—and—"

"Secretive," said Jesse. He stood up and began to extricate himself.

"Now, Jesse," said Clock, "I'm a public servant. There are laws about the right to privacy."

"Oh, hell, Andrew, if this damned woman got stopped for running a light, they'd shoot the plate number in to see if it was hot, wouldn't they? A plate number's nothing private." He draped one hip on the corner of Clock's desk here in the detective office.

"I haven't any legal reason to ask about it," said Clock.

"Oh, now, be obliging, Andrew. Remember I'm going to be your offspring's uncle, and I've got a lot of money to leave him—her—it. Ebenezer or Chloris."

Petrovsky laughed at the next desk. "Something in what the man says, Andrew. Money not to be sneezed at."

"Come on," said Jesse plaintively. "You've got that handy little machine, I've seen it. Feed a plate number into it and three minutes later back the record comes from the computer up in Sacramento."

"Ah, don't tamper with his conscience," said Petrovsky. "I'll get it for you—what's the plate number?" He went off down the hall, and five minutes later came back. "Who's to know, Andrew? No sweat. There you are, Mr. Falkenstein—Mrs. Gladys Cortland, Sherwood Drive, West Hollywood. No wants, no warrants, no moving violation tickets."

It was now three o'clock. Jesse, fired with the hunt, made good time through weekend traffic. His new objective was a tall condominium with professional landscaping around it. Mr. and Mrs. Douglas Cortland were listed in number twelve on the second floor. He ignored the elevator, took the stairs two at a time. It was at the back, probably overlooking the swimming pool. The hall was deeply carpeted.

When the door opened he faced a nice-looking woman, not young but still pretty: coiffed blond hair, a belted silk house robe showing a figure only slightly plump; she wore upswept crystal glasses. "Mrs. Cortland?"

"Yes?" She looked at his card. "Good heavens, has someone left me a fortune?"

"Sorry, no. But I think you knew Mrs. Claire Manning."

She looked even more surprised. "I do— Did? Is she gone?"

"Last month. I'm concerned with settling her estate."

"I see. And what is it you want of me?"

"It's a long story, but for various reasons we have to talk to all the people who—were in her orbit most recently. The will's being contested."

"You'd better come in," she said. "Did she have much money?"

"Quite an enormous bundle of money."

"For heaven's sake," said Gladys Cortland. "Come in. For *heaven's* sake. Well, you never know, do you? That house— My goodness. Douglas will be sorry to have missed you—he's out playing golf—he was interested in what I told him about her. Sit down, won't you? What do you want to know?"

"Well, how did you meet her, and why did you go to see her?"

She sat down opposite him in one of a pair of matching velvet chairs. This room was individual, restful, charming with small personal touches: a Degas ballet print above the mantel, an arrangement of pussy willows in a copper pitcher, on a low chest against the wall a sculpture of gulls mounted on an onyx base, frozen in flight.

"That's easy enough. But I don't know what you'll think about it. I was in Robinsons' last July tenth, buying a birthday present for my sister, and Mrs. Manning was at the same counter. We exchanged a few words while we waited for a clerk. Then later, we were in the same elevator up to the lunchroom, so it fell out naturally that we shared a table." She cocked her head at him. "And I just mentioned that it was the anniversary of my daughter's death—she was struck by a car when she was ten—and said I hoped she knew I was thinking about her. And Mrs. Manning looked so puzzled and surprised, and asked if I really thought she was still there, somewhere."

"Oh, my Lord," said Jesse. "I foresee the end of this. And that should have occurred to me, damnit. She probably hadn't been inside a library in her life, she had to have found out from somebody that there were books like that to read. But go on."

She raised her brows at him, amused. "You're not a skeptic?"

"Not me we're talking about. She'd never heard of such ideas, she didn't know a thing about evidence of survival, communication, the whole bit."

"I think from what she said she'd had a very orthodox upbringing—heaven and hell and judgment—and she'd just discounted it. We talked quite a long time, and she was interested. She'd obviously never given much thought to any of it, and what I could tell her—about some of the evidence—she was interested. She asked me to come and see her. I felt sorry for her rather, and if I could help her to some sort of conviction—"

"All right," said Jesse. "You needn't enlarge. You went to see her, and talked. You told her there was a lot of published material about all this, if she was interested in reading the evidence.

You went to see her twice and talked about it. What exactly did you point her toward, theosophy or what?"

She wrinkled her nose. "Not that. If you're familiar with the field, Myers and Lodge and Gardner. And some of the popular things."

"Smith and Steiger and *The ESP Reader*. Fodor. Garrett. Cerminara?"

"Cerminara certainly." She gave him a wide amused smile. "You're a very surprising lawyer, Mr. Falkenstein."

"Just interested in evidence. You just went to see her twice?"

"I was sorry for her. Yes. She seemed to be so devoid of any belief, she was bewildered that there were so many people interested and investigating—that anyone should think there was evidence for survival. I hope," said Mrs. Cortland, "I helped her a little. She was so old, she seemed so lonely. That awful house—it never occurred to me she could have much money. She told me she hadn't been to church since she was a child, but the church expected you to believe what it said just on faith, and she'd always relied on solid evidence you could look at and evaluate."

"Yes," said Jesse. "What the righteous orthodox always forget, all religion based solidly on the psychic phenomena." He picked up his card where she had laid it on the coffee table and wrote DeWitt's address on it. "Yes, some of the evidence can't be ignored. You may be interested to look up this fellow, friend of mine—serious experienced researcher. He's always looking for intelligent helpers, experimenting with his mediums."

Another dead end. But he might have expected somebody like Mrs. Cortland to show up; Claire Elizabeth had had to be led to those books.

She had had that serious illness just after meeting Gladys Cortland, and her mind had been on the subject—after she was home and able to go out, she went to the library for those books. Realizing she hadn't much time left. Wondering if she might find herself, somewhere beyond the veil, answerable to authority, asked to judge herself, what good and evil she had accomplished.

Was that when her mind went all the way back—to something —what?

Poor little Claire Elizabeth, after her busy, materialistic, productive life, wondering—

He thought wryly, something to put to a judge? Most of them orthodox, and it was a comment on a materialistic age—to the orthodox, interest in psychic research was evidence of mental instability. But if the twentieth century was going to add anything useful to history—anything philosophically important—it was probably the psychic researchers who would accomplish it.

EIGHT

On Sunday morning Nell and Fran departed with the baby and Athelstane up to the house in Coldwater Canyon to survey the redecorating as far as it had gone. Jesse was stretched out on the couch in the study somnolently listening to Bach when the doorbell rang, about noon, and he shut off the stereo in the middle of the *Toccata and Fugue in D Minor* and went to see who it was.

A neat smallish man in unobtrusive gray clothes was on the doorstep, felt hat in hand. "Mr. Falkenstein? Gil Allen with Garret Associates. I'm pretty sure I've nailed down your girl for you. Sandra Watkins."

"Already? I hadn't expected such speedy service." Jesse brought him into the living room. Nell had left the coffee on simmer and there were a couple of cups left. "That must have been the hell of a job—are you sure you've got the right one?"

Allen put his head on one side, exactly like an alert terrier acknowledging praise. "Not so much of a job, no. Things aren't usually very complicated in real life, you know. You go by probabilities. The probability was that she lived in or around Pasadena someplace, with the bank account there. If I'd had to go farther afield—but you start where you are, the easiest way. There are four Sandra Watkinses in the general area. So I had a quick look around—" Jesse could guess how, as the insurance investigator, collecting information for the city directory—"and the others looked ordinary, fairly unlikely for a blackmailer, though there aren't any rules. This one got her paycheck last Wednesday and took it into that bank. It came down to her in my mind, so I looked closer. She's living with a fellow named Mike Rogers, he drives a bus for the city. They're out three, four nights a week to a neighborhood beer joint—there are some regulars who congre-

gate there. Couple named Lindstrom who live in the same apartment building, old girl named Betty Paul and her current boyfriend Frank Wein. Lindstrom works at a garage on Green
Street, and I followed him to lunch yesterday—greasy spoon
down the street—and got talking to him."

"You usually work by hunches?"

Allen sipped coffee. "Unless it was something out of the ordinary, she was the logical choice. Anyway, Lindstrom hasn't any
imagination or two original ideas to put together. I said I'd been
in Eddy's Grill—the neighborhood place—the night before,
thought I noticed him with some people, thought one looked like
a woman I'd met someplace, Sandra Watkins. He said sure, that
was her. I didn't have to say anything else, he rambled on at random—nice folks, they got together to play cards, have a few
beers, and so on and so on, and pretty soon he said Sandra was
mighty lucky, everything so high and getting worse, but Sandra
has a nice pension of some kind comes in every month—"

"Now you have got to be kidding," said Jesse.

"People talk without using their minds, Mr. Falkenstein. I
thought of trying to get at somebody at the bank, but that isn't
just so easy. I'm pretty sure this is the one you're after, so how do
you want to play it? You want to handle it alone, or any more
work done on her?"

Jesse asked, "What's the setup?"

"She works at a dress shop on Colorado. She's no spring
chicken but puts up a pretty good front. They got in at midnight
last night, both feeling no pain."

"Think we could get a look at her?"

"Have a try," said Allen. "That your Merc in the garage? We
better take my car—that's a mite conspicuous for the neighborhood."

The neighborhood was old and run down, a narrow block up
on Raymond Street north of Colorado. Sandra Watkins and her
live-in boyfriend lived in a crumbling old apartment building
half a block from Eddy's Grill on the corner. Gil Allen parked his
middle-aged Chevy across the street, slid down behind the wheel
and said, "They may come out or not. Don't know their Sunday
routine. Give it an hour and see?"

They gave it more than an hour, until about two o'clock a man and woman came out of the apartment building and started off on foot. Allen let them get a block ahead before he started the engine; the Sunday streets were empty, and they were easy to spot. They went into a chain coffee shop two blocks down from the apartment. Allen pulled into the curb. "I'll take a closer look at her," said Jesse.

"Sure."

He walked across and into the coffee shop. They were sitting in one of the little booths against the wall. There was only one other customer in the place. Jesse sat down at the long counter just opposite their booth and ordered coffee. He could see them in the long mirror behind the counter.

She looked as if life had used her hard, her skin harshly wrinkled under defiant makeup; she was skeletally thin, cheaply smart in a black sheath and too much jewelry. The man was just a man, round-shouldered and getting bald, in unpressed work clothes.

They weren't talking much. A waitress brought them coffee and they ordered: the special, roast beef plate.

"You been drinking too much," said Sandra. "You oughta knock it off, Mike."

"Look who's talking."

"I'll knock it off too."

They sat in silence, like a dull married couple with little left to say to each other. The waitress brought their plates. Presently Sandra said, "You on late shift this month, leaves me kind of at loose ends. I'm goin' out to dinner with Betty tomorrow."

"Okay," he said inattentively.

"She was goin' to try to get tickets for that live TV show next Friday, that might be fun."

He grunted.

Jesse left his coffee half finished and rejoined Allen in the car. "I'll trust you to know what you're talking about. She's going out to dinner with Betty tomorrow night—probably back about the middle of the evening. He's working late. If she is X, I'd like a witness. Shall we welcome her home together?"

"Okay by me," said Allen.

When Jesse came in, Nell and Fran were back. They had made another pot of coffee and were on the couch with a great tome of a book filled with wallpaper samples. "You can let your-self go," Fran was saying, "on account of the solid-color carpet. A really bold stripe of some—"

"But anything very distinctive, you'd get tired of it fairly soon. Hello, darling, where have you been?"

"Consorting with a private detective," said Jesse gloomily. "He's probably spotted the blackmailer. I'll be out with him to-morrow night too."

Nell looked at him, amused and sympathetic. "You're rather taken with your Claire Elizabeth—you hate to think of her mixed up with something she was paying hush money over."

"Well, she was quite a girl," said Jesse.

"I didn't tell you," said Nell to Fran, "that I've been playing private detective too. I spotted something in that diary— I think it could explain the whole thing." She went on enlarging on it, and Fran looked interested. "I'll show you—" She went to get it, and bringing it back wrinkled her nose at the baby in the middle of the floor. "Heavens, you need your pants changed—" She scooped him up and handed the diary to Fran.

When she came back with the baby ten minutes later Fran, who had been poring over the diary while Jesse stared into space, said, "I don't see how you could be so sure about it, Nell. I don't read it that way at all."

Nell sat down beside her, pushing the wallpaper book to one side. "I suppose," she said vaguely, "if nobody minds ham-burgers, we can call Andrew and tell him to come here for din-ner. There are plenty of frozen French fries, and I can make a Caesar salad. What do you mean?"

"Well, look at what she actually wrote," said Fran. "It could mean something entirely different—"

Jesse wandered down to the bedroom to strip off his tie. When he came back, Nell was saying, "Well, you could read it that way— I never thought of that, Fran, clever of you—but she wrote, worried—"

"Well, you know, that kind of thing sometimes means—I sup-pose she was a normal girl and looked forward to having—"

"Oh," said Nell. "I see. But she did, later on."

Jesse was amused at the pair of them, black and chestnut-brown heads together, talking in shorthand. "It doesn't have to mean—" said Nell.

"What are you talking about anyway?"

"Your lady of the diary," said Fran. "Words of one syllable, what she probably meant was that her period was late again, but 'never know'—in other words it was always irregular. Some women have a thing called dis—dism—I can't remember the silly word—"

"Dismenorrhea, I think," said Nell.

"—And the reason she was worried about it, just a little, was that that sometimes means it's difficult for a woman to get pregnant. Of course, as Nell points out, she did, later on. But I don't see at all that that entry meant she was pregnant then, she just—"

Jesse dropped his pack of cigarettes and lighter. "Oh, my Lord!" he said. "Oh, my God!"

David Andrew, squealing, made for the cigarettes. He had one in his mouth and the lighter in one hand when the girls flew at him. Nell took the cigarette and lighter and Fran gathered up the rest of the cigarettes. "Really, Jesse—"

"Oh, my God!" he was saying. "She stayed for three months and left to get away from the associations—my God, am I wool-gathering?—it could be, it could be the answer—and wouldn't that have been a reason indeed, if her mind was starting to go even a little, for that damned will! It could damn well be! They'd been married five years before— And he was born in San Diego—"

"Now what are you talking about?" asked Nell.

"Manning," said Jesse. "My God, what Fran just deduced—don't you see, he could be that girl Alice Parker's son. Look at it—just look at it! Nothing says Claire didn't get pregnant—in 1923 or 1930—but five years— Most couples, if they want a family at all, start one in that time, and there was no reason they shouldn't have."

"Good Lord, you jumped a mile on this one!" said Nell, startled. She and Fran looked at each other. "But you're right—that could be so. But Jesse, would Claire—she was so madly in love with him—"

"But that's it, that's it!" said Jesse excitedly. "Can't you see it? They've patched up their marriage, they're going away to make a fresh start—and then Alice finds she's pregnant and goes to Bob

Manning. She'd know he'd be in some realty agency down there, and in those days it wasn't such a big town, she'd find him all right. And he seems to have been a responsible man, he'd agree to look after her. Suppose Claire knew by then she couldn't have children, and he wants his own child—can't you see them agreeing to take the baby? Manning is obviously his son, that's sure."

They looked at him, struck. "Yes," said Fran. "Yes. Just *because* she was so madly in love with him, she would. You just might have something there, Jesse. I'll say one thing, from what you know, she loved him a lot more madly than vice versa. And we can take it that Alice—lone lorn female—would have leaped at the idea."

"And how in hell I could ever trace the woman—if she's still alive— But all right, suppose that was so, can't you see the way her mind might have worked? He isn't a blood relation of hers— the money came from her father—it ought to go back to the family. It was logical after a fashion— What a mess!"

"But," said Nell, "there might have been a formal adoption. In fact . . ."

"It doesn't matter a damn," said Jesse. "There might not have been, too. But don't you see, if this is the truth of it, he's no blood relation, not her natural child, and it doesn't matter that she raised him as her son and thought of him as her son—until this hit her, when her mind began to hark back. He wouldn't naturally have first claim on her property—by God, what an unholy mess!—in fact, this third cousin would be her nearest blood relative. Of course, if there was an adoption, that would give him a much firmer claim, taken with everything else—the fact that he was brought up as her son and led to expect all the property— But now, by God, I'd like to find this Alice Parker and worm the truth out of her—if that is the truth. And I'd lay you any money it is." He was making for the phone down the hall.

He got the Gordons' apartment first. "One of you can go on a little trip," he told Jean. "Down to San Diego. I'm after some vital statistics. First, look for a birth certificate for John G. Manning, sometime in 1929, . . . got a pencil? Okay. Look for that, and if you don't find it, have a look for a baby boy born to an

Alice Parker, illegitimate, the same year. If you find that—or if you don't—have a look for the record of an adoption of a baby boy by Mr. and Mrs. Manning, probably within a year or so of the birth."

She said she'd get the early bus in the morning.

Birth certificates, thought Jesse, a hand on the phone. If this thing was true, obviously Manning had never seen his. No; he'd have missed all the recent wars, too young or too old, and he'd never have applied for a security clearance.

But he would lay a bet on this; and damn the consequences, the truth had to come out. He dialed his father's apartment. "You've got a number of pals up in Sacramento," he said.

"A few. What's on your mind?"

In the new house, whatever else they had, he was going to have a comfortable chair beside every phone. He abandoned the small stool, sat down on the floor with his legs stretched out and his back against the wall, and recounted the whole story. It took a while.

"Heaven help us," said Falkenstein senior, "you do get into such involved cases, Jesse. Just from a simple thing like contesting a will, too. Very mundane matter. It rather opened out and out, didn't it?"

"Isn't it still. What was in my mind—this Alice Parker."

"Pity it's such a common name."

"Yes, yes. She was intending to get a realtor's license. Of course we don't know whether she did, or whether she did and didn't go on renewing it—they have to be renewed every four years—but it might be one way to pick up her trail. They're all on file with the state, of course. Would you have some pal up there who'd get right on it and see if she shows?"

His father reflected. "There's Fellows. He's got an office full of girls with not a great deal to do."

"Good."

"You do realize that there'll probably be more than one. That she might have got married. That she might be anywhere in the state or out of it, if she's still alive."

"Have to start somewhere. Most married women use the initial of their maiden name in the middle."

"Well, it is a place to start, of course. How you get mixed up in these things, Jesse—"

"For my sins."

"I'll call Fellows tonight."

Jesse put the phone down to find Nell standing over him. "It's after six and Andrew just got here. I just have to cook the hamburgers when we're ready—come and fix some drinks."

They had been sitting in Gil Allen's car since eight o'clock, parked a space or two down from the entrance to the apartment on Raymond Street. This side street was very dark, the nearest streetlight half a block up. It was ten past nine when an old two-door Ford drew up in front of the apartment and Sandra Watkins got out of it.

"Thanks for the ride, Betty. See you Friday night."

"Okay, hon. Nighty-night."

"Night, Betty." The Ford slid away from the curb, and Jesse and Allen got out to the sidewalk. A few strides brought them up to her where she was just pulling open the door, fumbling in her bag for keys.

"We'd like to ask you a few questions, Mrs. Watkins," said Allen. She jerked around, startled, and he turned a pocket flash onto the badge in his hand, just letting her see it for a moment before sliding it back into his pocket. And if she took it for a cop's badge, could either of them help it?

"Oh!" she said.

"Suppose we go up to your apartment and have a nice friendly chat," said Jesse.

"What—about? I haven't done anything—"

"About Mrs. Claire Manning and the blackmail money you got out of her," said Jesse.

She stood absolutely still for a minute. Allen took her arm and turned her gently around to the stairs. "Let's go, lady."

She didn't utter a sound. Like a sleepwalker she turned and went across the little lobby, climbed the stairs; she stumbled on the top one and Jesse caught her arm. They went down to the middle of the hall and she fumbled blindly at the door until Allen took the keys and unlocked it; they went in and he felt inside the door, flicked on an overhead light. It was an expectable room: old furniture, disorder, a stale smell of beer and food and cheap cologne.

She sat down on the couch and looked at them. She was wearing the same black sheath, with a shabby red wool coat over it, and high heels. Under the harsh overhead light she was haggard. But she had been thinking on the way upstairs. She looked from one to the other of them and said, "You can't charge me with anything. It's too long ago."

"You're absolutely right," said Jesse. "You know she's dead, don't you?"

Slowly she nodded. "There was a double column about it in the *Times*. Well Known Woman Executive, it said." She opened her bag, took out a pack of cigarettes.

Jesse bent over her with a lighter. "And at least you decided to let it lay. You had quite a piece of change out of her altogether, didn't you?"

"You can't lay any charge."

"We don't want to," said Jesse. He sat down on the arm of the sagging old armchair beside the couch. "You couldn't be prosecuted. The original blackmail was too far back, the statute of limitations has run out on it. If Mrs. Manning wanted to go on sending you a present every month it was her own business. At least you aren't trying to carry it over to Manning—if you thought you had a chance." She shook her head dumbly. "No, the long ride on the merry-go-round is over."

She sat up a little straighter and took a long drag on the cigarette. "Yeah, over. I never believed it'd go on as long as it did, but she was a funny woman. So what do you want with me, if you can't arrest me? What the hell's this about? And—how did you know?"

"You didn't try to cover your tracks much—nobody knew about you, to look for you, until she was dead," said Jesse. "We're not cops, Mrs. Watkins. I'm a lawyer trying to settle her estate. All I want from you is the straight story. What did you have to hold over her?"

"That's straight—all you want?"

"Short of murder, it's all too far in the past to do anything about now. But I want to know—what did you hold?"

She said in a dull voice, "Can I get a drink?" She went into the kitchen, opened the refrigerator, ran water: came back with a tray holding a nearly full fifth of scotch, ice cubes, three glasses, a bottle of club soda. "Seeing there won't be any handcuffs." She fixed her own drink; neither of them followed suit.

"So?" said Jesse.

She took a long swallow, shuddered, lit another cigarette. Her eyes were slightly glazed, fixed on her glass. "I've been thinking all about it again—it was that headline, Well Known Woman Executive Dies. It brought the whole thing back so clear. It's funny to think I started to do it for Peggy. I never thought it would snowball. It was just a joke to start with, that first five minutes. Peggy Simpson, she was my best friend, and we both worked at Manning Realty then. That is, I still did. Peggy'd got fired because Mrs. Manning said her typing was sloppy—it wasn't fair, she was trying the best she knew how—and she needed the job. And it wasn't long after that I had to stay late one night. I was back in Mr. Acker's office finishing up copy for the newspaper ads, and she didn't know I was there."

She sipped from her glass. "And I didn't know she was there either, till I came past her office on my way out and saw there was a light on. And heard them talking. She was in there with a man, and he was giving her the business, making a real play, and she was playing right back—and at the same time he was talking business, I mean money business. It was funny, I tell you. Funny all ways." She stared at her drink. "I was only a kid then—twenty-two—and first I got an awful kick out of Mrs. Manning playing footsie with anything in pants—Mrs. Manning!—and I mean she was acting like a lovestruck teenager. Mrs. Manning!—always so stiff and sharp and all business—a regular iceberg, I'd have said. And then I began to take in what they were saying.

"He was talking about a new county building going to go up, he knew just where from somebody on the Planning Commission, but it was under wraps yet. If the guy owned the property knew, he could make a killing, but he didn't. This guy—the one in the office—happened to know he was strapped for money, and he'd let it go for fifty G's. But he—the guy in the office—didn't have it right then to spare, and he knew Mrs. Manning could put it up. Fifty-fifty, he said, and they could hold up the county for a quarter of a million.

"Another funny thing, you know—she was the eager one. All over him. I got the feeling he wasn't really so interested in playing house with her—but he wanted the loot.

"Well, when it dawned on me what I was listening to, I got my notebook out of my bag and started getting it down in shorthand—there was enough light from the streetlight outside the window. I used to be pretty good at shorthand then. She was promising to have it for him the next day. And then she said, not my house, and they were talking about a hotel."

Jesse sat listening to the dull voice. It wasn't anyone like Claire Elizabeth she was talking about. Nothing they knew about her—

"They were getting ready to come out, so I skipped back to the end of the hall and watched them go. She was hanging onto his arm good and tight. And I stood there in the dark and I didn't believe it—Mrs. Manning! But I thought for the first time, then, oh, brother, what I didn't have on her with all that! What I didn't have! They could both be charged and go to jail on a deal like that. And her going to a hotel with him— Her! Well, they say everybody's human but I never thought she was, very much. Anyway, not that way.

"I stood there and I thought, gee, something to hold over her all right— I thought, get something out of her for Peggy, she was out of a job—and something for me too. I mean, it was a jail charge but after all it was just the county's money, why the hell should I care if they pulled off the deal? But *her!* Acting so prim and fussy and particular—

"And I thought, could be the guy had a wife—there'd be something out of him too. All I had were my shorthand notes. I hadn't a clue who he was, never heard his voice before. But I knew that hotel, see. It was a little quiet old place around on Highland, and I knew they didn't lock up all night. I knew because the boyfriend I had then was playing sax in a combo, and he and a lot of other jazz boys lived there, didn't get in till late.

"I let them go, and I went home. But I figured they'd be sneaking out of there pretty early, and I set the alarm for four and went around there—I just lived up on Lexington. I had a cheap little Kodak, and Rex'd given me a flash attachment for it. It was lucky I had some film and a flashbulb. When I went in the lobby nobody was around at all, and I wondered how I could tell what room they were in, if he'd done the registering. But I figured they had to be about the last ones registered the night before, it had been about ten when they left the realty office. I looked at the register—it was open right there on the desk—and I'll be darned if she hadn't been the one to sign in. Did I know her handwriting! Stiff and straight as she was herself! Mr. and Mrs. Louis Domino, it said, room three-ten. I thought I'd better have that too, so I tore the page out real careful. And I went up and found the door and waited. I was jumpy as a cat, I'd never done anything like that before, but I kept thinking, that hypocritical old cat, to see her face when she realized—

"It felt like hours, and then I saw the door start to open and I got ready. I was a little way up the hall, and believe me I'd spotted the back stairs. They came out together and my hands were shaking like crazy, I was scared to death—I was going to say her name so they'd turn around but I didn't have to, I must've moved and knocked against a fire extinguisher on the wall and it made a noise, and they both turned around, and I snapped the thing—it went off like an explosion—and I never ran so fast in my life getting down those stairs—

"I don't know if she even saw me, to recognize me, right then. But she sure knew later on. I took that film to the drugstore as soon as it was open, got the print back a couple days later, and it was *good*—not very pretty but good. You could see plain who they were. He was good-looking. I hadn't gone to work since, for fear she had seen me. But I borrowed a typewriter from a girl I knew had one, and I transcribed my shorthand notes with two carbons. I didn't have any way to copy the register, there weren't any Xeroxes back then, but I could tell her I had it, and they could find out from the hotel it was gone. I had another print made, and I sent it to her with one of the carbons, and when I knew she'd got it I called her up on the phone, at her house."

Sandra Watkins poured more scotch into her glass and splashed soda. "She was— I thought, if a rock could talk it'd sound like that. A great big boulder. Funny. But I will say for her, she didn't argue or try to get out of it. She just said how much. And I'd thought about asking for a great big lump sum, but I thought it'd really be better—better all ways—to ask for something regular.

"And it was a good thing I did, too," she went on after sitting in silence for a long minute. "I split some with Peggy. But she died the next year—she had an appendix operation and they didn't have penicillin then and she died. I had a good job then at Chatham Realty. Then I got married to Fred, and he was a lush, he got me lapping it up too. I was pretty bad for a long while, but I got myself off it and divorced him. All that while, it was lucky I had that coming in.

"I even got her to up the ante. I didn't really think she would —but prices going up—I just wrote her a letter, like I did when I got married, and asked for more. And she sent it. The last ten, fifteen years, I figured she must be crazy to keep on sending it— nobody could have done anything to her for it now. But by then" —she held out her hands—"I'd got so shaky when I was on the stuff, I couldn't do shorthand or typing anymore, had to take what I could get—there were times I couldn't get any job. I wasn't going to get hooked up again, but Mike's a nice enough guy, somebody to be around the place when I get to feeling sorry for myself." She drew a long breath and looked up at Jesse. "Well, that's what you wanted to hear. You satisfied?"

He stood up. "It's all over, so I think you'd better give me what you were holding. If you've still got it."

She nodded. Without another word she went into the bedroom and they heard her open a closet door. She came back and handed Jesse a shoebox. He took the lid off.

Resting on a little sheaf of typescript, and another folded sheet, was a rectangular black-and-white snapshot. As she had said, it wasn't flattering, but it was plain. His eyes went first to Claire—looking so much, much older than in those snapshots taken at the beach by the Bakewells ten years before—the triangular face thinner, with hollows below the cheekbones, and the full mouth harder and thinner. She had been caught in a grimace of surprise, her mouth distorted.

Then he looked at the man, and said involuntarily, "My God in heaven!" It was a picture of Bob Manning.

"When you look twice, of course, you can see the difference. He wasn't quite as good-looking—shorter—different shape to his head. But the resemblance was uncanny." Jesse put the top back on the shoebox where it lay on Manning's desk. "We'll never know where she met him, but in his business he'd be associating with realtors here and there. I thought you ought to see all this."

"Yes," said Manning. He was standing at the window, his back turned.

"I think you could say," said Jesse carefully, "that she was hypnotized in a way. She had cared very deeply for your father. It must have been like seeing him come to life again, after seven years. I don't see how she could have helped knowing Domino's reputation, but at the moment it didn't matter to her—just as it didn't matter that he wanted money from her for a crooked deal. All she saw was Bob Manning come to life. I think—for just a little while—she just didn't care about anything but that."

"Yes," said Manning.

"She was thirty-seven, and she'd been a widow for seven years. We can understand her, can't we?"

"Oh, yes," said Manning. "And afterward, she despised herself so much for it—for the weakness that had led her into it—she paid this girl all these years to go on covering up. To keep me from knowing, really, because after it was too late for the law to be concerned, she'd have been afraid the girl would get to me if she stopped paying."

"The girl—who is now a raddled sixty—wouldn't have understood that at all, had any idea of going to you. She thought Mrs. Manning was crazy to go on paying."

"I wonder," said Manning after another silence, "if she did give him the money and take the profit."

"I think she did," said Jesse, "and that was when she—woke up and realized what she had done, and began to hate herself for it. To realize that Domino was just a crook on the make—that he'd seen he attracted her and used it to get money from her. She paid for it, Manning. All the rest of her life she paid, and not just in money. She'd never have been tempted to do such a thing if she hadn't loved your father so much. I think it's time she was forgiven."

"I forgive her?" Manning turned around at last. "I hope she could forgive herself—it wasn't anything to do with anyone else." He looked down at the box. "We'd better destroy this now. It's all a long time past, and better forgotten. It doesn't matter to her now."

Wilma Hansen opened the door and her mouth tightened when she saw him. "I suppose you have your faults, Miss Hansen," said Jesse, "but you were a loyal friend to her, weren't you? You knew something about Louis Domino, didn't you?"

She backed away, in tacit invitation, and he went in and shut the door. "You've—found out something," she said. "Prying and digging."

"How much did you know?"

She shook her head mutely and sat down. "I didn't know anything. But I knew there was something wrong. She wouldn't talk about him. He came to the office one day—after everyone else was gone—and she went with him. So much like Bob— But she wouldn't talk about him to me. She always talked to me about everything—we were best friends. All that time, my dearest friend. But—after she met him, she wouldn't let me mention his name. He looked like Bob but he wasn't anything like him—he was a bad man, and his reputation—but I couldn't get her to listen. She—pushed me away. I was terribly afraid—"

"Yes," he said. "It would have been like that."

"Thank God, it wasn't very long. But that week or so—it was a nightmare. She didn't come into the office— I had to take care of everything, we needed her signature, and I couldn't reach her on the phone— I knew there was something going on, I was afraid — I couldn't reach her," repeated Wilma. "And then she came in one morning and she looked like death, and she told Mr. Benson to sell the parcel of lots in Santa Monica. She'd been holding them for speculation—after the war values would shoot up high because of new building, she might have gotten a hundred and fifty thousand then. But she let them go for forty-five—I never knew her to do such a thing before."

"She had a reason," said Jesse.

She sat up straighter. "What did she do? I knew all there was to know about her all her life—I want to know."

He told her. "Ah, poor Claire," said Wilma sadly. "Just because he looked like Bob. But it's what I was afraid of then, something like that. And when you came asking the other day—I didn't want you to think anything wrong about her, I tried to make you think she hadn't liked him. But I don't suppose it matters now. You see, things always went too deep with her. If she could have—let things out—but she never could. She kept everything inside, always. When Bob was killed— We'd been out dancing the night before, to that old-fashioned dance in Exposition Park. Harry asked me to marry him that night, and I nearly said yes. Foolish—playing hard to get." For the first time he was seeing her, an old woman stripped to her essential self, not putting up any front; her pale eyes seemed to be focused inward. "I didn't hear about it, none of us did, until the next morning, when the police came to the office. I couldn't stop crying, but I had to go to her—Mr. Benson drove me up there. They'd only moved into the house the month before. And she was sitting there at Bob's desk—his new desk—just like a stone, not moving or crying. She never did cry, whatever happened. If she could have cried—just let me put my arms around her and cry and cry because it wasn't fair, they loved each other so and it wasn't fair they only had those few years— I tried, I said, darling, let it all come out— But she wouldn't let me touch her. She was like a stone. She said, we might have known—she said, it's too late—too late—we challenged the gods and they denied us. And she shut herself in the bedroom and wouldn't come out."

"It was a long time ago," said Jesse. "Maybe she's found him now, Miss Hansen."

"I don't know anything about that. If people do—go somewhere else, as themselves. I had to make the funeral arrangements. I got her a black dress and I went that morning and made her get up and get dressed—she was just lying there. And when it was all over—it was a cruel day, because it was sunny and warm and lovely there in the cemetery—and we came out to the limousine, she said in a perfectly ordinary voice to the driver, take us to Manning Realty on Santa Monica. She said, there's that lot out on Sunset, the Morgan couple were keen on it and

Bob said push them up to twenty-five hundred. She said, he'd never forgive me if I just let things go.

"And it was then I knew I couldn't leave her. She'd been through too much. We'd been through so much together, I couldn't leave her then. But now she's gone, it all seems to have been for nothing. It was all so important at the time, but if I'd married Harry—I might have had a family, something besides just a big annuity and going out to dinner with Mrs. Kane— Oh, for heaven's sake go *away!*" she gulped, feeling for a handkerchief. "I don't know what I'm saying—not making any sense— silly to get upset when she's gone and can't feel anything anymore—"

Jesse let himself out quietly.

Jean called him at the office at five o'clock Friday afternoon. "I'm sorry, Mr. Falkenstein, but there's no birth certificate on record for John Manning anywhere in San Diego County. I've been through Vital Statistics every place there are any, it's been quite a hunt. And there's no certificate for a baby born to Alice Parker. Or any adoption record for the Mannings."

"Well," said Jesse. "So you'd better come home." He smoked a cigarette, thinking about that. Finally he called C.M.R. Management and got hold of Manning just as he was leaving the office.

"My birth certificate?" Manning sounded harassed and bewildered. "What's that for? All these nitpicking legal requirements —damnit, I've had to scour three counties for a new security service for all the condos, the one we had going bankrupt overnight— What? Well, wait a minute, let me think—yes, that came up when I was in college and joined the R.O.T.C.—there wasn't any. Mother said they were living way out of town, just outside a place called Lakeside, and the doctor was an old country G.P. Probably he just forgot to register it. I know at the time Mother had to make an affidavit of some kind that I had been born—I suppose you know the sort of thing."

Jesse thanked him gently and sat looking speculatively at Sir Thomas. And that could have happened. But this just made him wonder a little harder.

Alice Parker, having her baby almost anywhere, here or San Diego or you name it—duly registered as Baby Boy Parker, father unknown, male, Caucasian, weight and height and appended footprints—did they do that in 1930?—and turning the baby over to the Mannings, and vanishing into limbo.

And what a legal mess, if that were so.

Let it go, forget it? Sir Thomas fixed him with a stern gaze. For better or worse, the truth had to be the ultimate objective. It might be unpleasant. And he thought of Webster—"There is nothing so powerful as the truth, and often nothing so strange."

And he thought, fifty years ago—

Tregarron called him just as he was leaving the office at six o'clock. "I have at last heard from Pollock," he said. "A very peculiar communication, Mr. Falkenstein—very peculiar, it strikes me. A telegram handed in at San Francisco at two P.M. today. It simply says 'Will be in your office 9 A.M. Friday May 9.' That is all. A week from today—"

"Well, at least he's shown up," said Jesse.

"He sounds remarkably brusque," said Tregarron. "And—er—affluent. If he has the funds to contest the case—whatever case you may bring—"

"Wait and see," said Jesse.

NINE

On Monday morning Jesse sat early at his desk looking at the list of names his father had dictated to him on the phone last night. Mr. Fellows' clerks had been industrious, up in the state Hall of Records.

There had been, of course, some criteria to limit the list: some specific data to narrow it down and eliminate the doubtless many Alice Parkers or Alice P. Somethings who had held realtors' licenses from 1930 on.

She had probably been in her mid-twenties in 1928; at least she wouldn't have been under twenty. He had specified birth dates between 1900 and 1910. Realtors' licenses included birth dates and current addresses and had to be renewed every four years. Of course, if she had ever held one she might have let it lapse, when or if she got married, for any other reason.

The clerks had turned up, from researches into the realtors' licenses on file, quite a list of possibles, and of course they were all over the place. Unfortunately, as Falkenstein senior had pointed out, Alice was a common name. There were realtors past and present (after all, the woman was no longer young, and the clerks had looked at lapsed licenses too) in the San Francisco, Yucaipa, Fresno, Eureka, Sacramento and Bakersfield areas—a few Alice Parkers and the rest Alice P. Whatevers.

But, as Gil Allen said, you had to go by probabilities. She had lived and worked here; if she had stayed in real estate, there had been enough scope on the job in the L.A. area, in the next ten to twenty years, that she'd have had the incentive to stay here. It might be an impossible hunt, but you had to begin somewhere. And the most logical first cast was right here.

In any case, it shouldn't take much time or a battery of questions to spot the right Alice Parker. The one simple question—

Did you ever know Bob Manning?—should provoke some reaction from the right one.

He had the morning free, and not much else on hand for the rest of the week; he thought, take a first cast around himself and if he didn't turn up any lead, hand it over to Gil Allen or whichever of his colleagues was available.

It was a formidable list.

One of the nearest to hand was Alice P. Jourdain, at an address over in Glendale—some of the addresses would be private, some business. Jesse had been early enough for once that he was leaving just as the Gordons were arriving; they greeted him with sarcastic surprise. "Once in a while I can get on the ball," he told them. "I'll be back for the one-thirty client."

The address in Glendale was a brightly painted little one-story building on West Glenoaks, Keen and Son Realtors. He asked for Mrs. Jourdain and she was pointed out to him, at a nearby desk. He gave her a card.

"I'm settling an estate, trying to trace one of the heirs." Simplest introduction. "Hope you don't mind answering a few questions?"

She looked up at him in surprise. She was a big-boned woman with short-cropped gray hair and a fine complexion. "About what?"

"Did you ever know a Robert Manning?"

There wasn't a flicker in her eye. "I don't think I ever heard the name. Why did you think I would have?"

"He was once connected with an Alice Parker, in the real estate business. We've been looking up realtors' licenses."

"My God, what a hope," she said. "My maiden name was Parr. You'll be a lot older than you are now before you find her that way. I can only wish you luck."

Jesse was dismally afraid she was right. And, he thought, that one had all her wits about her: but after all, an experienced lifewise female seventy or upward wouldn't blush and jump like a naïve girl just to hear the name, would she? After fifty-one years? If Alice Parker had married and had a family in that time, she wouldn't appreciate the past rising up to haunt her now; she might not be able to prevent herself showing recognition of the name, but aside from that she wouldn't give him the time of day.

There was an Alice M. Parker in Pasadena. And, he thought
further, life— On the other hand, she might almost have forgotten it herself, and Bob Manning, in all those years. It would have
been a thing she'd have wanted to push to the bottom of her
mind, get over it, go on to the next thing. And time had a way of
blurring old feeling, and passions out of the past.

The little discrepancy in the dates—he'd given some thought
to that. There wasn't much in it, a matter of a few months. If he
was reading this right, Alice Parker's baby would have been born
along in late summer or fall of 1928; if there had been an adoption (he now had Jimmy looking at L.A.'s Vital Statistics) that
could have been in 1929. Manning's supposed birth date was
January tenth, 1929. It all fit in. A thing she had left behind her
—but even now, wouldn't she be bound to show some reaction
to the name?

At a real estate agency in Pasadena, a brisk dark young man
said, "Miss Parker?" in an incredulous tone. "I'm sorry, Miss
Parker hasn't been with us for nearly ten years." He was a little
annoyed with Jesse for not being a client; but he looked up the
address for him—Euston Road.

It was a modest bungalow on a narrow street. He waited on
the tiny front porch, and the door finally opened. "Well?" she
said in a sharp voice. "I don't buy at the door." She made no
move to unhook the screen and take his card. She was an angular
woman with thin gray hair in a knot on top of her head.

"I'm a lawyer, trying to trace someone. I think it's possible that
you once knew a Robert Manning."

The screen obscured her exact expression. "No, I never did,"
she said smartly. "Sorry." She stepped back and shut the door.

And might not Alice Parker have turned into just such a sharp
vinegary old woman? Especially if she hadn't married? Turned
into the upright respectable spinster? Prompt to deny the name
—and after all this time, passions spent and forgotten, not even
reacting to the name?

The hell of it was, he hadn't a clue as to what she'd looked
like, and in that many years she would have changed, perhaps
drastically. Very few people were recognizable at seventy-five
from pictures of fifty years before. And he could guess what he
would hear from the Meiklejohns—she had blond (or brown)

hair, her eyes were blue (or brown), she was short, middle height, tall. The hair would now be gray or white, face shape altered by false teeth, the figure probably changed to dumpiness or scraggliness; there would be different mannerisms, habits, ways of dressing—everything changed. It was even in the cards that the Meiklejohns wouldn't recognize her; they hadn't known her well, or long.

At an address in San Marino, an old frame house back from the street in a jungle of shrubbery, when he pushed the bell a voice called out, "I'm coming! I'm coming—give me time!" In a couple of minutes the door opened and a stout old lady balancing on a walker appeared. There wasn't any screen door here. She looked pleasant and cheerful. He gave her his story, and she said, "Goodness me, young man, must have been a good many Alice Parkers around with real estate licenses, time to time. I guess I was foolish to hang onto mine so long, haven't been able to get about enough to do anything in that line for ten years."

"Did you ever know Robert Manning?"

Her eyes never wavered on him. "I don't call it to mind. Common enough name."

Jesse stopped for lunch in Glendale on his way back to Hollywood, and landed back at the office at one o'clock. The client was early, and he got rid of him by one-thirty.

Going at the thing this way was impossible. If he was going to pin any faith on that list, he had better turn it over to Garrett Associates right now and let one of their terriers go out full time to have a look at every Alice P. on it—and what time that would take, and what it would cost—

For which, if he found her, and if he was right about her, John Manning would scarcely thank him.

He called Meiklejohn and found him at home. "That girl," he said. "Alice Parker. You told me she left the firm you and Manning were with, was going to try for a job somewhere else—what was the name?"

"I think she said Sullivan and Hartley."

"Do you know if she did get a job there?"

"No idea. You're not thinking of trying to find her, after all this time? You do make life hard for yourself, Mr. Falkenstein."

"Would you have any idea where else she might have got a

job? Is there anybody from Sullivan and Hartley still around who might remember if she did work there?"

"Well, I can tell you that old Sullivan is still alive, or was up to last November—I happened to notice him at a restaurant we went to. He must have retired fifteen years ago, he used to bank with us. Well, now. The Parker girl—she had experience in realty, and she was a good girl, good typist and fair shorthand. She could have got a job with almost any realty firm, on her experience."

"Can you name some that were going about then?"

"My God, Mr. Falkenstein," said Meiklejohn simply. "Hollywood in the late twenties, early thirties even? The general area? It was booming—money flowing like water. There were dozens —maybe hundreds. Of course after the crash a lot of them folded, and through the Depression business was slow. But the bigger ones hung on—there was always a certain amount of business, the whole area developing as it was. Yes, I was in it up until I got in at the bank."

"All right, name me some companies going in the thirties."

Meiklejohn thought. "Nolan and Alford. Al Pierce Realty, that was on Sunset I think. Willoughby and Hanks. Sam Ogden—he got in on the ground floor before Bel Air started to build at all. R. M. Stanley and Sons. Hope and Osgood. They were about the biggest firms, all weathered the Depression."

Jesse had been taking rapid notes in his copperplate. "Thanks very much."

"I'd be interested to know if you find her," said Meiklejohn, "but I'm not going to hold my breath."

"Could you describe her to me?"

There was a moment's silence. "Well, as to that—I didn't know her well, and she wasn't around long—six months? She had brown hair, and I'd say she was middle height—had a good figure."

"Very useful fifty-one years later," said Jesse dryly.

It was, however, useful to have minions to deploy. The Gordons were busy on paperwork, on the various divorce suits. He told them to forget it for a while. "I want you both to go down to the City Hall and look at a lot of back city directories. Look for all these realty firms—how long ago they were still in business, and whether the owners are still around—and their addresses if they are."

"You can think up some tedious jobs," said Jean.

"Isn't there a realtors association of some kind? If the city directories and current phone books fail you, maybe they could help."

This might be a more direct way to go at it. But he would need the hell of a lot of luck. Considering the number of realty companies around, then and now—and she might have gone into another kind of job; she might have married and quit work.

But, the probabilities. That was the job she had experience at. Wherever she'd been working, say between early 1929 and the crash, might have folded: these were the big outfits which had crept through the Depression safely.

"You don't expect anything today, do you?" asked Jimmy.

"I should think you'd have got something by quitting time. You should get down there by two-thirty if you step on it."

They exchanged resigned glances, but went out with his list. Jesse, harking back to the days he was trying to build a practice, spent the afternoon doing their paperwork. But it didn't altogether take his mind off Alice Parker.

After all, they'd had the whole state of California to choose from. She might even have gone somewhere else, to have the baby. He didn't have any idea where she'd come from, whether she had a family. It was, in fact, the proverbial needle in the haystack, and he was seven kinds of damn fool to think he could ever trace the girl. But he could have a try, looking in the most logical places.

On Tuesday morning Jean presented him with a neatly typed page. "We nearly got locked in down there last night, poring over your darned dusty old directories. But there you are."

He was grateful, and said so. It must have been a hell of a job.

Sam Ogden had sold his agency in 1965 and retired; it now bore another name, but by the current directory he was still around, at an address on Londonderry Road above West Hollywood.

Hope and Osgood had been listed up to 1960, when it became Osgood and Chambers; Donald Hope was still present on Scenic

Drive in Hollywood. Willoughby and Hanks had gone out of business in 1959, but still listed at the same premises was O'Rourke Realty; S. C. Willoughby was living in Bel Air. There were nine more names. In the city directory listings for those firms, partners and staff members would be listed as well as owners. The girls had hunted those down in the current phone books. Stewart—Reid—Prince—Byrd—Walker—addresses all over, from Malibu to Altadena.

Jesse regarded the list sadly; but he had asked for it. At least it was nice weather, not too cold or hot or, in May, wet. He tucked the page away in his pocket, stopped to get the tank filled, and started out on the impossible hunt.

He found Joseph Sullivan first, in a spacious condominium in Santa Monica. Sullivan looked to be in his eighties, but was alert mentally and cooperative. "No, sir," he said promptly. "I can answer that definitely. No Alice Parker. Our staff usually stayed with us for long periods, and I have a good memory for names. That doesn't ring a bell at all."

At one of the older houses in Bel Air, a woman opened the door and he asked for Mr. Willoughby. "Why do you want to see him, please? Some questions—about his business? That's a long time back, Mr.—" She looked at his card. "I doubt very much if he could tell you anything—he's had several strokes. You can try." She led him in to where a very old man, wrapped in shawls, nodded on a couch. He looked vaguely at Jesse, and only bewilderment showed in his eyes at the questions.

"You see," she said. "I'm sorry."

He went back to Hollywood to look for Donald Hope. Hope was a peppery little man in natty sports clothes, who regarded Jesse with annoyance; he had been backing out of the drive as the Mercedes pulled up. "Nothing but interruptions!" he said. "I am due at a meeting in exactly thirty minutes, I can spare you five. Interference! People poking their noses into private lives! Now what do you want?" He scarcely listened to the question at first, and it emerged that his annoyance was directed at the D.M.V., which had just notified him that since he had reached the age of eighty, his license would be up for approval, with a road test, every six months. When he had blown off some steam at Jesse, he listened and said, "Would you settle for an Ann

Parker? Had a fine secretary by that name—with me twenty years."

"Sorry, Alice."

"Well, never was one worked for us. I'm sure of that." He sounded it.

Jesse drove back west and after a little hunt located Londonderry Road. The house was all glass and brick, with roofs going off at odd angles. The woman who opened the door showed him into a very large room sparsely filled with chrome and leather furniture; there was a rather wildly colored abstract painting over the stark mantel. Another woman swept in, large and commanding, in ice-blue silk with a double row of pearls around her neck. "Ah, there you are!" she said, beaming at him. "Now, we're going to make a clean sweep of all this—terribly, terribly outdated, I can't think what the Morrisons were thinking of, heaven knows they've got enough money— It has all got to go! The whole place must be done over, as I told Mr. Druce on the phone. Danish modern, with just, perhaps, a few little touches of country. I thought pale sandalwood paint for this room—what do you think?"

"Think you're mistaking me for someone else," said Jesse. "I want Mr. Ogden." He gave her a card.

"Oh," she said, disconcerted, read the card, burst into musical laughter and said, "Oh, dear, that's a good one, me asking a lawyer about interior decoration! But I'm expecting the man from Druce Interiors, you see. Sam? He's over at the Easterbys'. He refuses to do anything but sleep here until I get all this horrible stuff moved out. We bought the house furnished last year, but we've been in Europe for six months." She gave him the address —Mapleton Drive—and he had a hunt for that.

Sam Ogden was comfortably engaged in a game of chess with Mr. Easterby, in a small dark room crowded with early American furniture and frowsty with the smoke of two pipes. He was a big fat man with a shiny bald head. When Mrs. Easterby brought Jesse in, he frowned at the card, frowned at Jesse, grunted at the question. "Well, let me think. There was a Parker girl, just a while before I retired—nope, her name was Amanda. Parker. Parker. Nope, I don't remember her. Never was an Alice Parker with us."

Seven kinds of a fool, thought Jesse. It was rather remarkable, come to think, that there were as many of these people around as there seemed to be, people who had been adults, and older than the Mannings and Alice Parker, back in the thirties. But what guarantee had he that they were remembering accurately? It was a long time ago and there must, over the years, have been a lot of people working for all of these firms, people trying to make a living selling real estate, probably some of them giving up, getting into other lines of work, the women dropping out when they married.

Two of the other names had Santa Monica addresses appended, so he went on there. Ronald Kessler, once of Hope and Osgood Realty, was in the middle of lunch, and testy at interruption; Jesse had lost track of time, still minus his watch. Mr. Kessler must be eighty-five, a long, stringy, yellow-faced man, and Jesse noted in some awe that his lunch consisted of three hard-fried eggs and at least half a pound of bacon. Mr. Kessler's apartment had no dining room; he beckoned Jesse out to the kitchen and finished his lunch rapidly while he listened to the questions.

"No," he said when he had swallowed the last piece of bacon. "Definitely no. Being in the way of dealing with large numbers of people all my life, I have an excellent memory for names, and there was never an Alice Parker working for Hope and Osgood."

Jesse stopped for a somewhat less substantial lunch—he reflected that Mr. Kessler's arteries must be in good shape—and proceeded on after Rupert Prince, formerly of Willoughby and Hanks. It was evident that the statisticians were right and people were living longer, healthier lives these days; he had to pursue Mr. Prince—it wasn't far away and there was no point in making two trips—out to the Riviera Country Club where he was playing a round of golf. Mr. Prince didn't remember any Alice Parker.

At five o'clock Jesse, feeling stale and weary, came to the Malibu apartment of Mr. Kenneth Stewart. The Stewarts were both at home, a nondescript elderly pair contented as cats, just sitting down to preprandial drinks on a sunny little balcony. They offered one to Jesse, who refused it with regret; he had thirty miles to drive home through traffic.

Mr. Stewart had been with R. M. Stanley Realty, later had branched out on his own. "Now let's see," he said ruminatively. "That seems to ring a bell in my mind. Alice Parker."

"Why, of course, Ken!" said his wife. "You remember that girl." She turned to Jesse. "I used to be in the office then too, those early days—everybody scrambling to make a living how we could. I let my license go later on. Alice Parker, I remember her—it must have been around 1931 she was there. I seem to recall she was a nice efficient girl."

"Yes, I do remember her now," said Stewart.

"What happened to her? She left the firm? You know where she went?"

"Why, she got her own license and went in with a new agency out in the valley." They consulted each other on dates and agreed that that was about 1936. "It started with a T," said Stewart. "They went on to be a pretty big oufit—the whole valley was just starting to build up then—Teggner, that was it. Teggner Realty in Glendale."

Jesse got home at seven o'clock, starving to death. Hearing an account of his day, Nell said, "For heaven's sake. I never in this world believed you could find a trace of that girl."

"That's all I've found yet," said Jesse.

No, he had never expected to find a trace of her, and he was still feeling surprised that he had. However, even if he could follow her up further, find her if she was still alive, it wouldn't necessarily solve the trickly little problem. Suppose she was married and had a family? She wasn't, just for being asked the questions, going to say to a strange lawyer, "Why, yes, you're quite right, I had an illegitimate baby by Bob Manning and the Mannings took him." She wasn't going to say anything at all, tell them yes or no on that.

It had taken a lot of luck to get this far; it was going to take a lot more luck to lead him to her, wherever she was now. And this had to be the right Alice Parker, of course. The dates, the name, the job—they all fit. And say he found her, and saw her react to Bob Manning's name: all she had to maintain was that it was a common name, it was just coincidence that she'd worked in real estate, she'd never heard of the Mannings and didn't know anything about it. There'd never be any way to prove she did. But having got so far, he was bound to follow her up.

On Wednesday morning he had an early client: Leffingwell, who seemed determined to show up at inconvenient times. Jesse sent Jean over to Glendale to look at more old city directories there and find out whether Teggner Realty was still operating. He collected the relevant paperwork and when Leffingwell came in he told him that there didn't seem to be any record of his wife's claimed Mexican divorce.

"But their records aren't always reliable, of course. It could be that there was a divorce, it could also be that there wasn't. To be on the safe side, I think you'd better carry through with divorcing her now and have it all straightened out."

"Well, I want everything all legal," said Leffingwell anxiously. "Then I could be sure Betsy and I were hooked up all square, when we get married. That's how I want it."

Jesse explained the procedure to him; the hearing might come up sometime next month. Leffingwell told him all over again how that damned woman had treated him and how happy he was going to be with Betsy, and finally took himself out at eleven o'clock. Jesse sat and fidgeted, deciding that Teggner Realty had probably folded, merged with another firm or whatever, and anybody there in 1936 would have vanished without a trace, along with Alice Parker.

But Jean came in about eleven-thirty and told him that Teggner Realty had been in business until 1966, when it became Teggner and Sons, and she had checked there: the original Teggner was still very much alive, Keith Teggner, Senior, and living on Mountain Street in Glendale.

Jesse bolted out of the office, but by the time he got to the Valley it was after twelve, and he spent an impatient half hour over a sandwich in a hole-in-the-wall on the main drag before he went looking for Mountain Street. It was a curving, hilly street in the northern part of the city, with large old houses hidden up steep slopes from the street behind old trees. When he found the right address, painted on the curb, he couldn't see the house at all; there was a flight of cement steps curving through tall greenery up the hillside. He started up lightly, but they went on and on, spiraling up forever, and he had to stop to catch his breath. Smoking too much, he thought; it couldn't be approaching age. Compared to all these spry elders he'd been talking to—

He finally came to the house, stucco with a red tile roof, and pushed the doorbell, still panting a little. The woman who opened the door was gray-haired and neat in a navy pantsuit.

"Mr. Teggner?" said Jesse. He drew a deep breath and reached for a card.

"My goodness, you didn't climb all those steps, did you? You can drive right up into the circular drive from the side street."

Now I know, he thought. He asked, "Is Mr. Teggner in?"

She looked at the card. "Oh, yes. Come in. Dad, somebody to see you."

Teggner came down the hall to this unpretentious living room, presumably from a study. He was a stocky, short man who bounced as he walked. He looked at the card, told Jesse to sit down, and asked him what it was about. Jesse put the question.

"Oh, yes," said Teggner at once. "I remember her very well. A nice young woman—and a good saleswoman. She came in with us when we first established the agency—that was in 1936—and she was with us until 1950."

"Why did she leave and where did she go, do you know?"

"Her husband was transferred," said Teggner, adjusting his glasses. "She got married the year after she came in with us—her married name was Stiles, I can't recall his first name. He was with the Highway Patrol. And in 1950 he was transferred to another location, they had to move."

"You don't remember where?"

"I'm sorry, I'm afraid not. But I would imagine that she went on working in real estate, wherever it was."

Alice P. Stiles wasn't one of the names on the list from Sacramento. "Well," said Jesse. A phone rang somewhere.

"You seem anxious to find her. I'm sorry I can't tell you any more, but it's some time ago, of course."

Jesse sighed and got up. "Can't be helped."

Mrs. Teggner looked in from the hall. "Mr. Falkenstein, your office wants to speak to you."

Surprised, Jesse followed her down to the phone. "Thank goodness I caught you," said Jimmy. "Sergeant Clock just called,

he wants you to come in to the precinct. He said to tell you
they've picked up the punk."

He looked about as Jesse had expected, a fattish lump of a
young fellow in sloppy, dirty clothes, ragged jeans and an imita-
tion-leather jacket. He had a shock of stringy dark hair and
about four days' growth of beard. He wore a sullen expression
under the eyes of Clock and Petrovsky, in the bare little interro-
gation room.

Detective Mantella had taken Jesse down there, and Clock
looked up as the door opened. "Here we are, Jesse," he said. "I
don't suppose you can identify this bastard, but he had your
watch, of course. Come on, Thornton. I told you we picked up
your prints in the Yucca Street break-in, we've got you for that,
and that watch was in with the loot, so you might as well tell us
all about that."

"About what? What watch?"

"My watch, you stupid lout," said Jesse. "You're one of the
three jumped me and beat me up a couple of weeks ago, and I'd
like to know why—who set you onto me?"

Thornton looked at him from under scanty eyebrows and said
without conviction, "I don't know anything about it."

"Come on," said Clock. "It doesn't matter whether you tell us,
because it'll make another charge—we know it was you—but
you might as well tell us who the others were and who put you
up to it so we can drop on them too. Or do you want to take the
rap alone?"

Thornton thought about that for a while. "I don't know anything about—wait a minute, wait a minute, I'm *tellin'* you! It
was this guy, his name's Panther, that's all I know, honest. You
see him on the street, he does a little dealing. I bought the grass
from him, a couple times the angel dust. Look, all I can tell you
—me and Terry Hurst and Jim Clymer were hangin' around on
the Boulevard this Sunday, see, couple weeks back or around
there, and this Panther, he deals out of his car, he was supposed
to show up round on Ivar about noon, and Jim made a little buy
—he was the only one had any bread, see. And this Panther—I
don't know him good, he's a loner, Jim says, you don't want to
mess with him, he's got a temper on him. He's a big guy with

funny eyes and he's got a tattoo on his arm, big green dragon thing. He says to Jim, how'd we like to make a few bucks, and he tells us how." He jerked his head at Jesse. "This guy. Rough him up but good, and it was fifty apiece."

"I thought I was a little more important," said Jesse to Clock. "Only a hundred and fifty?"

"Just like that," said Clock. "He told you who but not why?"

"He just said, make it good, beat hell out of him. And we had to say something—he made me say it over till I got it right. The guy's not s'posed to do no more work for somebody, a name like Mann or something." Ed Thornton shrugged. "It was easy money." He looked at Jesse. "We'd 'a' hurt you a lot more only it went kinda wrong."

"Thank you so much," said Jesse.

"That day, it was still light when you got home. He give us the street and number. But it was too light. The next day, though, it was dark enough—we were a little ways up the street in Jim's car, and we seen you turn the corner, that big Merc you got showed in the street light, that's some car."

"And what went wrong?" asked Jesse. "Except with me?"

"We'd 'a' busted you up a lot more, but we heard the dog, see, sounded like a big dog, comin' right out—so we cut out."

"Now I know why I pay for three pounds of dog food per day." They went out, leaving him sitting there, and Jesse added, "I told you so. Now just what the hell is behind it? Who the hell is Panther?"

"We'll have a look in the monicker list downtown," said Clock, massaging his Neanderthal jaw. "The tattoo should help too. Put the word out to the snitches we want him, we should turn him up eventually. But, Jesse—little street punks like these—a small-time narco dealer—over your high-class contested will? It doesn't make any kind of damned sense."

"I know, I know," said Jesse. "Just tell me when you find him, I'd really like to know where he comes in. At the moment tell me something else. Do the LAPD and the Highway Patrol speak to each other?"

Clock grinned. "We often find ourselves covering the same freeway crashes. I know a few fellows at the Hollywood station, why?" Jesse told him. "You don't mean to say you've got any smell of that Parker woman? That looked just impossible. You could get a job with us."

"I'd rather cope with the incompetent judges than the Thorntons. Tell me where to go."

"You go to Captain Ellis Gay at the Hollywood station and tell him I sent you. He's a nice guy. I saved his life once, so he'll oblige you."

"You got the drop on some desperado just as he was about to shoot?"

"No," said Clock seriously. "We were trying to talk down a jumper, on the overpass of the Hollywood freeway at Fountain. Gay had hold of his arms, and when the guy went, he'd have taken him along too but I grabbed Gay's belt."

"I still think I prefer my own job," said Jesse.

Gay was cordial, asked after Clock, and beamed pleasedly when he heard about the expected offspring. "And what can I do for you, Mr. Falkenstein?"

"One Stiles, front name unknown. He was with you at least between 1937 and 1950. In 1950 he got transferred, I don't know from where, somewhere else. I'd like to know where."

"Well, that shouldn't be any problem," said Gay, who was a lean, trim man in his forties. "We've got a direct line to Sacramento, and they've got computers up there with all our records. Excuse me." He picked up the phone and talked a little while with Communications. "Give it half an hour, see what turns up. Tell me what Andrew's been coping with lately."

The information came through in slightly less than half an hour. Henry Stiles had been a member of the Highway Patrol from 1934 to 1961. He had worked out of the Sun Valley station until 1950, been transferred to the La Habra station. He had retired in 1961, and at that time he had been living on Jacaranda Place in Fullerton.

"God bless our wonderful police," said Jesse. "Thanks so much."

He went home and told Nell the latest news. "Well, I'll never call you a useless monster again," she said to Athelstane, who laid his ears flat at her tone and moved his tail modestly. "Saving master's life."

"Don't be silly," said Jesse. "If he'd gotten out of the gate he'd have pounced on them asking to play games. Now Sally—Sally would have clobbered them." They laughed, thinking of Clock and Fran's redoubtable black Peke Sally, who had once nearly murdered a burglar.

"But I can't believe you've found the Parker girl. It looked impossible."

"And she'll hardly be a girl now," said Jesse. "I haven't quite gotten there yet."

He got down to Fullerton in Orange County about ten o'clock, and with the help of the County Guide found Jacaranda Place. It was a frame bungalow with a neatly landscaped yard. A woman answered the door, placid, uninterested. "Oh, Stiles," she said. "It was her we bought the place from in 1969. I don't know nothing about her. But you might ask Mis' Wagner next door, she's lived here a long time and knows everybody. Maybe she'd know."

He tried Mrs. Wagner next door. She was a thin slip of an elderly woman, bright-eyed and quick-tongued. "Oh, my, yes, I could tell you," she said. "Her husband died of a heart attack in 1964, and then she had a stroke in 1969, couldn't live alone any longer. Her stepdaughter took her—she never had any children of her own, he was a widower with two little kids when she married him, his first wife died real young having another baby, and the baby died too. Her stepdaughter's Mrs. Gallagher, Mrs. Tim Gallagher, it's Costa Mesa but I don't know the address."

Was he at the end of the trail at last? He found a public phone booth and looked up the address. Bay Street. Whatever else he was doing he was piling up the miles on the Mercedes.

This was a sprawling modern ranch house on a good-size lot. He parked in front, went up a curving walk and pushed the doorbell. In a minute the door opened and he faced a nicelooking middle-aged woman with graying dark hair and very blue eyes. She smiled at him inquiringly.

"Mrs. Gallagher?" He proffered a card, and she opened the screen door to take it. "I'm settling an estate for one of my clients, and your stepmother has some information I need. It goes back a way in time, but if I could see her—"

"She couldn't help you at all," said Mrs. Gallagher gently. "I'm sorry."

"If you'll excuse me, I'd just like to be sure of that. It's rather important."

She surveyed him calmly, opened the screen door. "Maybe you'd better come in," she said. "I'm sorry, if it's important. You see, when she had the stroke she failed all at once. We can't afford a nursing home for her and the best of those places are none too good anyway. It's a chore to look after her, she's quite helpless, but my sister and I spell each other—she was very good to us when we were little, she was like our own mother, and the least we can do is take care of her now. It's just terrible to see her this way, she was always so able and cheerful and loving— but I guess we have to take it as part of life."

It was an orderly comfortable living room, a few magazines lying around, good furniture, but he saw only the old, old woman tied into the wheelchair. "She couldn't understand any questions or answer them," said Mrs. Gallagher. "She can't write or talk at all."

She was a shriveled puppet figure in the wheelchair, her cotton dress rucked up under the stick-like legs. Thin gray hair barely covered her skull; one arm was crooked stiffly upward from the elbow. Her mouth was fixed in a rictus of permanent little grin. But her eyes, terribly, moved and were aware.

It was impossible to tell if she'd ever been a pretty girl, even just attractive with the attraction of youth.

She grunted, a sudden crude sound.

He bent over her. "Alice," he said, "do you remember Bob Manning?"

He thought her eyes moved, and she tried to move the fixed raised hand. That was all.

He straightened. He had found Alice Parker, and she couldn't tell him anything. All passion spent—all the fires of love and youth long dead—she couldn't tell him what he wanted to know.

TEN

He moved the car a block down to be out of sight of the house, and sat there trying to think the thing out. What else could he do and what else should he do? See her doctor, ask if she had ever had a child? The doctor would refuse to tell him if he knew, there were rights to privacy and confidential doctor-patient relations, and quite right too. And if he could find out, and she had, there was nothing to say it was Manning's child.

This thing had opened out and out, all right, from one thing to another—from John Manning pacing Jesse's office that day, saying he would have to contest that will, that earthshakingly unexpected will. Just looking for evidence to back up the possible grounds for contest, the Unnatural Provisions, the possible mental incompetence—looking for the motive behind that will—he had traveled a long road with Claire Elizabeth, Bob Manning, the colorless Alice Parker. And where had he come to now?

Just on the surface facts, Manning had a pretty good case with the Unnatural Provisions grounds—not such good evidence on the incompetence. But the fact that Claire Elizabeth had been so far out of touch with the family, so long, that she'd had to hire a private eye to find which of them was alive—the fact that Manning had been raised as her son and natural heir to her property, made a good case for the court to set aside that will and let the previous one stand. But if, in fact, Manning was not her own son and there had been no adoption, that was a different story. And as an honest man committed to upholding the law, he was bound to broach the possibility when the case was aired, wasn't he?

He felt exasperated with Claire Elizabeth, the secretive silent old lady, the once-capable brain starting to malfunction, leaving this unholy tangle behind her. The deterioration so gradual that she hadn't realized it, using the less-than-rational logic; her growing secretiveness descending into deviousness—deigning to leave no explanations behind.

He had groped around himself, looking for that irrational motive: because if he could explain that, a judge and jury would have a clearer understanding of the extent of her incompetence, to base a judgment on.

Claire Elizabeth, harking back to her youth, knowing she hadn't much time left; and all her busy materialistic life she'd never given a thought to what might come after death, until death was close upon her. She would probably have had the orthodox upbringing—heaven and hell and judgment.

That letter from Anne—had it lain where he found it all these years, or had she just come across it again, to be reminded—of what? To feel remorse that she'd ignored it, relief that she hadn't?

He looked down the years at the gay, pretty redhead, Claire Elizabeth—"the prettiest girl I ever knew," came the echo of Kathleen Kindly's voice—at what life had done to change her into the stern old lady, lonely in that gloomy house she had left just as Bob had wanted it. The indulged father's girl who had married her Prince Charming in a romantic elopement—the girl who loved to sing and play ragtime piano—learning she had to grow up into real life. A little spoiled, enjoying her parties, and then finding that Prince Charming was straying—a little or a lot? —maybe the parties not quite enough for him. She did a lot of growing up right then, said Sally Meiklejohn's voice—yes, basically a good girl, a girl of character—and perhaps loving Bob Manning too well. What then?

Was he reading in a complication where none existed? Woolgathering over this business with Alice Parker? She might have vanished from their lives, they might never have seen her again —eventually marrying her widower, raising his children, and forgetting Bob Manning and what might have been an innocent flirtation. But—but—

Claire Elizabeth, inadvertently led to the books, the possibility dawning on her that she might not step out of life to annihilation but to a place where she'd meet the people gone before—Bob, who else? "I'm afraid to meet them," she had said. Why? Claire Elizabeth, harking back down the years to old times, old friends before she met Bob? Something had happened then, back in September of 1923—giving rise to the motive for that will? The lonely old lady, revisiting places where she had once been happy and had fun—and one place to remind her of a dark time, when she was led into venality because she had loved Bob Manning too well, too well.

But he couldn't get the whole business about Alice Parker out of his head.

Finally he started the car, drove the thirty miles back to downtown Los Angeles, and unprecedentedly walked into his father's office in the middle of business hours.

"The legal question, damnit—if there wasn't any adoption and he's no blood relative, I've got a moral responsibility to raise the question. But it's all up in the air, no way to prove it or disprove it—"

"Words," said Falkenstein senior, smiling faintly. They eyed each other against the background of the rows of law books, two tall, dark, lean men whose minds usually ran alike. "Forget the legal nitpicking. You're responsible to your client—and there is such a thing as natural law, the reason that statute exists about Unnatural Provisions. He was brought up as her son, she often enough indicated that she regarded him as her heir—that's clear enough, regardless of the circumstances of his birth."

"But if he's Parker's child, and there was no adoption, this Pollock is her nearest relative and Manning's case is substantially weakened. And I—"

"You don't know and nobody else will know now. Isn't it better to let it lie? Is the chance even fifty-fifty, she or Parker the mother? It's just as possible that he was Mrs. Manning's child, and the reason for the will was irrational remorse for some little thing that happened before her marriage, some belated sentimentality for old times."

"Yes," said Jesse unwillingly, "that's what I was thinking before this came up."

"Leave it," said his father. "If you want advice, forget it. You could be imagining the whole thing. There is a discrepancy in dates, but no possible way to prove it—"

"Unless we come across his birth certificate somewhere."

"And speaking of legalities, that affidavit—she had acknowl-edged him as her son."

"True."

"Leave it," said Falkenstein senior firmly. "You'd only cause a lot of mental anguish to Manning, to worry him the rest of his life. But you've got a good case on the Unnatural Provisions, the probable incompetence because of the evidence that she re-garded him as her heir—and those odd specified amounts cer-tainly constitute more grounds to indicate incompetency. You'd do nothing but harm to bring up a possibility you may just have imagined—because a thing is possible doesn't mean it's so."

Jesse heaved a long sigh. "I'll have to agree there. Probably you're right—my well-known tender conscience crying wolf. There could be other pseudo-logical reasons behind that will."

Falkenstein senior said thoughtfully, "She might have been more incompetent than anyone suspected—it could be there wasn't even an illogical reason behind it, Jesse."

On Friday morning, when Jesse came into Tregarron's office a little late, Adam Pollock was already there, and had reduced Tregarron to surprised twitterings. He stood up and gave Jesse a large, firm hand and a brisk no-nonsense shake. "This," he said, "is the hell of a situation. I'm very glad to meet you, Mr. Falken-stein." He was a tall, broad-shouldered, good-looking man with strong features, a sleek head of dark hair, bright brown eyes under thick brows. He was dapper in expensive gray herring-bone, snowy shirt, a boldly striped tie. He had a forceful deep voice with the casual manner of command in it, like a field general in civilian clothes.

Jesse murmured conventionalities.

"I was just telling Tregarron, I never had his letter until last week. The Highland Park house is only open in summer—my wife and daughters are in New York, where I'm technically sup-posed to live." He lifted his big shoulders in a rueful gesture. "Forget the fancy title they hang on me, the fact is I'm the head troubleshooter for Hilton, and I'm apt to get sent anywhere at any moment's crisis. The letter got forwarded to my New York office, but I've been in Paris and then London—they knew I'd be landing here for a couple of weeks so all the recent mail was waiting for me in San Francisco. I—"

"'Scuse me," said Jesse sleepily. "I've been reading some old letters, Mr. Pollock, some from your mother. They—she and your father—were in pretty low water back in 1930. You're not talking like a poor man. Family fortunes took an upward turn?"

Pollock grinned at him cheerfully. "Most people were in pretty low water back then, weren't they? Oh, yes, my father landed a job with Wedemeyer and Filer—brokerage on the Street—he was with them up to his death and ended up with a little pile—he always had an instinct what to buy, what to get shut of. I'd probably have ended up as a broker too, and right now be sitting around some high-class club worrying about my high blood pressure. But one of my college pals, Jay Ferguson—his father was pretty high up the executive list with Hilton—and we had a little in, started at the bottom and worked up. To our present thankless jobs. Jay's got the whole Honolulu setup to run—I'd rather be where I am, thanks."

"I see," said Jesse. "In fact, them as has gets."

Pollock was lighting a cigarette. "If you mean this goddamned stupid will, you can shove it. I'd never heard the woman's name. I knew vaguely that there was some distant cousin of my father's out here, but she was never mentioned in the family. When I walked in here half an hour ago and Mr. Tregarron explained the whole thing, I couldn't believe it. I can't believe it. The woman was obviously crazy."

"You do know Mr. Manning intends to contest the will," said Jesse.

"With my blessing," said Pollock. "I never heard of anything so damned unfair in my life. I want to meet Manning—we'd be fourth cousins or something, wouldn't we? Listen, what in hell do I know about real estate management?" demanded Pollock. "I've got enough occupation in life as it is, a job I like and plenty of money. Mother's got another pile which will come to me when she goes, which I trust won't be for many a year because she's quite a gal, Mother. Do you think I'm as crazy as that old witch, to let a lawyer stick me with a sizable fortune and shove me up into the ninety-eight per cent tax bracket? Nuts!" He had been waving a lighter around in extravagant gesture, finally lit his cigarette. "As far as I'm concerned you can tear up the damned will here and now."

"It's in probate," squeaked Tregarron at this piece of heresy.

"Can't do it quite like that," said Jesse. "We do have to go through the rituals."

"And what the hell happens if some damn-fool judge decides she knew what she was doing and hands it all to me? Real estate!" said Pollock as if it were a dirty word. "You might as well expect me to turn into an archaeologist—"

Jesse laughed. "Lot of money involved. Real estate can be sold."

"Hell's fire, man, don't you think I understand how Manning feels? His own business, that he's thought of as his in all but name all his life! I'd be the world's biggest bastard to grab that because some crazy old woman went farther out of her head and made that damn fool will."

"You're very generous, sir—but I must repeat, all the formalities must be complied with, and the probate—"

"You two can attend to all that," said Pollock. "I suppose, if some judge did accept that will, I could hand it back to Manning by deed of gift or something. I'd like to meet him. I'll be here until Tuesday or Wednesday, I didn't really have much business up north, but I thought I'd meet Mother and fly home with her. She's been on a world cruise, she's due here from Honolulu on Monday."

"Mrs. Anne Pollock," said Jesse. "I'd like to meet her, Mr. Pollock."

He looked at Jesse in a little surprise. "Certainly," he said politely. "I talked to her on the phone last week when I had Tregarron's letter. She was just as flabbergasted as I was about this will."

"I'd like to meet your mother," said Jesse, "because she knew her, you see—Mrs. Manning. They were girls together, back in Passaic."

"They were—I never heard her mention the woman's name," said Pollock, looking very surprised. "That's damn funny."

"And it's just possible that she might be able to clear up a few points for me, and tell us something that would explain—just what was in Mrs. Manning's mind when she made that will. It's all very fine for you to make the large gesture and say forget all about it—"

"Really," said Tregarron, "a most improper suggestion, sir! Laymen, of course, do not understand these things—"

"But the fact remains," said Jesse, "that the law being what it is, all the formalities have to be attended to. And if I had the faintest idea—or a better one than I have," he added, pushing Alice Parker out of his mind—"just why she did it, it would be something concrete to put before the bench. Judges and juries are sometimes a little obtuse. If we could spell it out for them it would be helpful."

"What on earth do you think Mother could tell you?" asked Pollock curiously. "She hadn't laid eyes on this woman in—how long?"

"Fifty-five years," said Jesse. "But you know, I think she may have something to tell us. If it's convenient for you both, shall we say ten o'clock Tuesday morning, in my office?"

Pollock looked more curious at this definiteness. "Well, it's perfectly all right with me," he said. "I suppose it'll be all right with Mother."

Jesse was somewhat surprised when Manning walked into his office at five of ten on Tuesday morning. "Don't mind me," he said. "Adam asked me to meet them here—I want to meet his mother, and if we're going to turn up anything more about the will— My God, Falkenstein, I feel ten years younger!" He almost looked it; he seemed to have broadened out, and the worry lines that had been deepening from nose to mouth had smoothed out. "That is one very nice guy, isn't he? He could have been any kind of bastard, glad to grab what he could."

"Yes, Mr. Pollock is something of a surprise."

"I can't get over it. This last six weeks I've felt I was in a nightmare—but now—Tregarron said the hearing will have to be scheduled anyway, but there shouldn't be any trouble now, do you think?"

"It ought to be clear sailing, yes, especially with the attitude Pollock's taking. Just the formality, nothing to worry about." He was rather annoyed that Manning had turned up, but let the devil take the hindmost: if he was going to hear another unpalatable truth, it was always better to have the truth out in the open. And he wondered whether his father would agree with that: probably argue that where the truth would cause needless pain, it was better buried.

Jean opened the door and announced the Pollocks, and Jesse stood up. He was interested to meet Anne: Anne of those earlier letters, of that dignified little letter of 1931. She came in first, with her tall son behind her; he came to shake hands with Manning, then introduced her to both men.

She must have been a very pretty girl. She was still a pretty woman in her late seventies, and he thought again of time: perhaps the quality of life had something to do with the way individuals aged—or did not. She still had nearly the figure of a girl, and was very smartly dressed in a silver-gray wool suit with a perky mandarin-collared white blouse, a big gold brooch on one lapel. Her hair was almost white and still curly, in a soft, short halo cut, and she wore pearl studs in her ears. She had a fine creamy complexion, the same bright brown eyes as her son.

He said, "I'm very glad to meet you, Mrs. Pollock." He smiled down at her. "I've been reading some old letters of yours."

She was surprised. "Letters of mine?"

"That you wrote to Claire Manning years ago. Up to about 1928. And one letter you wrote her in 1931."

She put a hand to her mouth in an involuntary gesture, a pretty hand with barely pink-tipped nails, a fair-size sapphire ring. "That—" she said. "She'd kept that? How funny."

"Did she answer it, and send you what you asked for?"

She sat down in one of the clients' chairs Pollock held for her. "No, Mr. Falkenstein, she didn't. I never heard from her at all. Good heavens, what those letters must sound like now— You must have got the idea that we were wild little idiots."

"I'd like to know," he said, "what happened to Rose and Mary. I've been reading their letters too."

"They're both gone," she told him quietly. "Mary never married—she stayed home and looked after her parents until they died. She took a correspondence course and qualified, and got a job at the library. She worked there until she retired in 1967, and she died last year."

"Deploring and disapproving to the end? That sounds like Mary."

She threw her head back and laughed. "You've been reading her letters all right! Poor dear Mary."

"And Rose eloped with Jack Shephard. What happened to them?" They were talking as if they were alone in the room.

"Rose—nobody could ever do anything with Rose. That didn't work out, of course—Jack was an idle weakling. She divorced him in, let's see, about 1935, and later she married an older man named Waters. I suppose they got on well enough—he had a good deal of money. She never had any children. They were killed together in a plane crash in 1960."

"I never heard anything," said Jesse, "about Susan, born 1905."

"Oh, I suppose not," she said gravely. "She died of meningitis as a baby. I'd nearly forgotten it."

"You understand, we'd like to get at Claire's motive—if it was a twisted motive of some kind, there must have been one—in making this will. You knew her when you were young together—and after she was married, a little while. You mustn't mind me poking into private family matters, lawyers have to learn discretion."

"I don't mind at all," said Anne firmly. "They're all gone and past caring, and I decided—when Adam told me about this—it's better to have the truth, all the truth, out in the open."

"Well, then—reading her diary that she kept then, and something in a couple of Mary's letters, I got the idea that something fairly important happened along in September of 1923. That she and Rose and Mary had 'sworn never to mention.' I don't think you knew about it, or did you?"

"Oh, yes," she said with a very faint smile. "I knew."

"I thought just possibly," said Jesse, "she might have had an abortion."

Manning said, "What?" in a startled voice.

"That's very perspicacious of you, Mr. Falkenstein," said Anne calmly. "Would someone like to give me a cigarette? Only it wasn't Claire. It was Rose."

"Oh, my God, of course. Rose the wild one. Out making whoopee at the speakeasies with Jack Shephard."

"That's right. He hadn't any money, of course. She could have got some from Bill—protecting the family honor, you know—but she was afraid he'd murder her. Claire and Mary managed to get enough somehow, and argued the family into letting them go to New York on a shopping trip. Jack found out where to go. It was awful at the time, but later—" She sat back and watched the smoke from her cigarette spiral up. "I wonder what Claire was like in her old age. She was such a pretty girl—and she knew it!" She smiled. "We never heard another word from her. Of course we had all felt rather bitter about it—" She paused, and smiled at her son. "You never heard anything about this, because the family had scattered by then and there wasn't any point in talking about it. And it's ancient history. But you see, Mr. Falkenstein, I can tell you why Claire made that will."

She didn't, immediately. "We were the ones with cause to feel bitter, but she was the one who seemed to bear a grudge—I don't know why. It wasn't like Claire, but she must have changed a lot. Bill wangled himself a commission during the war, and got out here on his way to the Pacific. That was in 1943. He said the way he felt, it was water under the bridge, and we were doing all right, and he was curious to see Claire again. The only address he had was wrong, but he found a Manning Realty Company and went there, and they told him it was her office, so he sent in a note signed Your Long Lost Cousin—and she sent back a message that she wasn't interested in seeing him. *Not* like Claire. But then the other thing wasn't either."

"And what was that?" asked Jesse.

She turned to Manning. "I'm sorry you have to hear this, Mr. Manning. But it's what happened, and it's probably what was behind this will. You see—"

The phone on Jesse's desk shrilled, and he said, "Excuse me," and picked it up.

"We've picked up Panther," said Clock.

"That's nice, but I can't talk right now."

"Just give you the gist. He's got a pedigree back to age nine. A vicious one, Jesse. And no bleeding-heart excuses like poverty or brutal parents. His grandmother raised him and she's loaded, he can always get money out of her."

"Interesting, but—"

"His right name's John Kane. We'll see what we get out of

him, I just thought you'd like to know. Call you at home to-night."

Jesse put the phone down. "Go on," he said to Anne.

"You see," she went on obediently, "Claire's father, George Tilton, had a lot of money—a lot for those days. And everybody knew he'd leave some of it to the Pollocks—to Bill and Mary and Rose. He was fond of them, they were family. Oh, he'd have left more to Claire, but— I thought afterward, she'd always had everything she wanted with no question, and maybe after she was married to Bob Manning and had to start living on what he earned, she found out how important money can be. Or maybe she was just greedy—because other things are more important. Uncle George was terribly straitlaced. And she knew him so well—she could always manage him—she probably knew how his will read. And she wrote and told him everything she knew— I can even guess how she put it, though I never saw the letter— she would wrap it all up, pretty and pathetic, my conscience has been bothering me and you really ought to know—that sort of thing. And except for the abortion, it was all so petty—the silly things people did then, that seemed so wicked at the time—Bill going to speakeasies in New York, and Mary taking dirty modern novels out of the library—which she never did as far as I know—"

"Oh, yes, I see," said Jesse with a long sigh. "Wait for it. This was when?"

"Just after Bill and I were married. About July of 1927."

"Oh, yes. It could be that she sensed Bob was losing a little interest, and she wanted all the money, thinking she could keep him that way."

"I don't know anything about that."

"But how it all does fit in," said Jesse. "What happened?"

"Uncle George was in a terrible state. I wasn't there, but Bill said you wouldn't believe the names he called them. And probably in time Bill could have gotten him to see reason—except for Rose—but there wasn't time."

"No," said Jesse. "He made the will leaving it all to her, and six months later he died."

"You see how it was. I didn't know she had any family, and when Adam called me in Honolulu and told me about the will, I thought, well, she'd got to feeling guilty about it in her old age, tried to make it up. But when I heard about Mr. Manning, well, it seems she was going a little queer—"

"No," said Manning almost violently. "She wouldn't have done a thing like that—she couldn't. There wasn't—that kind of meanness in her."

"I'm afraid she did," said Anne apologetically. "And when she was old and ill, she felt sorry, felt she had to—make up for it, make some restitution. But of course she wasn't thinking straight or she wouldn't have left it *all* back to us—but that must have been what was in her mind."

"Yes, I see," said Jesse. "That fits all the facts—that's got to be the answer. Thank you very much for being so frank, Mrs. Pollock."

"I can't believe she'd have done a thing like that," said Manning; he looked a little pale.

"Poor Claire," said Anne thoughtfully. "We ought to be able to understand her a little. For the first time in her life she didn't have all the money she thought she needed, and she knew how Uncle George would react." Manning was still shaking his head mutely. Jesse offered her another cigarette. "Poor Claire," she said again. "I keep thinking of her as she was, and of course she must have changed. She was such a pretty girl—" She turned to Manning, with instinctive sympathy, as if to turn his mind to another subject, and said, "I suppose she must have learned to wear the glasses, however much she hated them. She was always blundering into things because she wouldn't wear them, but of course they didn't make such attractive frames as they do now—"

"Glasses?" said Manning.

"She was so fearfully nearsighted—myopic. You must have known that." Anne looked puzzled.

Jesse didn't realize he was standing up until his desk chair ran away and hit the wall. He felt the hairs stir on his neck. He said, "My good God in heaven—my God—not as pretty as—and Kane —*Kane*—all our lives—all our lives—"

They stared at him in lively astonishment.

She fell back at the sight of him, with the two big men behind him, at her door. He said, "You knew all about it, didn't you? You knew she was—the other one—since when? Since when? And I kept prying into the past, and you were afraid—after all these years—that I'd find out something. Weren't you? You wanted to frighten me off. It was a stupid thing to do, Miss Hansen."

She had both hands to her mouth, ugly hands with prominent veins. Her eyes were frightened.

"Your neighbor Mrs. Kane has told you about her grandson, the police always picking on him—you could guess the kind he was. You paid him to scare me off the case. So stupid."

She collapsed backward onto the couch. "I had to go on protecting her," she said in a dull voice. "I thought I had to. But it's all over—and she's gone."

"Yes, it's over now. After all this time, it's over."

She folded her hands carefully in her lap. "It seems queer I was so afraid. I don't seem to care what happens to me now. It doesn't matter."

Jesse bent over her. "Where is she, Miss Hansen?" he asked gently. "Where is Claire Elizabeth?"

She looked up at him, and her mouth worked a little. She said, "Under the garage floor at the house on Edgemont."

It was in Clock's office that she gave them a statement, steady and stoic. "You've got to understand that Bob Manning never really loved that empty-headed girl. He fell for a pretty face, and he soon got tired of her. It was C—Alice he really loved. I'm sorry, I called her Claire so long—longer than I called her Alice. We were together all our lives—we were brought up together in the Ada M. Hershey Home for Girls in Los Angeles. She was nearly two years older than me, you know—you didn't know that. She was nearly five years older than—the other one. She was eighty when she died. We'd always been best friends, helped each other.

"She and Bob loved each other. They were both miserable, because it wasn't right, he was married and it wasn't his wife's fault that he'd come to love C—Alice. And after his wife found out and made a row about it, they talked it over and Bob agreed to —to try again to make the marriage work. He talked to Alice about it—he said he had to try, she was such a helpless little thing and he was responsible for her, he'd married her and sworn

to take care of her. They were going away together—to make a
fresh start. Alice—she'd have done anything for him. If that was
what he wanted she'd just bear it. We were living together then,
we had an apartment on Berendo Street, she was working at the
same realty firm where Bob did and I had a job at another one.

"But then he called on the phone—the next night it was—I answered it and he could hardly talk, he was like a wild man—she
was dead, he said, C—Alice had to come. I went too, she wasn't
fit to be alone. And there she was—the other one—on the living
room floor. That little fool of a redhead. Bob told us how it happened—she was so nearsighted, and she wouldn't wear glasses—
she was happy, he said, laughing and joking, and she tripped on
the coffee table and fell and hit her head on the piano— I know
that's the way it must have happened, because I knew Bob—he'd
never have touched her—it wasn't that he hated her, it was just
that he loved C—Alice.

"But anyone could see what it looked like. Some people had
known—about him and Alice. And Alice—it's funny, I can think
of her as Alice again—she said it wasn't going to happen, she
wouldn't see him in jail for murder, there was a way out of it.
They'd been going away, and nobody would miss her—just
think she'd gone with Bob. We all worked like slaves that night.
Bob knew I was safe—I was sort of Alice's other self, I'd never
do anything to hurt Alice. I never worked so hard in my life as I
did that night. We got her out to the garage, and we took turns
digging, and we put her good and deep. They had it arranged,
he was to go down to San Diego and after a while she'd quit
her job and they'd get married.

"Only the next day—the very next day—there was a letter
from a lawyer, to say C—her father had died and left her all that
money."

"Oh, yes," said Jesse softly. "That was a facer."

"There'd be things to sign—if she didn't write back, they'd
come looking for her. Bob was scared, but Alice pulled him together. She said they had to, they couldn't just give up now—
she'd be Claire, who'd know? There were friends wrote her from
back there, but we didn't think there was any other family. Anyway, that's what they did—Alice found her diary and practiced
her writing. The lawyer said it would take three or four months

before she got the money. We cleared out the house in a hurry—
there was an old trunk of hers, we just bundled most of her
things into it—they hadn't owned any of the furniture but odds
and ends, and that piano— Bob put it all in storage.

"And he went to San Diego, and after a while she quit her job
and went down there.

"And it worked all right, they got the money—a lot of money
—and they turned it all into cash, and that was just before the
crash. The first thing they did with the money was buy that
house, it was for sale. And Bob came up here in the middle of
one week and he put the cement floor in that garage—it had
been just dirt. He put the cement six inches deep, he said, to be
safe.

"And I was out of a job then, and I went down there to be
with Alice. I was with her when Johnny was born—it was awful,
we lived out in the country and the midwife got there just in
time—

"You see, they never dared to get married. She *was* his wife,
Claire Manning, and they publish these things in the papers,
somebody who'd known the other one might have seen it.

"And they had to come back here. After the crash. There
wasn't anything moving in real estate except around L.A. It was
the only chance to make any money."

"Money," said Jesse quietly. "Could you have any guess, Miss
Hansen, about those odd amounts of money specified in that
will?"

She jerked her head stiffly. "I saw that when John showed me
the will. The ten thousand and some, to John and Jim. Yes. That
would have been—just about what Alice and Bob had between
them—without the other money. From the other one's father."

Jesse sighed and shut his eyes. "And of course she never knew
what the real Claire had done to get that money. Not that kind
of meanness in her," he murmured to himself.

"They came back—and we started Manning Realty together.
Most of the people Bob knew—in the business before—hadn't
known the other one, but a lot of people knew she had red hair,
so Alice dyed hers. It wasn't too hard to keep away from the
people who'd known Bob and the other one, the place was grow-

ing—lots of people coming in. They made new friends—we were happy. We were! They loved each other so much—they were meant for each other. And Bob was so clever, they worked together and the business was picking up— We'd almost forgotten —it was the way I told you before—a happy time—they went dancing a lot, they loved to dance—

"That piano. The other one, she'd never have parted from it, they'd had to take it, for the look of the thing, but of course Alice couldn't play it—but it was valuable, of course. They'd just built that house. Such a beautiful house then. And—Bob—was—killed."

"'We challenged the gods and they denied us,'" said Jesse.

"Yes. Yes. She said that. So she wouldn't change anything in the house. And after that—after that—"

"Oh, yes, she was trapped. She hadn't any choice but to go on being Mrs. Claire Manning." My God, thought Jesse, hadn't she walked with a shadow at her shoulder, down all the empty years! And then at the last, afraid of meeting poor little Claire Elizabeth again, afraid of some judgment to be brought, trying to return Claire's money where it belonged. Knowing nothing of the family, hiring the private eye—

The queer, lonely, secretive, but still somehow gallant old lady, with the shadow at her back, trying to make amends.

"What are you going to do about it?" asked Wilma numbly.

"Probably nothing," said Clock casually. "It was all too long ago."

And she said, "It was a lifetime ago. Too long—and too short. It doesn't matter what you do or don't do."

They found what was left, four Traffic men taking turns with pickaxes and shovels. The cement was thick, and what was left was a foot under that, in hard-packed earth. There were just bones, and a few shreds of faded discolored green silk, remnants of shoes—and the pendant watch, all blackened and broken.

Clock said, "I doubt if the D.A.'s office will do anything about it. There's no way to show how she died. At the most the Hansen woman would be an accessory after the fact. There's not much in it."

Jesse agreed soberly. Manning would probably see to a private burial.

He came home late that Monday afternoon to find Nell poring over the wallpaper-sample tome, David Andrew grimly practicing walking, and a vaguely satisfying smell from the kitchen. "Everything's ready, just keeping warm," she said. He fetched Bourbon and soda for himself, sherry for her.

"I had Tregarron in this afternoon. That's all going to go without a hitch, we'll likely just get the will set aside. I think I agree with Father—no need to air everything. Let it go, what the hell. Justice done in the moral sense."

"Yes," said Nell. She looked at her glass. "Jesse. Do you suppose—they ever talked about it—two old ladies playing cards together—or if, in all that time, it had just gotten down to the bottom of their minds—*her* mind, so that she'd forgotten she'd ever been Alice Parker at all? All that time when—the way you put it—she was trapped."

Jesse laughed ruefully. "I wonder. And my Alice Parker just a coincidental Alice. Funny. But it's not an unusual name."

"You know," said Nell, "how she must have felt—about everything—living out all those lonely years— I think she stood enough to—to square it all up, don't you?"

Jesse stretched his legs out and sampled his drink. "I think," he said, "I'll have to agree to that, my girl. I think that's one account that can be marked *Paid in Full*."

2